Her Dom

Dominic Powers Series, Book 1

By

A.D. JUSTICE

You've been Dominated!

Lots of love

AD Justice

HER DOM

This is a work of fiction. Names, characters, places, and incidents are a product of the author's imagination. If the location is an actual place, all details of said place are used fictitiously, and any resemblance to businesses, landmarks, living or dead people, and events is purely coincidental.

Cover design by Kari Ayasha with Cover to Cover Designs.

Front and back images under license from bigstockphoto.com.

ISBN-13: 978-0692253724

ISBN-10: 0692253726

Acknowledgements

There are so many people who help make this journey into writing books enjoyable. I want to take a minute to personally thank those who specifically helped with this book.

- First and foremost, I want to thank my Lord and Savior for His continued grace and love.
- My husband and my boys, for believing in me and supporting my endeavors, my long nights, and the days I missed time spending with them.
- My friends who stuck by me, through thick and thin: A.M. Madden, Christine Davison, Tricia Daniels, J.M. Witt, Skye Turner, Ren Alexander and Tabitha Stokes. I love every one of you!
- My cover designer, Kari Ayasha, who created this gorgeous cover.
- . Every member of my Street Team, who tirelessly promotes my books and recommends them to their friends. I love my Wicked Devils!
- Every single blogger who supports authors just for the love of the books. You are all rock stars in my book!

Chapter One

Today has been the day from hell. There's no other way to describe it but as the shittiest day in history. Well, in my history anyway. I am the Chief Executive Officer of my company, Dominic Powers Software, also known as DPS. We develop the software programs that run most of the other *Fortune 500* companies. The software engineers that are the backbone of my company are the best in the world. Recruiting globally from the top universities, we bring the talent to the office here in Dallas, Texas.

My problem is that I'm hiring a Personal Assistant and, so far, not *one* person has been qualified enough to even wipe my ass, much less be my right hand. My assistant must be able to make executive decisions when I'm not available, know what my expectations are, and have the gumption to carry out my orders with employees at all levels of my company. After endless interviews and countless yawns, I'm almost convinced the ideal candidate doesn't exist.

There are department leads for each of the major divisions. We also have a Vice President, Darren Hardy, but his main focus is being our Chief Financial Officer. He has no interest in making decisions that don't require number crunching. His recent revelation is the reason behind my current search through an endlessly disappointing applicant pool. My phone buzzes as my secretary, Dana, calls from her desk outside my office.

"Not another one, Dana. I can't deal with one more Ivy League graduate with no damn common sense," I say as a greeting.

"Mr. Powers, your four o'clock appointment is waiting to speak with you. Her name is Sophia Vasco," she responds professionally. However, since I know her so well, I can hear the motherly admonition in her voice. She won't allow me to be rude and brush off the last interview of the day and I love her for it. She's saved me from myself more than once.

"Do I *really* want to talk to this one, Dana?" I ask, genuinely interested in her opinion.

"I do believe so, sir," she replies and I can hear the smile in her voice.

"Give me five minutes then send her in, Dana. Thank you," I instruct before hanging up.

I rise and walk toward the fully stocked bar at the other end of my executive office. After pouring a tumbler of bourbon, I quickly down the amber liquid, enjoying the sweet burn as it flows down my throat. One more quick shot and I'm ready for the last interview of the day. This candidate better be good because I'm quickly losing faith in being able to find a good match.

The familiar, three-rap knock alerts me that Dana is at the door and I call for her to enter. Dana walks into my office and gives me a knowing smile. She's been with me since the very first day I was able to afford a secretary. In her later fifties, she is old enough to be my mother, but young enough to understand what I'm looking for in an assistant.

Her smile tells me she approves of this candidate. I straighten my stance and walk across my office toward her. Approaching them, my feet halt in mid-stride when the latest applicant steps out from behind Dana. Beautiful doesn't even *begin* to describe the lady standing before me. There's an unmistakable air of innocence about her, combined with a determination and steeliness that's evident in her perfectly straight stance.

She's unlike any woman I've ever seen before, especially in this cutthroat business. I've never been caught up in a woman to the point where I forget my own name, or what my purpose is, but she has me completely and utterly enthralled. Her long, reddish brown hair cascades over her shoulders with wavy curls scattered throughout. She's petite but her high heels provide just the right amount of lift to make her perfectly fit my six-foot height. As she looks down at the floor, her black eyelashes are fanned out across her cheeks. When she looks up at me from under her lashes, her deep brown eyes are full of both anticipation and trepidation.

When her eyes meet mine, my breath catches in my chest and I have to consciously keep from audibly gasping. My need for control kicks in and I feel my blood pressure returning to normal. There's something about this one that Dana obviously identified—she knows me all too well. Resuming my trek toward them, I remind myself of why she's here to see me. This is an interview for a job in my company, as my right hand, not as my paramour.

I strive to be the consummate professional at all times and somewhere my psyche chastises me for my momentary lapse. By appearances, she is young, inexperienced, and innocent. None of these are traits that I hold in high regard in any woman. Her beauty had momentarily stunned me, but now that I'm thinking with my business head, I know

4

what needs to be done. Time to put her through the grueling interview process every employee of DPS has to face. We hire only the best and brightest here.

"Mr. Powers, this is Sophia Vasco. Miss Vasco," Dana says, emphasizing the *Miss* as a message to me, "this is the owner and CEO of DPS, Mr. Dominic Powers."

Sophia extends her hand while maintaining eye contact with me. Her boldness gives me an unexpected thrill and the front of my dress pants begins to become uncomfortable. I take her proffered hand and instantly feel the sizzle from the connection. Her handshake is firm, but her hands are soft, and my mind wanders to imagine how they would feel on me.

"It's nice to meet you, Mr. Powers. I've heard great things about DPS and I'm anxious to learn even more," she politely says.

I hear her words but I can't completely focus on them at the moment. The pitch of her voice is like silk and crushed velvet across my skin, simultaneously soothing my nerves and exciting my body. I'm still holding her hand, slowly moving in the normal handshake manner, but nothing seems normal about this meeting.

5

"Thank you for coming, Miss Vasco," I say, intentionally choosing my words just to observe her reaction. The timbre of my voice mirrors the one I use in more intimate settings. She doesn't disappoint me—the flush of pink in her neck quickly crawls up her cheeks as she lowers her eyes. A shy smile spreads across her face as she takes a moment to regain her composure.

Very interesting, indeed.

"Thank you for seeing me today, Mr. Powers. It's my pleasure to be here," she responds with a genuine smile that reaches her eyes. They sparkle with a hint of mischief and playfulness. I release her hand and have a sudden urge to grab it again.

There's something about her that causes my thoughts to stray from the task at hand. My momentary reclamation of my senses has passed, and I am once again thinking of the various things I would love to do to her. Things I'm positive she's never experienced before. At one point in my life, I would've been more than happy to teach her. In more recent times, I've been more than hesitant to even consider it.

"Thank you, Dana," I say, finally recognizing that my secretary is still present with us. She smiles that familiar smile—the one that tells me she thinks she knows exactly what I'm thinking but offers no input. I can say with all certainty that she has *no idea* what thoughts are really flying through my mind.

"Can I get you something to drink, Miss Vasco?" I ask after Dana has closed the door behind her.

"Please, call me Sophia. Just a glass of water, thank you."

"Very well, Sophia. Please have a seat and I will be right with you."

Walking back to the fully stocked bar, I feel her eyes watching me, sizing me up and trying to read me. I know she hasn't taken her seat yet because her back would be to me and I wouldn't feel her eyes on me, burning through me and creating a physical presence on my skin. She obviously thinks she has time to take me in before I finish making her drink. I'm letting her believe she can stare at me without getting caught, just to gauge her true reaction. Merely envisioning the imminent busted look on her face makes me smile.

Turning quickly, our eyes lock and her face heats to bright red after I catch her brazenly ogling me. "Do you want that water on the rocks, Sophia?"

The tone of my voice doesn't give away my delight but there is no doubt that my eyes betray me. The truth is I attract women most everywhere I go but I'm used to it by now. I am in no way conceited, but I know I'm a handsome man and I work hard to maintain my physical fitness. My personal trainer puts me through a grueling workout every morning, alternating weights and calisthenics, but it's paid off in ways most people have never considered.

"Um, whatever is easiest for you, Mr. Powers," she answers before she quickly takes her seat as I previously instructed. Her answer pleases me in ways that have nothing to do with business deals. That's the part that concerns me, however. I need someone who can be as ruthless in business as I am, who can represent me when I am otherwise engaged, and who can make the best decisions for my company.

I muse over this as I drop a few ice cubes into a tumbler and fill it with bottled water. My mind questions if she has enough backbone to stand up to the many executives I meet with on a daily basis. Executives of other *Fortune 500* companies who are accustomed to getting their way and having others jump at their command. Right or wrong, this is still very much a man's business world. Many business deals are brokered over a game of golf and a few stiff drinks. This tradition doesn't normally include women unless the executives specifically request to bring their wives along.

If she's trainable, she could be a formidable asset, though. They wouldn't see it coming from her and she would knock them off their game. Any weakness of theirs gives us the advantage in a negotiation. It's time for me to test her strengths and weaknesses by suddenly thrusting her into an uncomfortable and stressful situation. My interview process is unconventional in ways but effective as the company retention rate is excellent.

I watch the movement of Sophia's shoulders as her chest rises and falls with each breath. She's practicing a calming technique and preparing herself mentally for the difficult questions she knows are coming. Intently focused on her meditation, she doesn't hear me walk up behind her. Reaching over her to place the tumbler on my desk directly in front of her chair, I keep my voice low as I say, "Here's your water, Sophie."

She jumps slightly as my proximity startles her. Her eyes fly open and she inhales sharply—our faces are inches apart and her eyes flit to my mouth. She watches with baited breath as I intentionally lick my lips, her eyes tracking the movement of my tongue across my lips. Willingly or not, she can't deny that I affect her—the desire is there and I have but to ask and she would be mine.

Keeping my movements fluid, I quickly retreat from her space and walk around my desk. She clears her throat and takes a quick sip of water. "Sophia," she responds.

"Sorry?" I quiz, knowing exactly what she means. This is the first test. Is she too polite to correct a basic misunderstanding? Will she subjugate herself and give someone else the upper hand in her attempt to be nice, to not offend the other person? Or will she stand up for herself and tell me that I've misstated her name?

"My name is Sophia. I believe you said Sophie. I just wanted to make sure you knew so that you don't give the job to the wrong person," she explains amiably but pointedly. Score one point for *Sophia.*

"So it is, Sophia," I reply as I take my seat. "Easy question first. Tell me about yourself," I request as I lean back in my chair. This is actually a very telling question even though it's one of the least structured of the interview questions. The information this applicant chooses to disclose tells me where her true intentions lie. If she replies with personal information, it tells me that my business is not her main priority. If she replies with her business accomplishments, I know she's attuned to the needs of my business.

"I graduated from the University of Texas— double majoring in International Business and Management. Since graduation, I have worked in the software development field in increasingly responsible positions over the two years. My latest position was as a manager of a small team of software engineers. I was responsible for overseeing every aspect of a ten million dollar project with a *very* tight timeframe for completion and a high probability of failure. Under my leadership, the project was completed ahead of schedule, resulting in a bonus for the company *and* my team.

"While I have been successful in my current role, it is time that I expand my horizon, learn more and apply more of my skills and expertise. My current employer doesn't offer that opportunity and when I saw this position, I wanted to interview with you to determine if this is the right place for me."

Her enthusiasm and genuineness are obvious in the way she speaks, the tone and inflection of her voice, and in her mannerisms. But she doesn't show the desperation that so many applicants demonstrate. This question sets the tone for the entire interview and she hit the mark dead center. She focused on her education, her accomplishments, and the reason why she is interested in making a job change without automatically assuming that this job is a perfect fit for her. She understands that she is interviewing me just as much as I am interviewing her.

Impressive.

Throughout the rest of the interview, I learn so much more about Sophia and what makes her tick, what she likes, and her sense of humor. Even during a formal interview for a very high level position, she has managed to infuse her humor into it in a professional and genial way. I can't recall the last time I actually laughed during a formal interview or enjoyed it so much. My mind goes to the everyday tasks and plays through how the scenarios would change if I add her to the mix. The only downside I've been able to determine is that being in such close proximity to her for prolonged periods of time will be hell on my libido.

"As you know, this position works directly with me. If chosen, you would be my go-to person—that includes making business decisions when I'm not here, acting on my behalf, and taking responsibility for major interactions. I expect each task to be carried out to my strict instructions and I expect you to make the decisions *I* would make. That requires you to spend an extraordinary amount of time with me, learning my methods, vision, and long-term goals for the company. I have to be able to trust you *implicitly*. Do you foresee any problems with any of that?" I ask, holding her gaze with a burning intensity in my eyes and giving no room for her to break our eye contact.

"No, I have no problem with any part of those duties. I want to do the best I can possibly do for the company, for you and for myself. I would be honored to spend time with you, learning from you and perfecting my skills. I know there's a great deal I can learn under your guidance," she finishes and I'm glad my desk hides the lower half of my body from her view.

"If chosen, when can you start?"

"After a two-week notice. I wouldn't leave without giving them time to replace me, even if that's only on an interim basis."

I regard her for a moment, watching her as she waits for me to reply to her last statement. The truth is, I can't control my racing thoughts about late nights, early mornings, and out of town trips with the splendid beauty sitting across from me. None of my thoughts are what anyone would consider wholesome and I can't help but feel that I will ultimately lead her into temptation. I see myself as the serpent and I'm tempting her with the fruit of knowledge—knowledge of a life of which she has no clue. This life could very well be her unraveling, destroying her delicate nature and shattering her innocence.

The intense pull is too much for me to resist, even with my great arsenal of self-control techniques. The devil on my shoulder whispers to me, telling me to teach her everything she wants to learn. He says to let her be the guide and reassures me that Sophia will tell me when it gets too intense for her. He lies to me frequently and I can usually ignore him, but I have to admit to myself that this time I don't *want* to ignore him. I want to take him at his word and bring her neck deep into my world.

Giving her my best smile, the one that always works on the ladies, I watch the pink creep up her face again. I know she likes what she sees and it spurs me on in my plans for her. "I'm glad to hear that, Sophia. You're hired. Report here in two weeks at nine o'clock on Monday morning. Dana will get you set up with all the paperwork and then we will begin your training," I explain and finish my sentence in my head, *in more ways than one.*

Sophia stands, grasps my hand in hers, and says, "Thank you so much, Mr. Powers. I am very much looking forward to working with you and learning everything you want to teach me."

Score one point for Mr. Powers.

Chapter Two

Two weeks later, I arrive at my office very early. I've been working relentlessly on a large software project contract. There are people under me who normally handle the day-to-day management of contract negotiation, but this one is special. This contract is with a specific location operated by the government, but this particular facility has cornered the market in their niche. The sensitive nature of their business dictates that only the most senior level executives can see their confidential information. I'm mulling over certain aspects of the contract when Dana's three-tap knock interrupts my thoughts.

"Good morning, Mr. Powers. Here's your coffee, newspaper, and your schedule for today. Is there anything else I can get you?" Dana cheerfully asks.

"No. Thank you, Dana," I reply and pick the contract back up with one hand while holding the hot coffee in the other.

"Miss Vasco is scheduled to be here at nine o'clock this morning. After I get her set up, do you want me to send her in here to you?" Dana asks, a little too nonchalantly, even for her.

I arch one eyebrow and give her a look that relays my suspicion of her inquiry. "Yes, Dana, you may send her to me when you're finished with her."

Dana smiles and leaves me to finish my work. After a couple more cups of coffee, I think I finally have the contract where I want it, positioning my company to be the sole provider of software upgrades throughout their entire top-secret facility. Since they are actually a facility that is owned and operated by the government, the contract has to be approved through so many red-tape channels it's ridiculous, but it will be more than lucrative in the end. It will also give my company footing to take on more government contracts and effectively corner that market in the process.

Dana's knock signals that Miss Vasco has graced us with her presence today. "Come in," I call from my desk.

Sophia enters and closes the door behind her. She is dressed in a straight skirt, form-hugging shirt, and heels. Her hair is down, flowing over her shoulders and shimmering in the light. Walking directly to my desk, she looks as if she is more than ready and eager to get started with her lessons. *How fitting,* I think.

"Good morning, Mr. Powers. How are you today?"

"Good morning, Miss Vasco. Call me Dominic," I say with a smile, "I'm great today. How are you?"

She's a bundle of energy but I don't get the sense that it's nervous energy. She seems really glad to be here and ready to start in her new role. I briefly consider how fortuitous it was for her to walk into my office so unexpectedly, right when I was ready to throw in the towel on finding a suitable assistant.

"I am wonderful today," she gushes. "I'm so excited to work with you and learn from the best of the best." Her tone is honest with no hint of insincerity. I feel a gush of humility wash over me and quickly dismiss it. There's a reason why I've reached this status well before my current age of twenty-nine and reacting with ridiculous feelings are not part of that reason.

"Very well. Let's get started then," I say as I put the confidential contract away. "We'll start with a tour of the building. By the time we're finished with the tour, the management staff meeting will start and I can introduce you to the team."

Sophia nods in agreement and follows me out of my office. "DPS occupies the top five floors of this office building. We have the best view in the city," I explain with pride. The Dallas Arts district is one of the most coveted areas for business. "The top floor is, obviously, where all of the senior executives' offices are located. The four floors below us are all software engineers, divided by function and expertise." We continue walking through the expansive offices and I point out the office specifics she will need to know.

"These offices are so chic-modern while yours is more conventional. Was that by design?" she asks as we walk side by side down the corridor.

"Yes, it was. I like the big, heavy oak desk, the built in bar, and the clean, crisp look that shows my professional side. But since the programmers don't meet directly with the customers and they are tied to their desks, for the most part, I wanted them to have a more relaxed, comfortable atmosphere."

"I love the ambiance in here. You've made it very conducive to working long hours while your employees are shackled to their computers," Sophia says with a warm smile and appreciation in her tone.

The vision of a *certain* employee in shackles flashes through my mind and my eyes drink her in. I can picture her delicate wrists and ankles bound as she's writhing and waiting for me to take her to the places I alone can take her. The vision of her face in the throes of passion is all I can see now as she takes all the pleasure that I alone can give her.

I clear my throat lightly, and as if I'm on autopilot, my feet turn and carry me on to continue our tour of the offices. As we turn the corner heading toward the bank of elevators, I instinctively place my hand at the small of her back. The intimate act feels so natural that I don't even notice it for the first couple of seconds. When the electricity from our touch courses through my hand, I look down and suddenly jerk my hand away.

What the fuck is wrong with me?

"I sincerely apologize for that, Sophia. It's purely habit for me, but I assure you it won't happen again," I try to explain.

"I didn't mind, Mr. Powers," she replies demurely with her eyes cast down to her feet, her black lashes lying against her soft cheeks, and her fingers clasped together as she lightly wrings her hands in nervousness. "Honestly, it's alright."

With an incline of my head toward the elevator, we wordlessly walk the remaining few steps to it. I

19

press the down button and silently curse myself for the egregious mistake on my part. To avoid temptation again, I quickly thrust my hands into my pants pockets and resolve to keep them there as long as possible. When the elevator dings, I allow her to enter first and have to consciously fight with my hand to not touch her again.

On the next floor, we walk and I explain the basis for the office arrangement. "The programmers on this floor all handle some type of application programming. This type of programming has the end user in mind so it's much more user-friendly and gives the output they need in order to conduct business," I explain. "For example, some of the programmers have built a new accounting system for one of our customers. It helps them track and maintain their inputs and outputs much easier."

After I show her around this floor, I continue to relay the information to her about the way our business is structured. "The floor below this one houses the system programmers who build the actual operating systems. They control everything the computer does, how it reacts with the applications, and the most basic level of technical functions it's capable of handling.

"The floor below that is for game programmers. We also subcontract with several high-end game companies. Below that is the floor where all of our web designers are. They build and design complex web designs, including the language, graphics, and web-based security systems. Each floor is set up like this one, so it's just a matter of tracking down the desk of the specific person you need," I finish and glance around the floor.

"This is very impressive. I'm really looking forward to jumping in and getting my feet wet."

I don't need any mental images of anything related to *wet* right now. My imagination is active enough without the constant reminder that I can only look and not touch. I can look at her perfect, perky breasts, as they push against the fabric of her shirt and beg for my hands to take them. The rise and fall of her chest as she breathes normally mocks me. The pulse of her jugular vein in her neck beckons me to nibble on her perfect skin. Her beautiful brown eyes are expressive, and her modesty causes her to blush when she thinks she has been caught in an errant thought.

Glancing at the clock on the wall, I'm saved from myself when I realize it's time for our staff meeting. "Let's go. I will introduce you to the entire management team at once," I say with my panty-dropping smile and she follows me back to the elevator.

"Mr. Powers?" she asks tentatively.

Turning to face her, I smile encouragingly and reply, "Dominic. Everyone here calls me by my first name so it's really alright."

The slow, shy smile crawls across her face as she says, "Dominic," trying it on for size. "Are there set hours that I should plan on working or will it vary from day to day?"

"Hmm, that's a good question," I laugh. "The morning start time is normally the same. If we have an early morning breakfast meeting, I will let you know ahead of time. We will have a lot of late nights and several overnight trips. I'm afraid you'll be spending a lot of quality time with me, Sophia."

"I really don't mind, Dominic. I'm looking forward to everything you can teach me," she replies with her voice low and sensual. I can usually read people very well, but I can't decide if she is intentionally trying to seduce me or if she really means she wants to learn.

"I hope I live up to your expectations then, Sophia," I intentionally respond with an equally low and sensual timbre.

Her cheeks redden, heated with a mixture of embarrassment and excitement, in my opinion. She's inexperienced in many ways but she's very bright. What she lacks in practice, she makes up for in eagerness. If only circumstances were different, I could take that eagerness and really teach her the things I want her to learn. But not for my pleasure alone—I want to teach Sophia to heighten and increase *her* ultimate pleasure.

"I have no doubt you will, Dominic."

Her response is so earnest and humble that it heats me to my core. I'm positive she feels the heat radiating from my eyes as I stare at her. The trust she automatically places in me after spending only a few hours together astounds and dumbfounds me. I wonder if she's this way with everyone she meets or if it's just me.

I resolve to find out the answer to that during our two-hour staff meeting. She will be subjected to many different personalities in a confined room. The tension is palpable at times, especially when there are heated discussions and major differences of opinions. One thing about my staff is they are all passionate about their jobs. It makes me proud most of the time; at times, it's a pain in the ass to cut through the strong personalities.

Sophia and I make our way back to the top floor and to the staff meeting. Most of my management team is already in their regular seats and are ready to begin the meeting. A few stragglers come in at the last minute and quickly take their seats. Sophia is looking around the room, her eyes wide in apprehension and I briefly question whether she will stick around much longer. These men and women are loud, opinionated, zealous, and hard to handle at times.

"Everyone, let's get settled in and begin the meeting. I have an announcement to make first," I call out in my booming, take-charge voice. This quiets the room immediately and everyone moves to their seats. There are advantages to being the boss. My employees have been loyal to me and enjoy working for me, but I do expect a lot from them and I don't put up with any bullshit. They know this and they are of the same mindset, so it works like a well-oiled machine for the most part.

"First up, I want to introduce you to Sophia Vasco. She is my new personal assistant. She graduated in the top five percent of her class from the University of Texas in Austin. She's worked in the industry and has several successful multi-million dollar projects under her belt. Sophia's first day is today so cut her some slack for the next couple of weeks. After that, she will be my right-hand person and will make executive decisions in my absence. She will help with contracts and, for all intents and purposes, she will be me when I can't be here."

"Sophia, do you want to say anything?" I ask, intentionally putting her on the spot to gauge her reaction. An abundance of energy usually keeps me from sitting too long during staff meetings. Today, it's important to note the interactions Sophia has with my other staff members, so I move to the other end of the room.

"Yes, I do. Thank you for that introduction, Dominic. I am very excited to be here and look forward to getting to know each of you. As the department leads, I would like to set up one-on-one time with each of you to learn about your departments, how they work, what you're responsible for, and how I can help you in my current position. I look forward to working with each of you."

Color me impressed. Again.

Sophia is looking around the room and her eyes connect with mine. A slow, sensual smile crawls across my face. I sit on the edge of the credenza and cross my legs at my ankles. She is beautiful, elegant, graceful, and the master of our staff meeting. It's a new aphrodisiac for me. A stray thought forms that perhaps my former lovers should have worked for me. It would have created a new experience, without a doubt.

Two hours later, I am more refreshed and relaxed after a staff meeting than I ever have been before. Sophia jumped in and took control of any takeaways that I have. She is organizing several of the group initiatives we have underway and made several process improvement suggestions during the staff meeting. I am again reassured that my decision to hire her is sound.

We walk back into my office and I begin assembling various types of contracts, acceptable language and terms, and other related items so we can continue her training. Out of the corner of my eye, I see her begin to pick up a chair so she can sit beside me. I drop the papers on my desk and move swiftly to her side. My hand grasps the chair, grazing hers as I wrap my fingers around it, and a slight tremble rolls through her body. Her breath hitches and she peers up at me, her brown eyes asking the very question I've been avoiding all day. We stand frozen for several seconds, just staring at each other and allowing a million questions to run through our minds at once.

"No need to move that, Sophia. We can sit at the table together. But, for the record, if it did need to be moved, I would do it. I have no doubt you're capable, but in my presence, I will take care of moving any furniture or anything else heavy for that matter," I advise her, leaving no room for argument or discussion.

She blushes, appropriately chastised, "I didn't want to assume anything, Dominic. But I do appreciate your concern and chivalry. Not all men are like you." She finishes her last sentence on a whisper. It makes me wonder how she has been treated in the past. It's not something I want to dwell on right now—not the thought of her in another man's arms or how he may have treated her wrongly. But she is exactly correct in saying that not all men are like me.

I'm not sure she could handle the real me. The man that no one here has ever seen or has any inclination that he even exists. That thought actually makes my pulse increase. Worlds collide, though, and it's best that my employees never know about my proclivities.

"You're right, Sophia. Most men are not like me. That may be a good thing, for the most part," I tell her with all seriousness and sincerity.

She starts to speak but the pink in her cheeks quickly turns to deep crimson. Whatever is on her mind is obviously hard for her to voice. I feel the need to know what it is she's thinking, even if it cuts to the quick because I know I can't do anything about it. The glutton for punishment in me wants to wallow in it for a while.

"What were you going to say, Sophia? You look like you have something on your mind. You're me, remember?" I encourage her to speak her mind, using her new position as the reason why she should do so.

She's flustered as she opens and closes her mouth a couple of times without speaking at all. I begin to think she really won't tell me—that her shyness will get the best of her—and I will never know what was on her mind. Then she surprises me again with her words.

"I think the world needs more men like you, Dominic," she whispers. "Every woman could use a man like you."

I shake my head in disbelief at her words. "You've only just met me. You don't know what kind of man I am, Sophia."

"You're a good man. Anything else is just icing on the cake," she replies hesitantly, without meeting my gaze this time. It embarrasses her to say these things to me. I'm her boss. I'm her employer. But, that's not all I want to be to her and I feel myself getting closer to crossing that line.

Standing close to her, I can see the gold flecks sparkling in her brown eyes as they betray her thoughts. They reveal to me that she is interested in more than a working relationship with me. She is still shy enough that she wants me to make the first move, but her eyes tell me that she is more than receptive to me. Funny thing is, she believes she's hiding this from me. She doesn't realize that I already know or that I can read a woman's body as well as I can read the contracts lying on my desk right now.

Taking a deep, calming breath, I take a step to my desk and pick up the papers I had left there. Turning back to Sophia, I give her a crooked smile and extend my hand toward the conference table behind her. "Let's have a seat at the table and go over these contracts, Sophia," I say, steering the conversation away from what we were just talking about. I'm not ready to share that with her just yet.

I'm not sure she can handle it.

I'm not sure I can resist it.

Chapter Three

At the end of the day, I inwardly congratulate myself for not looking like a complete and total fool in front of Sophia. Her subtle perfume has assaulted my senses all day, infiltrating my nostrils, clinging to my clothes, and wafting around me as she moved. It has stirred up all manner of mental images of her—mainly with no clothes on. Her scent will stay with me into the night, long after she's left and I'm home alone.

"Come on, I'll walk you out," I say as I stand and stretch. It's been a long day of training, and not the fun kind of training, either. "We've covered enough for today."

"Let me grab my things from Dana's closet," Sophia says as she rises.

I watch her walk on her four-inch heels and appreciate the way the muscles in her legs and ass flex. I've spent nearly every minute of the day with her and there is nothing I don't like about her. She's smart, witty, personable, and so very easy to get to know. I grab my suit jacket and follow her out to Dana's desk area. She's rummaging through her purse to find her keys and I patiently wait for her to indicate she's ready to go.

The jingle of her key ring is my cue that it's time to start walking to the elevators. As I begin to turn, she looks up at me and I once again feel the unmistakable pull to her. She gives me her best, full-on smile and I feel my lips part in surprise at the beauty radiating from her face. This is going to be harder than I thought it would be, especially after I realized during the staff meeting that she doesn't react to other men the way she does to me. The blush of her cheeks, the demure smile, her downcast eyes, and the longing gazes happen *only* when she's interacting with me.

The sun is close to setting as we reach the parking garage. We're about to part ways, and even though I don't want to let her go yet, I can't think of a valid business reason of why we should spend more time together. I force myself to let her go, telling myself she will be back tomorrow and we can resume her training.

"Well, goodnight, Sophia. I will see you in the morning," I tell her with a smile.

"Good night, Dominic. I enjoyed today. Thank you for taking so much time with me," she replies with a heartfelt quality in her voice. She turns and starts to walk toward the street and I'm puzzled by her actions.

"Did you not park in the garage?"

She turns to face me again as she answers, "Oh, no. I don't have a car. I'm going to catch the bus."

"Where do you live?"

"Southwest of the city," she answers without giving the exact area of Dallas she lives in, but I'm fairly certain I know where. It's the higher crime area of Dallas proper and it's not safe for her to take public transportation to that part of town at this time of evening.

"Let me give you a ride," I say while using my thumb to point over my shoulder in the general direction of my car.

"I couldn't impose like that, Dominic. I'll be fine."

"I insist," I say with finality and fix my gaze on her until she resigns and does as I suggest.

With a deep sigh, she approaches me, "Dominic, I feel like I'm taking advantage and imposing on you at the same time."

"You're not. If I let you leave at this hour and take the bus, I'll worry about you all night. It's not how I was raised, Sophia. I don't believe in leaving you to fend for yourself when I'm in a position to help you."

This seems to placate her somewhat, but just in case, I continue, "If you deny me this, I won't get any sleep and then it'll be *your* fault when I'm grumpy all day tomorrow."

She smiles at this and giggles as my words really sink in. "Okay, Dominic. If you insist."

I smile and motion toward my car again. "Let's go. I will drive you home."

I open the passenger door and allow her to climb in. She gives me an odd look but I continue to patiently wait for her to sit until her shock passes. Once we're both settled into my Mercedes S550, her eyes grow wide as she considers all the gadgets and gizmos it has. She looks around nervously but doesn't touch anything. Her discomfort momentarily makes me feel self-conscious before she looks up at me in wonder.

"This. Car. Is. Awesome," she says, emphasizing each word before her face splits into a wide, appreciative smile. A fleeting thought takes hold in my mind. *You care what she thinks.*

"Where to, ma'am?" I ask in my best English butler accent.

She laughs heartily at my feeble attempt and gives me her address to put into my GPS. It's in the general area that I had originally thought and that worries me more. Not only is it a higher crime area, but she's also relying on public transportation to get her there. Dallas residents are known for being independent. Most everyone drives instead of using buses or other mass transit systems. As I'm pulling out of the parking garage, her stomach rumbles and I instantly know how I can keep her with me for a while longer.

"We haven't eaten in a long time, Sophia. Would you mind having dinner with me tonight? I really hate going to the restaurant alone," I say honestly. I've never admitted that to anyone else and I'm not sure why I said it to her, except that I really want her to say yes.

"Umm..."

"I'm sorry. I didn't ask if you're married or if you have a boyfriend who would be offended," I apologize, instantly filled with dread at the thought of her already having someone.

"No, no—nothing like that. It's just that...well...money is a little tight right now. So, I should pass this time." She's kept her eyes trained out the side window, avoiding all eye contact with me.

"Sophia, don't take this the wrong way, but I would consider it an insult if you paid for your dinner when I invited you to go with me. My mother raised me better than that. She's ingrained in me. I don't want to take your independence from you, but I just believe there are certain things a man should do for a woman, and paying for the meal when he invites her to dinner is one of those things."

"Dominic, I don't know any man who believes in that," she replies with a mixture of shock and incredulity. "So, moving heavy things, paying for dinner, and what else?"

"Opening doors—including car doors—carrying luggage, protecting her by making sure she gets home safely from work," I say with a pointed look, "and anything else that requires a real man's touch." The last part is very cryptic and I don't suspect she will assume anything more than what my words actually relay. I hope she doesn't look at the deeper meaning. Yet.

"I'm not accustomed to being taken care of like this, Dominic. Even with the simple things you're doing for me. It just feels strange," she confesses. "I hope I don't offend you."

"I understand that. It is hard to accept if you haven't been used to it before now. But, Sophia, I don't want you to feel bad about it because I actually do enjoy doing them. It makes me feel good to do these things, so don't fight with me on them," I explain, hoping she better understands.

"I will try to remember that. It may not always be easy for me, though. I guess I'm just used to being completely self-reliant."

I look over at her and smile, "Let's make a deal. I will coax you, but then you have to actually let me *do* whatever it is."

"Deal," she says with a smile.

"Dinner?" I ask again, testing her, but I also really want to have dinner with her.

"Yes, Dominic, dinner with you sounds very nice. Thank you."

"My pleasure," I answer and stop the route on the GPS to take her to one of my favorite places instead.

As I turn into the driveway to the Four Seasons resort, I feel the tension radiating off of her. I casually look over my shoulder and see her astonished look, her eyes wide and her mouth slighted parted. Oh, the thoughts that must be running through her mind right now. But I don't want to frighten her or give her wrong impression, so I decide to save her from her overactive imagination.

"There's an awesome restaurant inside the hotel. Have you ever been?" I ask casually.

"Uh, no, I've never been here," she replies as her eyes dart around the landscape, no doubt looking for the alleged restaurant.

"Relax, Sophia. I brought you here solely for the food. It is out-of-this-world *fantastic*. I think you will like it," I try to soothe her. "I'm not bringing you here for any other reason than dinner."

I catch her look of disappointment that quickly changes to relief, then to confusion, but she doesn't verbally respond. I can't help but laugh to myself. *Women.* They're offended when they think a man is hitting on them and they're offended when they find out he's actually *not* hitting on them. Her reaction makes me question how offended she would be if she knew about the images of her that have stayed with me since I first saw her two weeks ago.

After leaving my car with the valet attendant, I turn to her and say, "This way, Miss Vasco." Her smile is warm and the suspicion has left her eyes, I'm much too pleased to note.

Once seated, she takes a moment to really look around the restaurant and take in her surroundings. It's opulent without becoming ostentatious. The food is expertly prepared and perfect every time. I'm trying to watch her, gauge her reactions, and understand where she's coming from without being overly obvious about it.

"Sophia, tell me about yourself. I know a little about your work background, but nothing about you personally," I prompt after we've ordered our drinks.

She hesitates only a second before she begins. "There's really not much to tell. Well, nothing that would be considered interesting, anyway. I'm twenty-three and from a small town outside of Austin.

"My parents and little brother still live outside of Austin. I miss my brother. He's four years younger but we were always very close while we were growing up. I haven't seen him in a while. Anyway, I moved to Dallas about a year ago and you know everything since then," she finishes with a smile.

"So, no husband or boyfriend?" I ask with a casual aloofness that says I want to hear about her but I'm not overly interested.

"No, definitely no husband in the picture. No boyfriend, either—at least not anymore," she says before tasting her wine. "This is delicious. You have very good taste. Thank you for ordering for me. I never know what kind of wine to get."

The subtle change in topic does not go unnoticed by me but I can tell she isn't comfortable talking about this subject yet. That's just as well. I'm actually not ready to answer any similar questions from her. In fact, I know I need to rein in these wayward thoughts and feelings toward her. I just met her, and while I would like to get to know her better, we are not at the right time or place for me to even consider being anything other than business associates. In addition to that, I'm her boss, and that's really the only fact I need to consider.

"Tell me about yourself, Dominic."

"I'm originally from Denver but moved here several years ago. I'm twenty-nine now and started DPS when I graduated from college. I built it from the ground up myself after majoring in Software Engineering and Computer Science at the University of Colorado. My dad is a computer engineer, so he actually builds them and identifies the best components to go into them, so I have some knowledge of that aspect from just watching him work. My mom is a stay-at-home mom and was always there for my two sisters and me with everything we had going on."

"So, no wife or girlfriend in the picture?" she asks and quickly looks down at her hands.

"No, no wife or girlfriend in the picture," I answer truthfully.

The waitress returns to take our order and we've barely glanced at the menu. I look at her and ask, "Do you know what you want, Sophia?"

She looks up at me with her deer-in-the-headlights look. "Oh, um, no. I'm sorry. I haven't had a chance to look. What do you recommend, Dominic?" She stutters her response and her face flushes with embarrassment.

"Would you like me to order for you?" I ask, tilting my head to the side and narrowing my eyes at her. She suddenly seems very uneasy and unsure of herself.

"If you don't mind. I trust your judgment. The lunch you chose for us was delicious," the relief in her voice is tangible and my curiosity is piqued.

I order the special of the day and another glass of wine for us both. We return to a normal, get-to-know-you type of conversation that flows easily, and I am again reminded how easy our first day working together seemed. There were no awkward moments and no forced niceties or uncomfortable silence. At times, it felt like I was working with a friend I hadn't seen in a while. It felt comfortable but new at the same time.

This makes her uneasiness just now even stranger to me. I decide to dismiss it and continue our friendly dinner without any confrontation. I normally meet any challenge head-on and ask the difficult questions; however, her demeanor tells me she may take it harshly. The waitress returns with our meals and Sophia eyes her meal apprehensively.

"Do you not like Ahi tuna?" I ask, careful to keep my tone carefree since she looks a little scared. "You can order anything you like."

"No, I'm sure this is fine. I've just never had it before but I'd like to try it." I smile reassuringly, "If you don't like it, I really don't mind sending it back and getting whatever you want. Just say the word."

With my fork in hand, I begin to eat and notice, from my peripheral vision, that she's watching me intently before she picks up her fork and begins to eat, mimicking my movements. I freeze midair as an old memory resurfaces, giving me the oddest feeling of déjà vu. The thought is so preposterous that it's not even worth another second of my time.

"So, what do you think?" I ask between bites.

"This is so good! I don't know why I've waited so long to try it!" She begins to consume the rest of

41

her food and makes soft, mewling noises with each new taste. My own food waits as I watch and listen to her for a moment. Shaking my head and smiling to myself, I quickly reclaim my good sense and finish my meal.

"That was delicious, Dominic. Thank you so much for dinner," Sophia says as we wait for the valet to bring my car around.

"You are so welcome, Sophia. I'm pleased you enjoyed it."

The attendant pulls up with my car and I open the passenger door for her. She smiles and slightly bows her head before getting in. At least she doesn't argue over it this time. The GPS is once again guiding me to her address and I start to make small talk with her on the short drive.

"Do you live in an apartment or did you buy a house?" I ask.

"Just a small apartment. It's really not much to look at," she says with a hint of humility.

"As long as it keeps you safe—that's what matters."

My alarm rises when she doesn't respond to that statement. "Sophia, is it not a safe for you to live?"

"I'm not sure. There are some men that hang around outside the building and they make me uncomfortable," she responds, her voice low and fearful.

"Have they tried to approach you?"

"They...they make catcalls and stuff like that toward me. Say things that unnerve me," she answers but keeps her head turned away from me.

I don't like the feeling I'm getting about this place where she lives. My foot presses harder on the gas pedal and the landscape flies by outside. My parents have always been adamant about the ways a man should treat and respect a lady. It's innate to me now to stand up for those who need my help. The thought of *anyone* mistreating Sophia in any way makes my blood boil, but *especially* men who are obviously bigger and stronger and like to abuse their natural power.

When we pull onto her street, I'm instantly on guard and can't believe my eyes. Her apartment is in the worst part of town, amongst the gangs and the drug deals conducted in plain view on the street corners. Her apartment building is run down and covered in graffiti. Garbage and litter is strewn all about, dilapidated cars line the streets, and all eyes are on us. Sophia fidgets nervously in the passenger seat as she looks at the entrance to her

43

building—there are several guys blocking the door, daring her to leave the safety of the car.

"Sophia, you are *not* staying here. Is there anything in your apartment that you need immediately?" my tone is adamant and unyielding.

"Just my clothes and toiletries. There's nothing else of value in there."

"Then we will come back later and pack your things," I say definitively, not giving her an opportunity to say no.

"Dominic, I don't have anywhere else to go. And I need my clothes for work tomorrow," the panic in her voice is rising and the color has drained from her face.

"I'll take care of it, Sophia," I say, determined to keep her from that rat-infested, condemned building and from the men leering at her from the doorway. If their reaction is any indication, they no doubt have vile plans in store for her. That is something I am not willing to leave to chance. Within minutes, we are back on the highway and heading toward the North Dallas area.

Dialing the head of my security team through the Bluetooth in my car, Nick Tucker answers, "Yes, Mr. Powers?"

"Tucker, I have a new employee we need to set up in one of our condominiums. Can you send someone over immediately and have it prepared? She will also need some clothes and toiletries. Have Mrs. Hernandez meet us over there so she can get whatever Miss Vasco needs," I instruct.

"Everything will be ready by the time you get there," Tucker promises

"I also need a team to go to her current apartment and pack all of her belongs. I will send you the address."

"Yes, sir. We will handle it," Tucker responds and we disconnect.

"Dominic," Sophia whispers, "I can't accept all this from you."

"You can and you will. My company owns these condos and we use them for executives who are new to the area. They are very nice and very safe. You can stay there as long as you want. It's one of the perks of being my personal assistant," I respond with a smile.

Sophia rolls her eyes playfully and unsuccessfully tries to hide the smile that's playing on her lips. "Perk or not, I really *do* appreciate your concern and your help, Dominic."

"My pleasure," I reply. "I will send a car to pick you up in the morning, and by the time we are finished tomorrow, you will have your own company vehicle to drive."

She wordlessly gapes at me. The surprise of my statement has apparently rendered her mute. She opens and closes her mouth a couple of times but still makes no sound. Her facial expression and response is so damn cute, I can't help it when my smile overtakes my face and then I laugh heartily.

"Sophia, again, it's a perk of your position. Normally, these things are negotiated at the time the position is offered and the salary is negotiated. I assumed you knew that and didn't require a company vehicle. But, now that I know you *do* need it, I will have it delivered to you."

My words sink in and her demeanor changes. She nods her head and I assume she's assuring herself that it's just a part of the benefits package. Then, she quickly wipes her finger under her eye and turns her face toward the passenger window. The protective nature in me wants to console her, protect her, and reassure her.

The other man inside me is hard to contain at times.

Chapter Four

Tucker is waiting at the condominium complex, as he said he would be. I hired him from the best security firm in the country, Steele Security, out of Miami. He relocated here to Dallas to be my head of security and has been worth his considerable muscled weight in gold. As the head of security, one of his responsibilities is to make sure each condo is secure and ready for the next tenant. He's even stricter on security measures than I am, so I have no doubt that Sophia will be fine here.

"Hello, Mr. Powers," Tucker says as we exit the car. "We have swept the condo and it is secure. Miss Vasco is all set to go up. She's in unit 2220. The kitchen is fully stocked and Ms. Hernandez is waiting inside for her."

Tucker hands Sophia two keys to her unit and gives her the paperwork with the security codes.

"Memorize these and destroy this paper. Your safety will be compromised if anyone else gets these codes, Miss Vasco."

Sophia looks at the information and stutters, "I - I will. Thank you."

"Thank you, Tucker. I will escort Miss Vasco upstairs," I state.

Tucker nods to each of us and walks away toward his full-size truck. Tucker is a big man—taller and much thicker than I am. He has a distinguished military background and is loyal to a fault. I placed him in charge of a team of men that he personally handpicked and they answer directly to him in the event of any issues. I have never had to step in and handle any error on a security measure. Tucker is swift and thorough in all his dealings.

"He's very serious," Sophia whispers when Tucker gets in his truck and is out of earshot.

"He is. He's the best at his job and it's what I pay him to do," I reply. "Ready to see your new place?"

Sophia nods enthusiastically and a beautiful smile splits her face in two. She is truly breathtaking when she gives her all-out, high-wattage smile. Her white teeth gleam in contrast to her tanned skin, her eyes sparkle, and she makes me want to smile in return. "I know I was a little hesitant about this, Dominic, but this place is amazing. I can't thank you enough for this."

My responding smile can't be contained, "Let me show you around, Sophia." Taking her elbow in my hand, I gently steer her toward the front door of the high-rise building. We enter the lobby and I hear a muffled gasp from Sophia. Her hand is covering her mouth, which is gaping open, and her eyes are huge, trying to take in all the luxurious surroundings. It's the stark opposite of the building she is currently vacating.

The lobby of the executive condominium building is very opulent. The walls are covered with English oak panels with fluted marble columns evenly spaced throughout the room. Couches, chairs, coffee tables and two enormous fireplaces also fill the space. A separate room provides a comfortable sitting area for chauffeurs. The armed security guard behind the desk is in plain clothes, and behind the wall is a hidden room where more security personnel monitor the security camera feed from the grounds.

At the elevators, I show her how to enter the security code to gain access to her floor. The elevators are locked from floors twenty and above for our employees' safety. Sophia stands close to me in the elevator and her intoxicating perfume once again permeates every cell in my body. When I eventually identify the scent, I realize I will never again be able to smell *Flowerbomb* without thinking of her.

Finally on the twenty-second floor, she excitedly looks around the vestibule. The condos are large so there are only a few doors on each floor. Just outside the elevator doors on each floor is a round table with an elaborate flower arrangement in the center. There are various types of houseplants, paintings, wall sconces, and a mixture of other elegant decorations to give each floor a more regal touch.

When she finally works up the nerve to open the door to her new place, she takes a couple of steps inside and stops cold. Watching her with amusement and admiration, I can't help but feel a little satisfaction at giving her such happiness. She suddenly bolts into action, darting from room to room to take in everything about her new home.

A sudden, high-pitched squeal from the master bedroom sends me into action. I race toward her, ready and willing to defend her and fight off whoever has joined us uninvited. When I reach her, she's standing frozen-still in front of the walk-in closet. Her hand is still on the doorknob and I quickly push her behind me to shield her from whatever is inside. When I get a full, unobstructed view, I realize there is no one and nothing inside the closet.

I turn quickly and look her in the eyes. "What's wrong, Sophia? What happened?"

"The closet...it's *huge!*" she exclaims, her voice infused with sincerity and amazement at once.

After a second or two of allowing my pulse to return to normal, I find myself once again laughing. She is so amusing and easy to please. I hang my head, my hand still on the doorknob and my shoulders shake from intense laughter. "Well, I'm pleased that you appreciate your new closet," I finally manage to say while shaking my head.

When I look up at her, she's beaming—her face is glowing and she's smiling from ear to ear. Her eyes sparkle with happiness and appreciation. Once again, I feel fortunate to be the person who could bring her such pleasure with something so simple.

Mrs. Hernandez, my household manager, joins us in the bedroom. "Hello, Miss Sophia. My name is Christine and I understand you need some help getting clothes and other toiletries," she smiles warmly at Sophia.

Sophia looks questioningly at me, as if she's waiting for me to answer Mrs. Hernandez for her.

The many contradictions I have seen and felt with Sophia over the past twelve hours are mind-boggling, but I can't help but be drawn more and more into her with each revelation. This woman is hard and soft, strong and weak, happy and sad, a mystery and an open book. I give Sophia a single nod and she answers Mrs. Hernandez.

"Yes, I'm afraid I do. What do you have in mind?" she asks somewhat timidly.

"All you need to do is give me your sizes and your preferences. I will take care of the rest for you," Mrs. Hernandez reassures her.

"If you're sure," Sophia responds, but her eyes catch mine and I know she is also asking me.

"Mrs. Hernandez *lives* to spend money, Sophia. She doesn't mind at all," I respond and give Mrs. Hernandez a playful wink.

Mrs. Hernandez takes Sophia into the kitchen and expediently makes a list of the necessary items. I continue my slow perusal of the condo, telling myself that I'm double-checking after Tucker but deep down I know better than that. I'm stalling and waiting to be alone with Sophia again for some reason. The masochist in me wants to be tortured by something I know I can't have.

I rejoin them just as Mrs. Hernandez is leaving the condo. Sophia is still gushing at her, convinced she is being a burden and that Mrs. Hernandez has better things to do.

"Christine, I really appreciate this. Thank you so much for your help. Are you sure you don't want me to go with you?" Sophia asks, but I'm sure it's not the first time.

"No, dear. You've had a long first day. Just relax and your clothes will soon be delivered," Mrs. Hernandez assures her before she turns to leave.

Sophia gestures toward the kitchen, "Tucker was right—the kitchen is *more* than fully stocked. Do you want some coffee?"

"I should probably get going and leave you to get acquainted with your new place," I tell her as I casually glance around. When my eyes land back on hers, I see some apprehension in them.

"Don't you need to be here when Christine gets back?" she asks.

"She won't be back. She will pick them out and a courier will deliver them to the guards downstairs. They will call first and then bring them up here for you."

"Oh, well, okay then. Thank you so much for everything, Dominic. Really—I don't know what else to say," Sophia tells me, the glistening from unshed tears of gratitude in her eyes.

"It is truly my pleasure, Sophia. There is really no need to thank me. You are welcome to stay here as long as you need or want," I reiterate. She sees me to the door, and despite the security in place, I still encourage her to thoroughly lock up and double check if anyone knocks on the door.

An hour later, I'm at my house having a nightcap when my phone rings. A quick glance at the screen tells me Sophia's calling. I answer it on the second ring, "Sophia? Are you alright?"

"Yes, Dominic, I'm fine. I'm sorry to call you so late, but the courier just dropped off enough clothes and shoes to fill up the huge walk-in closet in my bedroom! I'm afraid there must be some mistake and I wanted to alert you as soon as possible," she says, talking as fast as she can to convey her entire message to me.

"There is no error, Sophia. Those are all your things now. Take them, enjoy them, and wear them to work," I assure her, knowing she can hear my smile through the phone.

"No one has ever done anything like this for me, Dominic. This is beyond a perk of being your employee," she replies, her voice taking on a low, sensual quality.

"I *told* you Mrs. Hernandez lives to spend money, Sophia. She's just giving you a wide variety to choose from before work in the morning," I jest, trying to lighten the mood and turn the conversation from the direction it's headed.

She takes a deep breath and releases it with a mixture of a soft, sweet sigh and hum that shoots directly to my groin and causes an immediate discomfort. This attraction is undeniable, from both sides, but the thoughts she invokes in me are from a different time. Those thoughts are from a different lifestyle that I no longer live in. The mental pictures are exquisite and I can feel the desire to return to that way of life increasing, beckoning me and pulling me into its claws.

"Okay, Dominic, if you say so. I've said *'thank you'* so many times in the last eighteen hours but it just seems so lacking. I can't tell you how much I appreciate all you've done for me. In the short time I've known you, you've done more for me than anyone else has my entire life," Sophia says and her voice cracks on her final words.

"Get some rest and enjoy your new place tonight, Sophia. I will see you in the morning," I respond softly, purposely not responding to her declaration.

"I will. Goodnight, Dominic."

"Goodnight," I say before disconnecting.

I know what I'm doing next. I am heading straight for a cold shower and then to bed. Alone. *This fucking sucks.* After my shower, I crawl into my king-size bed and allow my thoughts to go where they want. Immediately, my mind settles on Sophia and the long day I spent with her. How is it she is affecting me so much all of a sudden? Over the past few years, I couldn't count the number of beautiful women who have thrown themselves at me. I've been told enough how handsome I am, what a great catch I'd be, and what a wonderful husband I would make.

I know I'm above average height. My muscular build coupled with my stylishly messed hair, piercing blue eyes, and eternal five o'clock shadow has turned more than a few heads of all types of ladies, from the very bold and brazen to the shy and reserved. That used to be a great turn-on and ego boost for me, but not anymore.

One year, four months. Sixteen months. Sixty-four weeks. Four hundred forty eight days, give or take a day. That's how long my current self-imposed dry spell has lasted. For the first time in all that time, I am considering breaking that dry spell for a very lovely, very sexy, and *very* seductive Sophia Vasco. These are my last thoughts as I drift off to sleep.

At 4:44 a.m., I wake with a start and sit straight up in the bed. My heart is pounding in my chest and the blood is as loud as a freight train in my ears. My pulse is racing out of control. Instinctively, my hand covers my heart and somehow my brain registers that my skin is clammy and sweaty. *Fucking nightmare!* It was all so damn real—I could see, feel, smell, and hear it all. Every last detail of it mirrored the memories I have worked so hard to forget for the past year. The events of the past that came closer to breaking me than anything else in my life.

Except, this time, Sophia was the one in my nightmare.

What the hell is happening?

I'm back at the office early this morning to review more aspects of the confidential contract before Sophia arrives for work. I couldn't go back to sleep after my early morning mind-fuck, so I dressed and decided to do something productive to get those images out of my mind. The contract is somewhat helping to take my mind off of the nightmare, but not nearly enough.

After reading and rereading the same paragraph three times, I put the contract away and start preparing for Sophia's training today. There is still so much to do to get her ready to fill in for me when needed. The company lawyers are coming by today to discuss some of the legal ramifications she has to consider. They've already properly chastised my ass for hiring her before contacting them and it's been duly noted. One more thing to add to the list of ways she's knocked me off my game. My only defense is this is an at-will employment state, so there are no real 'contracts' when it comes to employment.

Today, Sophia will meet with all the department heads and the CFO to start understanding their roles. Once she feels comfortable with their key responsibilities, I will have her start attending my meetings and conference calls. After this rigorous training program that will put her through the ropes and test her stamina, she will be ready to assume more responsibility.

I, however, will be ready to combust.

I hear her voice outside my office door and have to admit I'm ready to see her again. The triple cadence rap on the door brings a smile to my face.

I lean back in my leather office chair as I call out, "Come in."

Dana opens the door and Sophia sweeps in. Mrs. Hernandez has outdone herself in her recent shopping excursion. Sophia looks absolutely stunning in a fitted navy dress and off-white belt-sash with matching shoes and purse. I pause to give her an appreciative once-over. Her beauty completely steals my breath away.

"Good morning, Dominic," Sophia says with a sweet smile. "You're here early again."

I respond with a noncommittal shrug of my shoulders. "It's a dirty job, but someone has to do it," I joke. Dana brings us both coffee and we ready ourselves to begin another full day. I explain my plan to Sophia and she's very eager to get started. After taking her down the hall to Darren Hardy's office, I resume reviewing the contract.

My office phone rings and I automatically recognize the number on the caller ID. It's Rich Daltry, one of our major potential customers and the owner of a large video game corporation. His company is very influential and important to my company. He has previously informed me that he wants me to attend an in-person meeting at his headquarters in San Diego. I have a sneaking suspicion that's why he's calling now.

"Dominic Powers," I answer.

"Dominic. Rich Daltry here. We are ready to move forward with the contract negotiations. Can you come out to San Diego in two weeks?" Rich takes control of the conversation without so much as saying 'hello,' first.

"Hi, Rich. Good to hear from you. Let me check my schedule and see if we can make that work," I reply calmly. A few clicks on my computer later, I'm looking at a jam-packed calendar for the next two weeks, especially considering I'm still training Sophia. "I can make it in three weeks, Rich. Will that work for you?"

"Yes, yes, that's fine. The sooner you can get here, the better, Dominic," Rich replies. We each transfer the call to our secretaries to make the arrangements and get the details sorted. I also tell Dana to include Sophia in the travel plans before I hang up the phone.

A business trip with Sophia is both exhilarating and concerning. On one hand, I will have time alone with her. On the other hand, I will have time alone with her. I will have to endure it regardless of what happens.

Chapter Five

The past three weeks have flown by so quickly it makes my head spin. In this short time, Sophia and I have built an easy, cohesive working relationship. She has picked up even the minutest details of the job and has proven her worth time and time again. After her meetings with each of the department heads and the CFO, she helped revamp workflows, increasing productivity and employee morale effortlessly. Everyone here loves her and loves working with her.

Our personal relationship has been changing, evolving, and becoming more complex. There have been conversations about inane topics that felt like so much more was actually being said. Last week, I met with her to review her performance over her two-week training period. Our conversation took an odd turn as we were discussing business but there was a hint of something more just under the surface.

"Sophia, I must say that I am very pleased with your performance. You have exceeded my expectations," I complimented her.

"Thank you, sir. I have worked very hard to make sure I did the best I could do to please you," she replied sincerely while keeping her eyes somewhat downcast.

"You have done that, most definitely. I've also received praise from several other department heads for your contributions and suggestions."

"That is very good news, indeed. Is there anything more I can do for you?"

"Just keep up the great work, Sophia, exactly as you've been doing. Keep learning and rising to the occasion."

She nodded in agreement and kept her eyes slightly downcast, intentionally avoiding meeting my gaze directly. "I am only here to please you," she replied, her voice low and unsure.

I was speechless at her revelation. It stunned me in many different ways. If another employee had said something similar, I would've quickly dismissed it as insecurity in a new position and making sure the boss's expectations were met. But with Sophia, there is always something more to what's actually being said. It's in the double entendre words and the way she phrases them.

It also conjures more images of her that I really don't need to have. Images of her naked, kneeling and submissive in front of me, and eagerly waiting for me to vocalize my desires dominate my thoughts. At the time she said she was here to please me, I was in a completely different frame of mind—and anything job related was the furthest from my mind.

The last three weeks have slowly worked on changing my resolve. Sophia's eagerness to please, deference to my wishes, and obvious admiration of me have stirred feelings I thought were long dead. Her natural personality and actions bring out the man in me that I used to be. She makes me want to show the real man underneath the normal, CEO façade—the man that deep down I know I was born to be.

Today, knowing that we are preparing for our trip to San Diego, I feel more anticipation than ever. She has made it clear that she wants more from me than a working relationship without actually saying the words. The sly looks, the intentional touches, and the *accidental* body brushes all point to one thing. She's trying to tell me she's interested without being overly forward. Mrs. Hernandez outdid herself with Sophia's clothes because every outfit she's worn has been subtly provocative, and Sophia seems to be taking full advantage of that.

I suppose it could be me, just being impatient and ready to move on. My dry spell coupled with all the time I've spent with her has been hell on earth. We've worked late together a couple of nights in the past week. At first, I considered having her come to my house to work, where it would be more comfortable and we could have a working dinner. I changed my mind after I almost claimed her soft, plump lips as my own when she bent too close to me while we were reviewing a contract.

But this morning, we fly from Dallas-Fort Worth to San Diego and we will be there for four days and three nights while we hammer out the details and negotiate with *D-Force Games*, Rich's company. He insisted that we also tour the facility, get to know the employees, and spend time with their executives to understand their vision and mission. I would normally politely decline such a demand, but, like me, Rich isn't one to take no for an answer. Plus, his company is vitally important to the future growth and expansion of my company. So, I will indulge him this once and even I have to admit that it's primarily because Sophia will be with me.

Tucker picks me up first and we drive to Sophia's apartment to pick her up on the way to the airport. She gives me a sly smile as she climbs into the backseat with me. Her beauty still takes my breath at times, just feeling the warmth radiate from her smile.

"Good morning, Dominic," she purrs.

"Good morning, Sophia," I reply. "Are you ready for our short business trip?"

"I'm looking forward to it. I hope to learn a lot from you and hopefully come to a mutually beneficial agreement," she says, but I feel an underlying tone to her words.

We arrive at the private airstrip between Dallas and Fort Worth and Tucker stops at the steps leading up to the private jet. Sophia looks around, anxious and excited, her eyes wide and more expressive than usual. She is obviously unaccustomed to this type of travel and is enthralled with every detail of it. I give her a reassuring smile, understanding what she must be feeling, and allow her a moment to take it all in.

"This is an incredible jet, Dominic," she earnestly pays a compliment.

"Wait until you see inside," I reply with a mischievous grin. "There's a bedroom, a fully stocked bar, ultra-plush leather captain's chairs and two full-size leather couches." I intentionally keep my voice sensual, seductive, and suggestive, emphasizing certain assets of the plane and allowing her imagination to take over her thoughts. I know she immediately picks up on my innuendos when she smiles shyly and averts her eyes. I'm intrigued when she doesn't blush with embarrassment this time.

Fuck, this week is going to be harder than I originally thought. The visions of an eager and willing Sophia invade my thoughts. We will be away from any other prying eyes and office gossip. Even though it's a working trip, we could very well make it a mini-vacation, of sorts. This is in complete contradiction to how I normally behave. Business is business—no mixing pleasure. No considering anything other than a platonic, business relationship with my employees.

But this lady...Sophia Vasco...is different from any other woman I've met. This isn't a stupid, fucking cliché. This isn't an adolescent infatuation that I just need to work out of my system with a quick romp between the sheets. The man inside me, the one I've hidden from existence for the last sixteen months, *senses* her, *feels* her, and wants to *own* her. She walks up the jet stairs ahead of me and the rhythmic sway of her hips has me entranced.

She abruptly stops on the step above mine, turning to face me, and I find myself face to face with her, barely avoiding a collision. My hands reach out automatically to steady her, holding her hips in a way that is usually reserved for more intimate settings. Our lips are so close that the slightest movement from either of us will result in a kiss. Sophia sharply inhales a ragged breath but her eyes never stray from mine.

Her brown eyes darken with desire and her tongue flicks out, wetting her lips and silently inviting me to lean in just a little closer. My jaw is clenched so tightly that it hurts, but that's not where my mind is focused at the moment. My thoughts run away with me as I consider the possible outcomes of my actions if I act on it. Mike Smyth, the pilot, saves us both as he interrupts the moment from just inside the cockpit.

"Susan, can you make sure they've restocked the bar in the back? I think there were some bottles running low on our last flight," Mike calls out to the flight attendant. I drop my hands from her sides just before he steps into the galley. Seeing us on the landing, he is obviously surprised and unaware of the internal conflict brewing, "Oh, hello, Mr. Powers. You're all set to board. We're just making some last minute *libation* checks," he says with a smile.

"Thanks, Mike. Appreciate it. We'll go ahead and take our seats," I reply, regaining some semblance of decorum. Throughout the entire exchange, Sophia keeps her eyes trained on me. Clearing my throat as a subtle warning, I steel my resolve and extend my hand toward the door of the plane. "Time to board, Sophia."

The disappointment in her eyes is unmistakable. The moment of temporary insanity has passed and I'm more convinced now that I need to keep my distance from her and reexamine why these feelings, thoughts, and nightmares are resurfacing after all this time. I really just need to be alone, take a breather, and consider all the aspects of this clusterfuck, but that won't happen for the next four days while we're on this trip.

Shit.

Sophia takes her seat in one of the plush-leather captain's chairs. I sit across from her and immediately regret my decision to not sit beside her. When she crosses her legs, her skirt rides up higher on her thighs, exposing more of her smooth, silky skin. My eyes are glued to her legs, and as she shifts in her chair, her skirt moves ever so slightly higher. At this pace, her lacey panties will soon be showing. Should that happen, I will be compelled to throw her over my shoulder and carry her to the waiting bed in the back of the plane.

When I finally tear my eyes from the part of her body I would really love to lose myself in, I see her eyes are beyond heated. Her breaths have increased to the point of nearly panting, and without a doubt, I am in deep shit. There's no way this attraction will fizzle out. These feelings will not just go away. These thoughts won't just stop. This itch must be scratched in the most sensual, intimate, and carnal ways possible.

Fuck me.

All of the pre-flight checks have been completed and the flight attendant has recited the required safety standards. After a smooth takeoff, we reach cruising altitude, and after getting our drinks and a light snack tray, I excuse the flight attendant from her duties for a while. Having changed seats, I am now beside Sophia instead of across from her. I pull out the small table that's tucked away between our chairs and we share the food. The flight only takes about three hours from wheels up to wheels down, but it's three hours of having Sophia all to myself that both concerns and excites me.

We settle into a comfortable companionship, enjoying the food and the pitcher of mimosas the flight attendant left with us. I don't know if it was the extra glass of mimosa she had or how we just seemed to click all of a sudden, but Sophia seems so much more relaxed with me. As she starts opening up to me, I begin to see a whole new side of her.

"So, tell me about your brother, Sophia."

Her smile conveys her love for him. The look on her face tells me that she misses him more than her words can tell, but there's a deep sadness in her eyes that she tries very hard to hide. I wonder if she's trying to hide it from me—or from herself. She takes another sip of her mimosa before she answers me.

"His name is Shawn, and like I said, he's four years younger. He's the best." Then she adds, almost absently, "I miss him so much."

"Why haven't you seen him?" I inquire, intrigued and confused. If she's so close to him, and loves him so much, why wouldn't she still see him now?

Her eyes fly up to meet mine and the color briefly drains from her face. Her mouth is gaping open and her eyes are wide, like a deer caught in the headlights and physically unable to move out of

70

the way of danger. She quickly recovers and drops her eyes to her glass, her finger tracing the rim as she speaks softly.

"I haven't seen him in quite a while. My...uh...my parents and my brother both vehemently disagreed with some choices I've made in my life. They have effectively disowned me. To be honest, my parents and I never really saw eye to eye. I spent my whole life fighting with them, but my brother held my heart. When I lost him, I really felt it. It really hurt," she continues, speaking to her champagne flute.

"I'm really sorry to hear that, Sophia. That must be really hard on you, being in a different city with no family support," I offer understanding, although I really want to ask about those choices she's made that ended with her being disowned. Even with her revelation, or maybe because of it, it just seems inappropriate to ask for details just yet. "Perhaps enough time has passed for you to try to speak to them again. Help them understand where you're coming from and why you've made the decisions you have. Distance helps give a new perspective on things." Being a man, I instinctively want to offer advice to fix things as quickly as possible.

The gloomy smile she offers me says it all— she's tried and she's been shot down, pushed away, and told to never return. It happens all too often in families—more than most people realize—but I wait and let her tell me the story and withhold my own thoughts for the time being.

She slowly shakes her head from side to side, "No. I can never go back there. I've come to terms with that and it's been damn near impossible." The back of her hand whisks a tear away, and before I can move, more quickly take its place.

Rising quickly, I kneel in front of her and pull her into my arms. She tries to hold her tears back, but they keep coming, and soon the sobs are wracking her small body. I pull her closer, willing my strength to flow into her and help her through this pain. It suddenly occurs to me that this is most definitely inappropriate contact, but then her arms wrap around my neck and she plasters herself to me. I bury my face in her hair and whisper soothing words repeatedly while gently stroking her hair.

Her sobs subside but she doesn't let go of me, or I of her. We stay connected, on more levels than one, for several minutes before I feel her slightly loosen her hold. She doesn't let go completely—leaving her arms around my neck—but she pulls her face back to look directly at me. Her pain and insecurity shine in her eyes, begging me to accept her and not shun her as her family did. I know these signs—I've seen them too many times before.

I search her eyes and her face for a cue from her, a sign of what she wants next. Her soft lips touch mine, and at first, she gives me a sweet, chaste kiss. Then, she increases the pressure and slightly parts her lips. When her tongue lightly rakes across the part in my lips, asking for permission to enter, I can't stifle my approving groan. Her tongue slides into my mouth and glides across my own. Her taste is intoxicating, and before I know it, my hands are threaded in her hair, tilting her head, and deepening the kiss.

As I take control of the scene, I feel her body willingly submit to me. She becomes pliant under my touch and molds to fit me, giving herself over to my will. The old feelings buried deep within me stir and I hear the man locked up inside me prodding me to claim her, own her, and make her say she's mine. He's always there, just under the surface of my calm demeanor, waiting to come out and take over. I've held him back for sixteen long months— but if I continue this, he will definitely reappear. She brings him out in me more than anyone else I've ever met before. He will want to make her all *his*.

When she moans softly into my mouth, electricity shoots through me, and every nerve in my body is on high alert. Every strand of her hair floating across my fingers excites me even more. My fingers close on her hair, pulling it into my fists, she melts under the slight pain of my pull. Using my body, I ease her back in her chair and my upper body covers her. Every feeling is unique and exquisite—almost like it's the first time I've felt it. Her breasts press against my chest, and for a split second, I consider removing my hands from her hair.

It's this thought that brings me back to Earth. Actually, I'm crashing back to this airplane that's cruising at about thirty thousand feet. This is crazy—she's my assistant, my employee, and she's distraught. This is not the right time to act on inappropriate feelings and thoughts. Releasing my hold on her hair, I deliberately slow the pace before ending the impromptu make-out session. When I pull back, I see the most beautiful sight.

Sophia's face is flushed, her lips are swollen and red from our kiss, her hair is slightly messy—but just enough to be sexy—and pure, unfiltered desire is uncontained in her eyes. My knuckles lightly stroke her cheek and I watch her reaction as she realizes what just happened. I have a feeling I will have to calm her and reassure her, although I'm not sure how because I feel anything but calm and reassured myself.

Chapter Six

Sophia is in somewhat of a daze and I watch with fascination as realization dawns on her. The emotions playing across her face betray her private thoughts—lust, confusion, comprehension and finally, humiliation. She bows her head and avoids my eyes, her face turning a deep shade of crimson red, and I am convinced she is about to start crying again.

"Hey," I say softly, "It's okay. Really."

She shakes her head and replies, "No, no, I was completely out of line. If you fire me now, I completely understand."

"Sophia," I can't avoid the slight admonishment in my tone, "I'm not going to fire you. In case you didn't notice, I was a willing participant. *I* should be the one apologizing to *you*."

I sigh heavily and continue with the part I don't really want to say but I know I should. "If you feel uncomfortable working with me now, I can transfer you to another area to report to someone else. I don't want you to feel pressured or awkward at work now."

Sophia's deep brown eyes finally rise to meet mine head-on. She stutters for a second before getting her words out. "I - I don't want that! Dominic, don't you know? I love working with you, learning from you, and just being with you. What happened just now-," her voice trails off, her brows furrow, and she looks down at her fidgeting hands.

"You regret it? It's fine, Sophia. You can say it."

"Regret it? No! I've *wanted* to do that for so long now," Sophia says emphatically as her eyes search mine for affirmation. "I just can't believe I really did that. That just isn't like me at all, being the aggressor. It's embarrassing," she says as she first lowers her eyes then her head.

Gently grabbing her chin, I lift her face as I say, "Sophia, you shouldn't be embarrassed. If I hadn't wanted it to happen, it wouldn't have. Now, we have to focus on where we go from here."

"Where do you want to go?" she whispers to me.

"That's up to you. I am obviously attracted to you, but I'm also your employer. This is uncharted territory for me, but I'd rather you make the decision for what's best for *you*," I purposely answer cryptically.

"Really? You care about what's best for *me*?"

Now my brows are furrowed and I narrow my eyes at her, "Of course. Why wouldn't I want what's best for you?"

"I just don't think anyone ever has considered that before," she says absently, momentarily deep in thought somewhere else. "I'd like to see where this goes. I already know I like spending time with you. I'd like it to be more."

"Sophia, there are things you need to know about me, beyond how I am during our working relationship," I know I'm not telling her everything just yet, but there some things that are ingrained in me now.

"Okay," she says apprehensively.

"One, I only want committed, monogamous relationships. I don't share and it won't end well for anyone involved if that were to happen," I purposely wait, because this is a deal-breaker for me. I realize it's a shocker for most women—that a man would willingly choose a monogamous relationship instead of playing the field.

77

"I won't have to share you?" she asks incredulously, and I narrow my eyes at her choice of words.

"No, no sharing either way. I won't share you with another man and there will be no other women for me. If you aren't onboard with that, there's no point in continuing this conversation," I say decidedly.

She blinks her eyes in shock before agreeing. "Yes, I'm onboard with that. I just wasn't expecting that. Most men want to be a free agent, especially in a new relationship."

"I know they do, but I don't. I have certain expectations and there's no way they would be met if we're not equally committed."

"What expectations?" she asks, now narrowing her eyes at me, tilting her head to the side and watching me carefully.

I can't help but smile at the look on her beautiful face. Her brown eyes are so expressive and she definitely doesn't have a poker face. Just when she thinks she has me figured out, I throw her a curve ball and she has to rethink her position. "Sophia, my parents always taught me to take care of women. Not that they're weaker and can't take care of themselves, but that it's a man's responsibility to love, cherish, and protect the

woman he cares about. I take that very seriously—
it's deeply ingrained in me now. If you can't believe
in me and trust me to do what I think is best for you
and for us, we won't work."

"Are you saying you get to make all the
decisions for me?" I instantly recognize that there
is no judgment in her tone of voice. She is simply
asking for clarification.

"Yes and no. There are obviously times you
will have to make decisions without me, but I would
expect that you would make the choice that you
know I would approve of. If you go against me, it
goes against my ability to protect and care for you."

Sophia pulls her bottom lip between her teeth,
her eyes taking on a distant look, and I know she's
deep in thought. Her apprehensiveness and body
gestures are giving away her feelings. She's
conflicted—on one hand, she wants to question
me, but on the other hand, she isn't sure if she
should.

"What if I mess up?" she asks and immediately
casts her eyes downward. Seeing her muscles
tense up, I know she is more than nervous—she's
scared. Her body is cringing at whatever thoughts
are flying through her mind and my mind conjures
images of someone abusing her.

"We will talk about it, Sophia," I respond and wait for her to look at me again.

"Are you a Dom? Would I be your submissive?"

Her question shocks the hell out of me. I was *not* expecting her to ask that of me at all. I'm not ready to share this part of my life with her. Am I a Dom? Yes, but I haven't taken a sub in the last sixteen months for a reason and I honestly wasn't thinking about making her my sub.

"Why do you ask that, Sophia?"

"Just your mannerisms—the way you phrase things, the way you take control. You just remind me of a Dom. Then, when you said you would make the decisions for me, I was pretty sure of it," she searches my face and eyes as she answers and then holds her breath as she waits for me to answer and I notice a slight cringe—that fear again.

"You've been trained as a sub?" I ask, but I already know the answer. Now it's my turn to hold my breath as I wait for her answer.

Ever so slightly, she nods her head in affirmation. I exhale and feel my shoulders slump. This definitely changes the dynamics of our newly budding relationship, if that's where we're actually headed. If she has already been trained as a sub, she will expect the Dom in me to take charge, to

80

take complete responsibility, and to treat her as a sub. It's not that the Dom in me has disappeared— he will always be there. He is me, I am he, and I can never be separated from that mindset. I've managed to keep him locked away and I had no intentions of allowing him back out to play. My self-control has held the desires and natural tendencies at bay for the most part.

"That's what you feel you need to be fulfilled? A Dom?" I ask her, mainly to test her submissive mentality. I'm fairly certain I already know the answer to that question.

"I don't really know any other way, Dominic," she answers, her voice low and unsure. She's waiting for a cue from me on how she should react. The submissive in her wants to please me and needs confirmation that her answer is what I want to hear.

So many things become clear to me now. The instant attraction I had to her—the Dom in me sensed her, felt her, and wanted to make her belong to him. This is the reason behind the reoccurrence of the dreams—nightmares—I've had since I met her. It's also why she avoids eye contact with me at times and why she responds differently to the other men on my staff. She doesn't see them as a Dom, so she doesn't treat them with the same reverence.

"That really wasn't an answer to my question, Sophia. Is that type of relationship the only way you can be happy?" Keeping my facial features neutral, I insist she answers me truthfully with what *she* wants and needs rather than only thinking of what *I* want. The two men inside me are warring against each other and my own desires are unclear. The devil on one shoulder urges me to take her, make her mine, and bend her to my will like a true Dom. I am not allowing her to make the decision regarding which course we take. I simply need to consider all the factors and ramifications of my decision.

"What do you have in mind?" she asks.

Clever girl.

I give her my domineering look and she visibly shrinks back in her chair. My eyebrow is arched and my eyes are piercing hers, waiting for a satisfactory answer. Funny how quickly the little gestures just come back to me without even consciously thinking about them. Sophia feels it, too—her back straightens, her hands are clasped in her lap, and her eyes do not meet mine. Like the alpha male in a pack of animals, the others avoid direct eye contact unless they are intentionally challenging him.

"I would prefer it. It's what I'm used to and it's how I know how to be," she finally responds truthfully.

I reclaim my seat beside her and consider the phrasing of my words before I respond. "I admit I wasn't completely expecting to hear this from you, Sophia, but it's also not something I haven't already considered. If I decide we are taking this route, there are guidelines you will have to agree to meet," I state matter-of-factly.

"Like a contract?"

I nod my head, but a thought occurs to me and I quickly amend my original intention. "I've used contracts in the past, Sophia, but I want to try something different with you. We are consenting adults and we can agree on the terms. We can each state our hard and soft limits and just respect them. We don't need a contract to do that.

"Besides, I don't want our relationship to be about a contract. This has been on my mind for a while now. My position on it has changed considerably. In my experience, too many people get hung up on the fact that a contract is even there. It becomes the primary focus when all I want to focus on is getting to know you in every way and earning your trust."

Sophia gapes at me in stunned silence. She tries to speak but can't find her voice. Tears fill her eyes and she swallows hard, trying to push the overwhelming feelings back down into her chest. She's trying to hide them so she can just go along with what she thinks I want. Little does she know now, she has so much to learn about me.

"What about the punishment part?" she asks meekly for the second time during this short conversation. That alone speaks volumes to me. The quiver in her voice tells me this is a sensitive area she wants to know about but she's been afraid to ask. Rather, she's been afraid of the answer.

"Sophia, I'm a little concerned about your past training. You seem to have the wrong idea of punishment in your head and we need to fix that. My expectations will be clear—and you will have to be clear on yours. We can compromise and come to an agreement. I won't do anything that you don't agree to. If you say no, that's the final word.

"But know this, I can read your body, even now, and I know what you're thinking before you do. When you're simply afraid of the unknown, I will push you past your limits if I'm certain it will bring you pleasure. I'm not into causing you pain just for the sake of pain, though. In fact, I am certain you will *want* the kind of pain I can offer," I explain, hoping she understands the difference. I want to get in her mind and find out where she's been, where she's at, and where I can take her next.

"You won't make me do things I don't want to do?" she asks for reassurance.

I shake my head, "Never. If you have to safeword on me, it means I'm not doing my job in taking care of you. I've already told you that I take that job very seriously. I enjoy doing it—taking care of you, giving you pleasure. Taking you to new heights gives me pleasure. I just need you to trust me, but I will *earn* it from you."

She is so visibly relieved at my answer, it makes me furious inside to think about some other man taking such obvious advantage of her. The light in her face is back, her smile is warm and inviting, and the muscles in her body are relaxed. Her hands are no longer clenched together, and while she still has great posture, her shoulders aren't nearly as tense as they were just minutes ago.

"I love the sound of that, Dominic. While we have some time alone, can you start telling me what *you* need? Should I call you Sir?"

I control the intensity of my voice. I do *not* want to be called *Sir* under any circumstance in a relationship. I can barely stand it when people outside of my circle call me that, but definitely not Sophia. "No," I state simply, not feeling the need to provide any explanation.

Her brow furrows as she considers other titles. "Daddy?" she asks tentatively, her face twisted as if she's just bitten into a lemon. I withhold my belly laugh—I don't want to her to be offended or feel foolish for asking.

"No, not that one, either. Just call me Dom. Even if we're in public, no one will question it since it's a shortened version of my name. No one else is allowed to call me that, by the way, so it's really a term of endearment for you to do so," I explain with a smile. Taking her hand and gently brushing my lips across her hand, I place a kiss each of her knuckles. She melts under my touch, becoming more pliable and open to me.

"What will my pet name be? What will you call me?" she asks on bated breath.

"The name I give you will have meaning and won't be just a generic nickname. It may take a little time for me to decide on it, but it'll be yours and yours alone," I tell her and she readily accepts it.

"That is one of the most romantic things I've ever heard."

I shake my head in disbelief. "Sweetheart, you haven't heard anything yet. We are just getting started."

My Angel just pops into my head without warning. It has a certain ring to it. I may have to try it out on her soon and see how she reacts. The name is important because it's a symbol of the trust, the intimacy, and the promise we've made. It shows she is mine and I am hers. I want more than just a submissive that is at my beck and call, though. My pleasure comes from giving her pleasure, from her willingly submitting to me even when she's unsure, and from her giving me her complete and total trust.

I'm entering this lifestyle again. It's not that I'm becoming a Dom again. No man *becomes* a Dom—he either is one naturally or he's not one at all—but I'm living the lifestyle again for her. I'm taking a chance I never thought I'd take again–for her. She has an air of delicateness and innocence about her that makes me want to shelter and protect her. Even though she's been somewhat trained as a sub before, she doesn't have the slightest presence of any sub I've met before. She's very intriguing, mysterious, and different.

I am so ready to get to know *My Angel* much more intimately now.

"I'd like to get to know you now, Sophia. First, the question I'm not supposed to ask. How old are you?" I ask with a mischievous smile. Yes, I do know her age because it's in her personnel file, but this is in a different context and I want her to share herself with me in every way.

"I'm twenty-three years old. You've already told me you're twenty-nine. So, is it my turn to ask you a question?" she asks with an equally mischievous smile.

"Sure, you can ask anything you want," I answer truthfully. However, that doesn't mean she will get an answer I'm not ready to give her.

"How long have you been a Dom?" she asks innocently.

"All my life." She doesn't look pleased with my answer and I smile, "My turn again."

She nods, "Okay."

"How long have you been a sub?"

"About a year," she reveals and immediately drops her eyes to her lap.

My voice deepens, threateningly and menacingly, to convey my displeasure, "Keeping secrets and lying are part of my hard limits, Sophia. Not just in the bedroom but in every aspect of my life and business. There is *no room* for negotiation in this."

"I'm telling you the truth, Dom," she says emphatically. Her eyes fly up to meet mine and they are open wide, hiding nothing from me. Her arms are at her sides, conveying she is being open with me. Her use of my new nickname does not go unnoticed by me. It just rolled right off her tongue, right out of her mouth, as if she's been mine for years.

"Why did you look away when I asked that question?"

She inhales deeply and looks down again. Rising from my seat, I kneel in front of her again. Using my thumb and index finger, I gently lift her face to look at me. Placing my hands on either side of her face, her small stature is immediately obvious, and a dark thought forms in the back of my mind. I speak gently but clearly to emphasize my point. Any mention of her former Sir upsets her and I have a growing concern that I know exactly why that is.

"I don't know about your former life, but with me, I prefer for you to look me in the eye. We can talk about anything at all—just don't hide from me," I gently explain. A tear escapes her eye and I catch it with the pad of my thumb. "I won't intentionally give you any cause for tears of pain, Sophia. You can trust me, you'll see."

Sophia's tiny hands fly up and encircle mine, even though they are still tenderly holding her face. Her tears increase and I take a moment to examine her fully. There is real anguish in her eyes and she is no longer able to hold it in. We haven't even begun to discuss her former life—how she was trained and what she expects—and she is already reacting emotionally toward me.

"Talk to me, *My Angel*," I whisper to her, my face close to hers as I use my proximity to reassure her, shield her, and protect her. The tears are still slowing, but she slightly cocks her head to the side and furrows her brow. Her eyes dart back and forth between mine for a few seconds before I see the light bulb click on inside her.

"My pet name?" she whispers back.

"Yes, love. You are *My Angel,* if you want to be."

"I do want to be," she replies as she grips my hands tighter.

"You don't know the stipulations yet," I remind her.

"You said you won't hurt me, that I can trust you to not push me too far, right?" Her voice is still watery and scared, but the tears are slowing and she's beginning to calm down.

"That's right. I will push you, Sophia, but never more than I know you can take. And never, ever, to hurt you—physically *or* mentally," I confirm.

"Then the rest will sort itself out. I'm yours, Dom," she says softly before leaning in to kiss me softly on the cheek. It wasn't an overt, take-charge, enticing type of kiss. It was a gentle kiss of sincere gratitude.

Chapter Seven

There's not much time left in our flight to San Diego and I have so much I want and need to learn about Sophia. I've held him at bay long enough. Dom is ready to come out, take charge, and coerce the answers out of her. He wants to make sure there is no doubt of who she belongs to by the time the first wheel touches the tarmac. While I've held off on this for good reasons, we are entering into this relationship differently than the norm.

"Sophia," I intentionally use her given name to convey I'm being serious, "I need to understand what methods were used to train you. Were you with the same Sir the whole year?"

"Yes, Dom, I've only been with one man and he was the one who trained me," she answers easily as she shifts in her seat so that she can face me.

"Tell me about his expectations, his stipulations, and the same for yours," I request. This is actually not easy for me to ask because I've never wanted to think about what is mine being with another man.

"Mine?" she asks, clearly confused. Her eyebrows are drawn down, her eyes are crinkled at the corners and she's looking around, but I know her mind is searching for an answer.

"Yes, Sophia. What stipulations and expectations did you put in the contract? Or did you not have a contract?"

"There was a contract," she answers slowly, "but it wasn't for me or my stipulations. The contract was only for him, Dom. It said what all he was allowed to do," she looks worried. "I'm sorry, Dom, please don't be mad. I'm not trying to hide anything from you. I just don't know how to answer your question."

"It's fine, Sophia. I believe you. I'm just trying to understand, okay? There are no right or wrong answers, so you don't have to worry about what you say. I just need to clarify something. The contract you had with him—it only addressed his needs, his desires, and his expectations? It didn't have anything about what you wanted or needed? What you were or were not willing to do?"

93

She shakes her head slowly, "No, Dom. There was nothing about me in it. Was there supposed to be?"

I take her hand to reassure her, "*My Angel*, the contract should've *only* been about you. Your wants, your needs, your desires should have been the *first* things addressed. Your submission to him is just that—*yours*. I know this next part will be hard to talk about for you, but I need you to do it...for me."

"Alright," her voice sounds unsure—scared—again.

"Tell me about the punishment part of it. You've been very worried about that, I can tell. I need to know why," I say gently, as if I'm trying to soothe a frightened child.

"He just gets mad, you know," she shrugs her shoulders, "when I don't know what he wants right away. I hate the whips the most," she says as a slight shudder runs through her.

"Sophia, he shouldn't touch you in anger—ever. Any punishment is agreed upon before it's given, and it's only given in love and correction. Never in retaliation. Never when you don't know what it'll be," I try to explain, but she gets that confused expression again. It's almost as if her mind is engaged in a battle between what he has put in her head and what I'm trying to tell her.

"I'm going to start from the beginning and teach you *my* way, Sophia. You're mine now, so it's only right that I should be the one who gets the pleasure of teaching you and guiding you. Don't you think?" I decide to change my tactic and not make her choose between us yet. He is still in her mind, controlling her, and exacting his type of abuse over her. I have to break that hold if we have any hope of moving forward at all.

"Um, okay, if that's what you want. I will let you teach me, Dom," she says sweetly. The words flow over her beautiful plump lips. The ones that are begging me to kiss them and make them succumb to my will. I reach up and languidly brush a strand of hair behind her ear, allowing my knuckles to graze the smooth skin of her cheek.

"First, let me tell you what I like and you tell me what you like," I say to her, easing her into the conversation and helping her feel comfortable talking about this with me. The fact is, any sub knows what this lifestyle is as about—as long as we come to an agreement, there are mutual benefits to it with no pretense of waiting an acceptable amount of time to have sex the first time. But with *My Angel*, I want it to be different. She is different and I know it. I'm convinced she hasn't really lived as a submissive and I'm not sure she's in the frame of mind to handle the true nature of a sub life. I don't want to overwhelm her.

I continue, "I've already told you, I like for you to look me in the eye. It's fine that others see it as a sign of respect to keep your eyes averted unless told otherwise, but this is *my* thing. I can read your body, but when you look me in the eye, *you* know you can't hide things from me."

"The way you dress is also important to me. Every Tuesday, Thursday, and Saturday, I want you to wear skirts, heels, and no panties," I say with a devilish grin. She looks shocked at first but recovers quickly.

"Even at work?"

"Yes, even at work. Our work relationship will be somewhat separate. I've never been intimate with anyone I've worked with, so this will be different for me. Not that we need to hide it, but I expect complete professionalism at work when we are around others," I explain. "I reserve the right to change that when we're alone, though."

She nods and smiles in agreement, "I can do that. What else?"

"We're not defining punishment yet. This is not up for debate. We will discuss anything that would normally warrant punishment, but I'm convinced you have a completely different idea of it than I do. You need to learn *me* first," I explain with as much understanding and compassion as I can infuse into my voice.

"I will take charge in the bedroom and you never have to worry about me hurting you. I'm not into that. The greatest pleasure I get is from taking care of you—in many ways. Which leads me to my next demand. You will take care of yourself in every way. You will not do anything that has a high probability of putting your life or health in danger."

"That's a little vague to me. Can you explain?" she asks, tentatively.

"If you've had a drink and then get behind the wheel of a car, you know that significantly adds to the chances you could be seriously hurt. If you text and drive, you know that adds to the probability of a wreck. If you don't eat healthy food, or don't eat all, you know that is bad for your health. Those kinds of things are not alright," I state emphatically and there is no doubt that is the end of the discussion.

"Okay, I understand. What do we do now?"

"Now, you tell me what you like or don't like," I cajole.

Momentary confusion flashes across her face before she responds, "I like what you like, Dom."

"That's the response for a Master, *My Angel.* I'm not your master. This is a two-way relationship. I will read your body and know what you need. I will test it, tempt it, taste it, own it, and command it, but I also like to know ahead of time what you like and don't like. It just helps me pleasure you," I respond, gently stroking my fingers across her cheek.

"I don't like being suspended, or gags, or being humiliated," she replies, her voice barely above a whisper. I have a sudden and unyielding urge to hunt down her last Sir and put my fist through his face. The images her fear and inflection of her voice bring to my mind are enough to make me want to kill someone.

"Tell me what happened, *My Angel,*" I command, taking her hand in mine to give her reassurance that I'm here for her.

She squeezes my hand and turns her face down and away in shame. "I was left suspended and gagged with no way to call for help. It scared me and he punished me for not trusting him to know what I needed."

My anger flashes to the heat of the sun in an instant. If I had been home instead of on this airplane, I would go hunt the motherfucker down and show him what it feels like. No *real* Sir puts his submissive in that predicament. No *real* man would treat his lady like that. She is to be loved, revered, and taken care of at all times. The level of abuse that she just described makes me want to repay the favor to this bastard—an eye for an eye, a gagged suspension for a gagged suspension.

For Sophia's sake, I rein in my extreme anger so she doesn't mistake it for something she's done wrong. "*My Angel*, listen to me, sweetheart. *That* is abuse—plain and simple. I would *never* do that to you, under *any* circumstance. I understand your hard limits and I will not push you to do that."

"But, will you be happy with me if I don't?" her voice is shrill, her eyes wide, her breaths increased, and she is clearly terrified.

"Yes, love, I will still be very happy with you. I don't need those things, Sophia," I comfort her. She immediately looks relieved and simply nods. "Anything else you want to tell me? Likes or dislikes?"

Her face turns the most beautiful shade of red and her straight, white teeth shine in her shy smile. "I like having my hair pulled during sex," she admits.

This makes me smile—the fact that she's becoming comfortable enough with me to have this conversation. The sign that she is beginning to trust me with information that she obviously deems to be embarrassing to admit. "I think I can help you out with that, Sophia."

She giggles and I instantly fall in love with the sound of her shy laugh. A thought occurs to me— maybe she will always be somewhat wary of sharing this type of admission. The shame her family cast on her caused deep-rooted issues with trust, acceptance, and belonging. Obvious abuse at the hands of a man she willingly submitted herself to only added more validity to those feelings.

"I feel like I'm starting all over, Dom. This can't be what you were looking for," she admits with a somewhat defeated tone.

"I was only looking for a new employee, Sophia, but when you walked in, I knew I had been looking for you...waiting for you...my whole life, " I openly admit.

She gasps and I reclaim her lips, covering them with mine and devouring her mouth as if it were my very lifeline. Our tongues move in sync, lightly grazing and skimming the other's, and I feel her body once again melt under my touch. When I pull away from her, I know there are two more ground rules I must add.

"I have two 'must haves' I need to tell you about, *My Angel.*"

"Alright," she answers on a ragged breath.

"There can be no deception of any kind—no lies, no omissions, nothing fake at all. And you cannot withhold your body from me, unless we've discussed it ahead of time and there's a good reason for doing so," I level her with my gaze, showing my complete and total lack of joking about either stipulation.

"I agree, Dom. I agree to those," she responds and I can sense she is waiting for me to once again take her mouth with mine, taste it, own it, and command it at my will. I am only all too eager to do just that.

The plane is finally touching down in San Diego and our meeting with Rich Daltry is the furthest thing from my mind. I have Sophia to myself today and tonight and I plan on making the most of every minute. We are two consenting adults and we've just spent the last three hours talking about what we do and don't like during sex. I'm well past ready to move our relationship into the next stage, but for her sake, if she wants to take it slower, I will oblige her for a little longer.

Fuck, I hope she's ready because I have a hard-on that would cut diamonds.

The car is waiting at the private hangar and we wait in the backseat as our bags are transferred from the plane to the trunk. I can't help but take the opportunity to test the waters with Sophia.

"We are staying at the Hotel del Coronado," I lean over and speak low into her ear. Her skin prickles with chill bumps rippling down her arm, making the tiny hairs stand at attention. My fingers follow behind her reaction and her body trembles at my touch. "Have you ever been there?"

She shakes her head first then audibly answers me, "No, I've never been to San Diego at all." Her voice is barely above a whisper, but is rich with need, want, and desire. Knowing I have a similar affect on her as she does on me makes our union even sweeter. Even if I have to teach her every step, every touch, and every look, it'll all be worth it.

"I think you will like it. It's very nice, upscale and it's directly on the beach," I continue, using my nose and chin to move her hair so that my lips gently glide across her neck. Her reaction is immediate and it spurs me on.

"I've heard of it," she answers breathlessly. "I've heard the hotel rooms are heavenly."

"That they are," I respond while intentionally kissing her neck this time. "But, we're not staying in a regular room."

"Ooooh?" she asks, although it comes out as more of a moan than she intended. It's sexy as hell and it shoots straight between my legs, suddenly making my pants entirely too tight.

"Mmmhmm," I murmur with my lips against her sweet skin. I flick my tongue out and enjoy tasting her while we're still alone in the car. "We're staying in a three-bedroom cottage in their Beach Village."

"Three bedrooms?" she asks and she can't hide the disappointment in her voice.

I smile against her skin and pull her earlobe into my mouth. "Mmmhmm," I murmur, intentionally waiting a few seconds before I continue. "Gives us plenty of space to stretch out."

Sophia smiles and lifts her hand to my face before running her fingers through my hair. "You're teasing me, Dom. That's not nice," she says in mock admonition.

"You don't want three bedrooms?" I ask, teasing her, testing her, and loving her reaction to me.

"Three bedrooms are fine—as long as you don't mind that the other two won't be used without you," she purrs back at me.

"Are you sure you're ready for this, Sophia? We can wait a little longer—I can wait for you to be ready, to be sure this is what you want with me. Another week or two won't kill me."

In all actuality, it *may* kill me. Waiting for her another *hour* may kill me, but it's something I'm willing to do if it means she feels safe, secure, and protected with me. If it means that she will never compare me to her former...I can't bring myself to call him a Sir because a real man would *never* treat her the way he must have. But if it means she sees he was never what I can be to her, it's worth the wait.

My inner Dom resurfaces and changes my tune. She *will* feel safe, secure, and protected with me. The only comparisons that will be made will be how lacking she finds him. And she will see that he isn't even a real man, much less a real dominant—he's a real dick who preys on women. I will be everything she's ever needed, nothing she's ever had, and the only thing she will never be able to live without again.

I *am* her Dom. She will feel me when I'm not even there. She will hear my words whispered in her ear even when she's asleep. No man will ever come close to touching her again after I've shown her what I can do.

She is mine.

Claim staked.

Territory marked.

Chapter Eight

Sophia rushes from room to room in our plush beach cottage. Her excitement is palpable as she checks each room while I tip the bellhop after leaving our luggage. A squeal echoes through the room and I keep walking toward her direction. She's standing in front of the huge picture window that overlooks the Pacific Ocean.

"Oh, Dom, this is wonderful! I've never been anywhere like this before! Thank you so much for bringing me with you!" She throws her arms around my neck and hurls her body into my arms. I instinctively pull her closer to me, tightening my hold. Her breasts are pressing into my chest and her plump lips are so close to mine, the temptation is too much to resist.

Leaning my head down slightly to meet hers, I kiss her gently at first while relishing in her taste and touch. With building urgency, the spark from our kiss ignites into an all-consuming fire, and for the first time in memory, I am slightly uncertain of maintaining my control. Only slightly, though. She makes me want to throw complete caution to the wind and figure it out as we go. Then, the next second, she makes me want to bend her over, pull her hair, and tell her to hold on tight.

Option two is my preference.

Lifting her higher off the floor, she wraps her legs around me as I push her back up against the wall. Her hands are in my hair and every time she pulls on it, the mixture of pleasure and pain only heightens my senses even more. My crotch is perfectly aligned with the sweet spot between her legs. Lightly grinding into her, I can feel her warmth envelop me. The moan that escapes her lips is intoxicating and I push into her again, only this time I intentionally grind into her harder than before. The thin material of our clothes is all that's keeping me from burying myself deep inside her and not stopping until she's screaming my name repeatedly.

My mouth is devouring hers, and every time my tongue slides across hers, I imagine myself licking her pussy, lapping up the juices that flow from the evidence of her arousal. I fantasize about her thighs framing my face, lightly scraped and red from the scruff of my five o'clock shadow. While my fingers plunge inside her, my mouth would find the sensitive skin of her inner thigh and I would leave my mark on her. My teeth would lightly sink into her skin as I bit, licked, and sucked until she is branded by me.

My hands are under her ass to hold her up. She's so thin, she hardly weighs anything at all. I can easily bear her weight and carry her to the bedroom without even breaking a sweat. I pull back from our kiss and peer into her eyes. They're like melted chocolate, asking for more and submitting to me at the same time. For now, it's still too early to carry this any further.

The ray of sunlight streaking through the picture window grabs the natural red tint in her hair, making it shimmer and glisten. Lowering her feet to the floor, I use my body to hold her against the wall and gently run my fingers down the length of her hair. I lean in and gently kiss her lips that are still swollen from our passionate kiss.

"We're in no hurry, Sophia. We have all the time in the world for this. I want to get to know you. I don't want to rush this and risk building your trust in me," I whisper to her lovingly.

"You're not rushing me, Dom," her voice pleads with me to continue.

I'm in control and won't let her lead us down this path. When I'm convinced she's unable to wait another second, I will be more than willing to fulfill her every need. Smiling, I gently stroke her face and peer intently into her eyes. "*My Angel*, let go of your fears. I'm not going anywhere. I can wait for you—until you're ready."

Her eyes well up with tears but she is able to hold them back. Her emotion is raw and real. She's both shocked and relieved that I saw past her bravado. There's not doubt that she wants me, but there's also no doubt that she's not in the right frame of mind just yet. She has to start trusting me—to not hurt her, to not leave her, and to give her what she needs.

"Let's go to the outdoor restaurant and have some lunch, maybe a walk on the beach. Then we'll see where the rest of the day leads us," I offer. "We have time later to review for our meeting tomorrow. I'd like to enjoy time alone with you."

"I would like that, too, Dom," she replies and I take her hand in mine. Her hand is so small and feels so fragile in mine. The abuse she suffered at the hands of the man who was supposed to care for her is the only thing holding me back from making her fully mine right now. She needs time to see me differently, but damn if I don't want to show her how good we can be together.

Later.

I tug on her hand and gently pull her to the door. She takes a few steps and then stops. "Dom, don't I need to unpack our suitcases?"

"No, *My Angel*, the concierge will come in and unpack for us while we're gone. They already know which ones not to touch," I explain patiently.

"I didn't mean to question you, Dom," her tone apologizes.

"You can ask all the questions you want or need to. Correction will only be dealt with if you continue after we've discussed it and I've given my final answer. Understand?"

She nods her head in agreement and smiles broadly. Her beautiful brown eyes glitter with happiness and my chest swells with pride from knowing I put it there. Simple words, natural gestures, and sincere feelings—it's amazing how many men just don't get it. I can be Dominant and loving, in control and flexible, and hard and soft—all at the same time. If this is what she needs to make her feel the real me and know that my promises are absolute, I can give this to her every day.

As we walk together from our cottage to the large dining patio area, she naturally falls in step with me, moving into my side as I wrap my arm around her. Several other men notice her as we move through the crowds. She's stunning and the other men turn their heads to watch her move past them. Sophia, *My Angel*, is oblivious to all of them. Her sole focus is on me and her behavior pleases me immensely.

"Do you see all these men staring at you? Wishing they were the ones with you?" I ask her, simply to pay her a compliment and reassure her of how beautiful she is. I feel her entire body tense beside me and her hands fidget nervously.

"I only want to be with you, Dom," she answers solemnly, as if she's been scolded for misbehaving.

I stop walking and tilt her face to look at me as I speak to her. "*My Angel*, it was a compliment. They can look all they want. It's me you're with and it's me who you will *always* be with. You can be proud of your beauty and proud to be in my arms. You never have to be ashamed of it with me."

Her whispered reply nearly floors me. "And you won't share me?"

What the fuck has he done to her?

"I will *never* share you, Sophia. And you will never have to share me with anyone else. I give you my word," I ardently reply. "You can believe me."

"I do. I won't question you again," she quickly states.

I give her a single nod to acknowledge her leap of faith. Slowly lowering my hand to hers, I let my fingers flow across her skin until our fingers lock. Our eyes stay glued to each other's and our looks become more heated. The simplest touch ignites an inferno in me that can't be quenched with anything but her—*all* of her. She's craving an intimate touch to reassure her that she's wanted, needed, and loved.

She will get so much more than that tonight. Sophia needs to feel like this will last and that it's not a fleeting notion that will drift away on a whim. I'm here to stay and soon she will no longer doubt it. When she falls asleep tonight, she will be in my arms, fully sated, decidedly tired, and completely loved from the top of her head to the tips of her toes.

The bright San Diego sun warms us as we enjoy a bottle of wine and the delicious food. The patio dining area is beachfront and I notice that her eyes keep straying to the waves rolling onto the shore. She doesn't ask, but I know that longing look on her face, and it's killing her to not be near the water.

"So, Sophia, tell me why you love the water so much."

She quickly hides her shocked look and responds, "I've always loved the water. It feels like home to me—it calms me, gives me a feeling of peace, and I could just sit for hours and watch the waves roll onto the shore."

"Let's take a walk on the beach then," I say after signing the check for our meals.

"Really?" she asks excitedly.

"Of course. If you love it that much, I can't deny you this simple pleasure." We quickly make our way to the beach and kick our shoes off. Sophia hums in pleasure as her toes sink into the sand. I take her shoes and place them in a secure spot close to our cottage. Hand in hand, we walk to the shoreline and she immediately puts her feet in the water. She stands completely motionless, just allowing the waves to wash up over her feet before rolling back out again. She then closes her eyes, tilts her head back, and basks in the feel of the sun and the surf. *My Angel* is absolutely stunning.

Quickly fishing my cell phone out of my pocket, I snap a few pictures of her before she opens her eyes. She has a completely serene, carefree countenance about her and I have to capture it before she realizes I'm watching her intently. My phone is back in my pocket by the time she opens her eyes and she's none the wiser. I'm met with her dazzling, full-face smile that I can't help but return.

"Walk with me," I request, offering my arm for her to hold and she quickly takes it. We being walking and immediately fall in step with one another, as if we were performing a routine we had practiced over countless hours. Walking along the shoreline, she shrieks when a rogue wave washes up farther than anticipated and splashes up her legs. Her skirt is short enough that the water didn't reach it, but her legs are soaked and her laughter is infectious.

Before I know it, I've joined in her fit of laughter even though, at this point, it's unclear of what we're really laughing about. I just know it feels good to let go, really relax, and enjoy this with her. My impression is she hasn't had the luxury of laughter in quite a long time. Another large wave comes rolling in and she jump-steps her way just out of its reach.

"You're already wet. Why don't you just jump in?" I tease her.

"You first, Dom," she replies coyly.

Taking her hand, I say, "Come with me." Her confusion registers on her face but she doesn't question me. In some ways, I feel her trust in me growing. Seeing confusion rather than fear in her eyes confirms that even though she doesn't know my intentions, she is comfortable enough with me to comply without being apprehensive. Small steps. One at a time, and soon enough, we will be at the point of our relationship where we need to be.

She wraps her little fingers around my hand and lightly squeezes. When I look over at her, she's smiling from ear to ear and has a bounce in her step. "What are you so excited about, Sophia?"

"I'm so glad you brought me here. I've also been thinking—," she starts before I cut her off.

"Uh oh," I reply in jest and she lightly hits me on the arm as she laughs.

"I was *about* to say that I've been thinking and I'm really happy that we're redefining our relationship, but now I may have to take that back," she pretends to pout and turns her head away to ignore me.

We've been walking while talking and we're rounding a corner into a sandy alcove that's secluded from the rest of the beach. No one is around and the best idea has just appeared in my mind. While she's looking away, pretending to be insulted, I ease my phone and wallet out of my pockets and place them on a large boulder that juts out toward the water.

Scooping her up in my arms, I rush headlong into the ocean and dunk us both in the water. As we break the surface of the water, she sputters water and gasps with her eyes as wide open as her mouth. I can't help but laugh at the shocked look on her face. She weighs nothing in the water's buoyancy, and I quickly turn her so that she's facing me with her legs wrapped around my waist. My arms fold around her and hold her close to me.

"Have you lost your mind?" she asks with a laugh when she finally overcomes her shock. "You are *crazy*!"

"That I am, Sophia. I'm quickly becoming crazy over you. The past three weeks and working all these crazy hours with you have been wonderful and *pure hell* at the same time."

"I know exactly what you mean," she whispers.

The droplets of water are scattered over her face and I watch as one bead rolls down her cheek and onto her lips. Just as she flicks her tongue out to lick it away, I capture her mouth with mine and she easily surrenders to my unspoken demand. Slipping my tongue into her mouth, I slowly glide it across hers. Sophia tries to increase the speed but I maintain my pace and give her no other option. I feel when she acquiesces to me and the Dom in me is pleased with her.

In fact, I'm pleased enough with her submission that I reward her with what her body is craving. Increasing the pressure and the urgency, I devour her mouth, lightly nipping on her bottom lip, pulling it into my mouth and lightly sucking on it. It's only a preview of what I plan to do to her but she understands my message. She moans softly and her body somehow melds into mine even more.

Moving along her jaw line, I kiss and lick her perfect skin. She tastes sweet and salty—her natural sweetness mixed with the salty ocean water is inebriating. When I reach the junction of her jaw and her ear, I gently pull her earlobe into my teeth and easily graze over it. "You taste so good, *My Angel*," I whisper to her. Her skin prickles again and I love knowing I have that affect on her.

Tilting my head, I dive in, sucking her neck along the side, casually moving from just below her ear down to her clavicle before moving back up again. "*My Angel*, I think you're wearing too many clothes," I whisper seductively to her.

"Here?" she glances around somewhat nervously, but also a little excited at the possibility. One thing she must learn is that when it comes to sex and business, I am always Dom and I won't tolerate non-compliance.

117

"Here, Sophia," I reply, my tone now resolute and I level her with my domineering look.

Realizing her gaffe, she lowers her eyes and asks submissively, "What do you want me to take off first, Dom?"

"How about I help you, *My Angel*?" I offer and her small, sexy smile returns.

"I would *love* for you to do that, Dom."

Chapter Nine

Gripping the hem of her shirt in my fingers, I pull it up and she raises her arms so I can pull it over her head. She takes it from my hand as I reach around and unhook her bra, never moving my eyes from hers. I watch as her pupils dilate, conveying her anxiety, but she doesn't object. I slowly pull the straps off her shoulders and ease her bra down her arms.

Taking both her shirt and her bra from her hand, I pitch them onto the rocks jutting out in the bend of the shoreline, safe from being washed out by the waves. Her legs are still wrapped around my waist while the top half of her body is completely bared to me. Her breasts are small but ample enough for my tastes. In this cool water her nipples are erect, but I suspect the reaction is also from her own desire.

I keep my eyes locked on hers as I lower my mouth and pull one nipple in. She gasps and inhales a sharp breath as her fingers weave through my hair. As my lips close around it, she arches her back to give me full access to her body. I snake one hand up her back and into her hair. Fisting it, I pull on her hair to tilt her head back while at the same time my teeth graze her sensitized nipple.

Sophia squirms in my arms and I release her nipple and softly admonish her. "Be still, *My Angel.* No squirming yet," I murmur to her. "It distracts you from the pleasure and I want you to feel every single thing. Understand?"

"Yes, Dom," she replies breathlessly.

"Good girl," I praise her. "Let's try that again."

Before she can respond, I have the other nipple in my mouth and repeat the process. Soon, her hair is in my hand, and with a slight tug, her head drops backward and her back arches, thrusting her breast into my mouth. Her fingers curl into my skin and the scratch of her nails on my skin is an aphrodisiac to my system. The sudden need to feel her skin against mine is all consuming.

Breaking my ministrations on her breast, I quickly snatch my own shirt off and throw it onto the rocks. Pulling Sophia in closer to me, her nipples graze across my skin and ignite my hunger for her even more. Her swollen breasts are simultaneously soft and firm, and while they definitely have my attention, there are other body parts that require much more attention right now.

"You can still say no, *My Angel.* It's your choice if we proceed or not. But know that if we do, it will be on my terms. You will have to trust me," I offer her one last chance to slow this down.

"I don't want to say no, Dom," she concedes. "I want this. With you."

Sliding my hand down and unzipping the back of her skirt, I lower her legs so she can stand. The water is not quite waist deep when I stand fully erect, but it's perfect for the access I need. As I push her skirt down over her hips, I hook my thumbs in her panties and drag them both down her legs. I continue to watch her every movement—her breathing, her eyes, her facial expressions, and the tenseness of her muscles that may give away her real thoughts.

Through it all, she is right here with me. She's excited about the public display of real affection— she's aroused and she's submissive to me. *Fuck, I didn't intend to have this type of relationship again, but she has made me miss it.* Sophia has awakened the man I've tried to pretend I didn't need to be. This is happening, and instead of being filled with dread, I feel full of life.

She steps out of her skirt and panties and I chuck them both onto the rocks. "Looks like I may need some help, *My Angel*," I smirk at her and look down at my soaked dress pants. I quickly grab the condom packet out of my back pocket. I had placed it there earlier when we arrived in the room, obviously with high hopes, but I'm very glad I have it on me now.

Her dainty hands swiftly unbuckle my belt. In no time, she has removed my pants and boxer briefs. Our clothes pile on the rocks is out of reach, making the possibility of getting caught even more exciting. There would be no denying what we were doing and there would be no way we could get to them in time, much less get *into* wet clothes.

What is it about a public place, a private act, and the mere possibility of being caught? The thrill, the rush, and the heightened senses, that's what. It's as if every nerve is firing at the same time, resulting in every sensation feeling unique and ethereal. It's the forbidden, the taboo, and the sensual all wrapped into one. It's living life on the edge and making the most of every moment.

Covering her mouth with mine once again, I claim her as mine simply by the way I own her response. She softens under my touch, becoming pliable and responsive to my every unspoken and spoken command. Our naked bodies are pressed as close together as they can get while standing. I easily lift her so that her legs are once again wrapped around me.

Walking into deeper water with her attached to me, our mouths fuse together as our tongues perform their erotic dance. Once the depth of the water covers us to my waist, I stop and pull back to look her directly in the eyes.

"*My Angel*," I whisper ardently, "you are about to become *mine*. *All mine*. All of you—your mind, your body and your heart—will belong to me. And, Sophia, I don't give up what's mine."

In response, she reaches her small hand down between us and wraps it around my cock. She gasps in surprise when her fingers don't meet and looks up into my smirking face. "Don't worry, *My Angel*, I promise to make you feel good."

She begins moving her hand up and down me but I'm already so hard it's almost unbearable. Her hand floats down along my arm until she finds the condom wrapper I'm still holding. Taking it from me, she slowly rolls it on me. Hoisting her higher, she positions me at the entrance to my heaven on earth and lowers onto me, inch by inch. When she stops midway, I soothe her with my words while I hold her up with my arms.

"Take your time, *My Angel*. Just relax and let me fill you, cupcake," I say as a term of endearment.

Sophia begins to move again, lifting up by using her legs as leverage, then back down again. Each time, she takes me deeper inside her and a little closer to the hilt. When she's finally able to take all of me, she croons a mixture of a sigh and a moan. Pulling my hips backward, I quickly thrust forward into her, flexing my hips and hitting the perfect spot in sweet succession.

Her inner muscles clamp down around my cock, squeezing me and increasing the friction even though we're still in the water. My mouth finds her neck and I lick, suck, and bite it as I continue to surge into her. Wrapping my hands around her shoulders, I push her down as I flex upward, driving into her harder and harder.

When my mouth reaches her ear, I murmur, "You feel so fucking perfect, *My Angel*. So sweet, so damn good." With that, she screams out my name with complete abandon, having forgotten we are in a very public place. That's actually the last thing on her mind as she climaxes, her body squeezing me like a silk-swaddled vice. Everything about her feels amazing—the way her body fits mine, the feel of my cock buried deep inside her, and the way she responds to my touch and my voice.

Sophia's coming down from her high but I'm just getting warmed up. All the things I want to experience with her start flying through my mind and I have to consciously fight to stay in the moment and not plan out the rest of the day and night. She finds her rhythm with me and soon we're both gripping each other tightly, and just before we each climax, I cover her mouth with mine and capture her screams.

That one time is definitely not going to be enough to sustain me for the rest of the day and into the night. I hold her close to me, stroking her hair and back as I bend my knees so that the water covers us up to our shoulders. "*My Angel*, you are so beautiful. You feel so good. I think I'm already addicted to you after just one time."

She strokes the back of my neck and twirls her fingers in my hair. Her head is lying on my shoulder and she's snuggled into the crook of my neck. It occurs to me, yet again, how perfectly she fits me and how she stirs my deepest feelings. Her tiny voice breaks my thoughts.

"Dom?" she inquires. "Can I ask you a question?"

"Yes, *My Angel*," I answer. "Anything."

"Why do you call it 'cupcake'?"

"What?" My tone relays my total confusion. My eyebrows are drawn down, and I'm looking at her like she's lost her mind, or maybe I have, as I'm trying to figure out what she's asking me.

"Just a few minutes ago, when you said you wanted to feel my cupcake. I just wondered why you call it that," she asked, embarrassed and not looking at me.

I search my memory. *When did I say I wanted to feel her cupcake?* Then it hits me and I burst out laughing. My whole body shakes and I can't stop it. She's just so damn cute and this is the icing on *my* cupcake.

"I actually said, 'Let me fill you, cupcake,'" I answer, emphasizing the words. "But now that you've given me the idea, I actually like it. Now I can have my cupcake and eat it, too," I explain with more laughter.

She blushes bright red but laughs with me. "Well, I'm glad I'm so amusing to you," she says playfully, pretending to be offended.

"You are *very* amusing to me and I think that's a great idea. Now, when I want to see that beautiful blush color on you when we're in public, I will just remind you of how much I love your cupcakes," I half-tease, knowing full well that this

126

term is now sticking with us for good. "I like icing on my cupcakes, too," I add for good measure. She buries her head again but I feel her body shaking from laughter.

Coaxing her from the water back to the beach where our clothes wait is a bit more challenging. She is convinced that as soon as she steps foot outside the water, a hoard of people will come around the bend and see her. Being ever the gentleman, I stay low in the water as far as I can go, then jump up and run to the rocks. After grabbing our clothes, I run as fast as one can run in the Pacific Ocean and dive into the water beside her. We manage to get dressed and find that putting wet clothes on underwater is actually easier than putting wet clothes on out of the water.

Good to know for future reference.

We walk back to the hotel in soaking wet clothes, talking, laughing, and just generally enjoying each other's company. My arm is draped around her shoulders and her arm is wrapped around my waist. I lean over to her ear and whisper, "Don't forget, *My Angel*, you are all mine now. There's no turning back."

Instead of tensing up, like I expected her to, she leans into me even more and wraps her other arm around me, circling my waist. She stops walking and positions herself directly in front of me.

When she tilts her head to look me in the eye, I see it glistening in her eyes. I know the look, I know the expectations her mind has set, and I know exactly what she's thinking. She loves me.

"I don't want to turn back, Dom. I *want* to be yours. I don't ever want to leave you. Thank you for being so understanding with me," she says earnestly. "I'm sorry for letting you down at first," she says while fighting back tears. "I never want to disappoint you again, Dom."

I stroke her face and lean down to kiss her tenderly. "You didn't disappoint me, *My Angel.* That's part of my responsibility—to help remind you, guide you, and teach you. I agreed to that when I agreed to this lifestyle. There are two areas where I am always *Dom*—the bedroom, or wherever bedroom things may happen, and in my business. Remember that, and most anything else will work itself out naturally."

"Okay. I can do that," she answers. "Does that mean I can't kiss you first?"

"No, not at all. I love when you're affectionate with me. What I mean is, you need to learn to trust that I won't hurt you—physically *or* mentally. Anything I do to you will bring you great pleasure, if you just submit to me and relax."

She hugs me tightly and her hand darts to her face. I know she's wiping away tears, comparing me to that fucker who hurt her. If I ever get my hands on him, he *will* know what real fucking pain is. He *will* know what it's like to be submissive at the hands of another who only wants to cause harm. He *will* learn his fucking lesson.

We draw curious looks from people as we walk by in our fine clothes, soaking wet and plastered to our bodies, but neither of us really cares. In my life, if I have learned anything, it's that people will think good or bad of you based on their own experiences, their own beliefs, and their own prejudices. I'm not changing who I am to try to fit someone else's mold, so the only opinions that matter are from those whom I love and who love me. Since none of these people fit into that category, Sophia and I stroll across the sand to our cottage like we own the place.

"*My Angel*, it's time for a hot shower, don't you think?" I ask her in my bedroom voice as we enter our temporary abode.

"Oh, yes, I *definitely* think a hot shower is in order!" The gleam in her eyes lets me know that she's also ready for round two.

Giving her my naughty grin, I quickly toss her over my shoulder and sprint to the master bathroom. She squeals with laughter and playfully swats me on the ass before grabbing it and squeezing it in her little hand. This surprises me at first but I quickly find that I like it. Actually, I fucking *love* her hands on me in any way I can get them. Once in the bathroom, I set her on the counter and turn the shower on to let the water get warm.

Situating myself between her legs, I cup her face in my hands and gingerly kiss her lips. Then I work my way along her jawline and all over her neck. There are certain places on her neck that cause chill bumps to spread down her arm and leg on that side of her body. It's fascinating to watch her body's reaction and I do it several times over.

Sophia is watching me curiously as I stroke the most recent round of chill bumps on her arm. "You like that, don't you, Dom?" she asks, her tone that of being proud of bringing me such strange pleasure.

"I do like it—a lot. It's like you're connected to me, Sophia. I can touch you or whisper to you and your body instantly responds. It knows you've always belonged to me.

"Let me get you out of these wet clothes, baby. You must be freezing and I'm playing with your chill bumps. That's not very gentlemanly of me, is it?" I ask with a smile as I remove her wet shirt and bra. "Now I can *really* enjoy looking at you. It was a little hard to get a good look with you plastered to me in the water," I say with a wink at her.

"Can I help you out of that wet shirt?" she asks shyly. "I didn't get a good look at your tattoo or your awesome body with you crushing me to you in the water," she retorts with a smile and squenches her eyes at me.

I put my hand on my chin, as if I'm in deep thought, and reply, "I really can't think of a single instance where it would be *inappropriate* for you to take my clothes off of me." I drop my voice an octave and finish, "Have your wicked way with me, *My Angel*."

Chapter Ten

Sophia pulls up the hem of my shirt, but she's too short to pull it all the way over my head. Reaching up, I grab my shirt from behind, yank it off, and cast it aside. Her hands roam over my chest, her fingers gliding across my skin as she intently studies my tattoos. She rubs her hand over my chest, shoulder, and arm as if she can actually feel the tattoos as something separate from my skin. I watch her with what I'm sure is the same curiosity as she watched me just a minute ago.

"This is gorgeous," she compliments my ink. "How long did it take to get all this done?"

"It was over a period of time, baby," I patiently explain. "I didn't get them all at once. Just kept going back and adding to it."

She traces it back up my arm, across my shoulder, and onto my chest again. Her other hand rises and the contact of her skin on mine is again like an electric charge running through me.

"You work out a lot, don't you, Dom?" she asks as she runs her fingers across my abdominal muscles.

"Yes, I do. I have a personal trainer who puts me through the ringer every day during the week. I usually take weekends off."

"What about this week?" she looks up at me through her eyelashes as her hands keep traveling south to my pants.

"I'll get up early and use the hotel's gym. You'll still be asleep," I say, tucking a strand of hair behind her ear as she unbuckles my belt, unbuttons my pants, and then slowly unzips them. Letting go of them, they fall to the floor and I step out of them.

I then pull her up to stand and encircle my arms around her to unzip her skirt. I follow it over her hips and down her legs to the floor, until I'm kneeling in front of her. I look up at her as I remove her panties and she steps out of them. Wrapping my hands around her, I grasp her ass in my hands and knead it as I tenderly kiss her stomach.

"Sophia, *My Angel*, I'm ready for more of my special cupcake," I tell her, my mouth still against her skin as a smile crawls across my face. She whimpers in response as my tongue flicks out across her hipbone.

Standing, I lift and carry her into the luxurious open shower area. After placing her on the built in bench seat, I use the handheld showerhead to wet her hair. After placing it where the warm water will cascade over her and warm her chilled skin, I lather her hair with the amber wood and vanilla scented shampoo and rinse it, watching the suds and water flow over her beautiful skin.

Picking up the matching soap, I lather a washcloth and begin washing her body. She opens her eyes and watches me, but the look on her face says she's slightly uncomfortable. I kneel in front of her, gently lift her leg, and wash her while keeping my eyes trained on hers.

"Tell me what you're thinking, *My Angel*," I state. It's not a question.

"I'm thinking I should be doing this for you instead of you doing it for me," she answers honestly.

"I see," I reply cryptically while I keep rubbing her skin with the perfumed soap. "Sophia, do you think I would do this if I didn't want to? If I didn't enjoy it?"

She looks taken aback for a second when she stammers, "I never really thought of it that way,

134

Dom. I'm sorry I disappointed you again," and drops her eyes to the floor.

"Sophia, I'm not disappointed in you. I will tell you when you disappointment me, so you never have to question that. If I don't say it, I'm not thinking it. Deal?"

She wipes at her eyes and nods her head in agreement. "Deal, Dom."

"As far as showering, washing you, bathing with you, it is a pleasure for me to do it. Put everything else out of your mind. Do you like it?" I ask, sincerely wanting to know her answer.

"Yes. It makes me feel special," she meekly replies.

"You *are* special to me, *My Angel*. I want you to feel special, I want to do this, and I want you to allow yourself to enjoy it. For me," I add.

"Yes, Dom," she says, and I can tell she wants to add more, so I give her a moment to pull herself together. "You're just so different. Is this real? Is this how it really should be?"

"This is just the beginning of how it should be, baby," I soothe her. "There's so much more we can experience together and it's all for your pleasure. I've told you, if you don't like something, we can stop and never do it again. Or, you can say no and we will never do it at all."

She shakes her head, as if to clear the thoughts that are trying to take over, and cups my cheek in her hand. Lightly stroking my face, her fingers scrape against the scruff of my eternal five o'clock shadow. "You are too good to be true," she whispers. "Can I kiss you now?"

I smile warmly at her, "That's another question you never have to ask, baby. You can *always* kiss me." Leaning in to each other, we meet in the middle and our warm, gentle kiss quickly turns red-hot and demanding. She wraps her arms around my neck and pulls me closer to her, our wet bodies again warmed by our mutual desire.

I push her back against the tile wall and break our kiss to move down and explore her body. "You are so beautiful," the words each punctuated with an open mouth kiss to her body. Taking one nipple between my thumb and index finger, I gently roll it back and forth as I continue my southward journey on her body. "Mmmm, I think it's time for dessert and my choice is cupcake," I say enticingly as I spread her legs farther apart.

Without any preamble, I take her clit into my mouth and swiftly suck it. She cries out and sits straight up in response. Her hands fly to my head and she clenches my hair in her fists. My fingers grip her hips and I pull her ass to the edge of the bench seat to get better access.

"No squirming, *My Angel*. Sit still and just feel it," I instruct her. She bites her lip but nods her head in agreement. I lap her from bottom to top and back again. She sits still, except for the slight pull on my hair, and I smile against her inner thigh. With a little more force and tenacity, I taste my cupcake again. "This is the best cupcake I've ever eaten, Sophia."

I feel a slight shake as she laughs but it's quickly replaced by her pulling my hair as my tongue dives in to thoroughly enjoy my special bakery delight. After a couple of minutes, *My Angel* can no longer sit still and her hips begin moving in time with my tongue. As I insert my finger inside her, she moans loudly and uses my hair to pull my face closer to her. My slow movements rapidly increase tempo as I insert a second finger. Crooking my fingers, I scrape against the spot that drives her wild time and time again.

"You're holding out on me, Sophia," I murmur to her. "I know you're ready. Let go, baby."

When she finally does, it's a beautiful sight. She rides her climax out as wave after wave hits her. She cries out my name and pulls my hair harder. Her face is flushed with desire and her body is quivering. When she finally opens her eyes again, I pull my fingers out of her and place them in my mouth, licking off the remnants of her arousal. "That's the best cupcake I've ever had," I assure her.

"Oh, Dom. That was amazing. I don't even know what to say," she says breathlessly, her chest still heaving as if she just finished a strenuous exercise. Her eyes are glazed over and her body could be boneless for the lack of control she has over it.

"I should tell you, *My Angel*, that I *am* clean. I have tests every six months, standard requirement of my life insurance policy," I state, hoping she tells me what I already know.

"I'm clean, too, Dom. I've been tested regularly, but the last one was my pre-employment physical."

"What about birth control?" I ask her the one question I don't have an answer to yet.

"Yes, I had it implanted in my arm about six months ago. It lasts three years."

"I really just want to feel you. Are you okay with me not using condoms? It's up to you and I will do whatever you want," I promise and wait for her answer.

"Yes, Dom, I'm fine with you not using them."

Her Dom

I shower faster than I have ever showered before in my life, thoroughly washing myself as Sophia watches me. Even though the ocean scene was incredible, I really want to get her somewhere I can just take my time with her. She looks at me quizzically and then I explain, "We've had enough water sex for today. I really just want to get you in my bed."

"Well, why didn't you just say so?" she asks playfully.

After picking up her towel, I thoroughly dry her beautiful body, taking time to worship every part of her with kisses, soft touches, and assurances of how she makes me want to lose control. She gives me full access to her and it does not go without notice that she accepts my adorations without hesitation. All she needed was to understand that it was important to me and she is more than willing to comply. It's in these moments with her that I know this life is the right choice for us.

I quickly dry myself and lead her to the bedroom. The king-size bed is oversized, extra-plush, and directly underneath the ceiling fan, making it the perfect location for what I have in mind. The headboard is attached to the wall, so my suitcase of tricks will have to wait until I can improvise. It's actually best for now since Sophia needs to feel more comfortable with me before I try to introduce any type of restraints.

However, a blindfold is not a restraint, so that can be one step in my *"learn to trust her Dom"* mission. I position her in the middle of the bed and step back while maintaining eye contact with her. "*My Angel*, I need you to lie here for me while I get something from the suitcase."

A quick flash of worry moves into her eyes and she quickly hides it. "Tell me what you're thinking, love."

"I'm afraid, Dom. I'm sorry. I'm trying," her tone pleads for understanding.

Smiling, I lean over and kiss her, lingering for just a moment before lightly brushing my tongue against the part in her lips. She needs to remember the passion, the desire, and my promise to never hurt her. I'm purposely not moving too fast with her since another man scarred her and the emotional trauma is not easily overcome. By not responding verbally, I'm giving her a moment to come to a decision on her own.

Will she trust me?

Will she tell me to stop before we even start?

Her eyes tell me she wants me, she wants to trust me, and she really *is* trying her best. I want to reward her for that. After gently stroking her cheek, I walk over to the suitcase that the staff didn't unpack. Leisurely unzipping it, I intentionally take my time going through the items until I find the one I want. My back is to her and she can't see the contents, so she can't see which one I've chosen for her. As I turn to face her, I quickly put that hand behind my back and walk back to the bed.

She's waiting right where I left her only a moment ago. She isn't entirely relaxed, but she's not about to bolt from the bed, either. Giving her another sensual kiss, I rub my free hand across her body and down between her legs. Ending the kiss, but keeping my lips against hers, I whisper, "*My* cupcake, *My Angel*," just before I push my finger into her wetness.

She moans in pleasure, closes her eyes, and lifts her hips to meet my hand, asking for more, allowing me to do what I will to her. Her mind is more relaxed now as she focuses on the pleasure. I'm slowly replacing her initial reaction of fear to associate this with the most pleasurable experience she's ever had before. Reconditioning her to put the past experiences behind us and just enjoy what we can have together.

"*My Angel*," I whisper softly as I add a second finger and she suddenly soaks my hand. "Does my voice do that to you, love?"

"Yessss," she hisses in response. "Yes, Dom. It's so deep and masculine, but soft and sensual at the same time. It drives me crazy."

Slowing my pace and allowing her to come back to earth, I continue speaking to her in hushed tones. "Open your eyes, love."

She obeys and this time there is no fear in them. No apprehension and no worry to be found. She is now completely open to my suggestions and me. "*My Angel*, do you know what I've picked for you today?"

She shakes her head from side to side. She's curious, but she's also fighting all the negativity that fucker put in her head.

"Have I hurt you?" I ask. She shakes her head no again.

"Did I promise I would never hurt you? That I would never do anything to hurt you physically or mentally?" I ask. She nods her head yes.

"Do you believe me?" There's only a split second hesitation before she nods her head yes again.

"This is what I've chosen for you, *My Angel*," I say as I produce the scarlet red silk sash. "I would love to blindfold you, if you will trust me."

"You're not tying me up?" she asks meekly.

142

Her Dom

"No, love, just covering your eyes. Your hands will be free to take it off any time you feel the need."

She nods in agreement, "I trust you, Dom."

"Sit up on the side of the bed," I instruct and she complies. Moving behind her, I place the sash over her eyes and pull the end around the back of her head to tie it securely in place. Then, I lean over and place open mouth kisses on her neck and across her shoulder. "That's my good girl," I praise her, "I'm so proud of you."

Moving back to her side, I scoop my arms up under her hips and easily lift her. Depositing her back in the center of the bed, I cover her body with mine and let her feel my rock hard cock glide across her leg as I position myself between her legs. Sophia lifts her head, offering her mouth and wanting to kiss me. For her leap of faith, I reward her with another kiss.

"You can relax, love. You are mine and I take care of what's mine."

Making my way back to my cupcake, I lick and devour it like I'm a starved man. Her icing only makes it better and I relish every taste of her, every one of her cries of pleasure, and every time she writhes from my touch. Moving up her body, I leave love bites in my trail until I reach her breasts. As I

143

lick and bite around the swell of her breast, I thrust my cock deep inside her.

I almost come undone from the feel of her soft sheath as I fill and stretch her to accept my size. Thrusting forward to the hilt once again, she's unable to contain her screams. At the same time, I increase my bite pressure on her breast, leaving my mark and claiming my territory. The mixture of pain and pleasure creates another wave of orgasms. Over and over, as my hips surge into her, and my teeth find her delicate skin, her body clenches around me and begins to milk me. Unable to hold out any longer, I grab her legs and push them forward to penetrate deeper as I come with her.

"Fuck, baby, you feel so good," I utter while thoroughly kissing her. I remove the blindfold and my chest swells with the look she gives me. Her eyes are filled with complete and utter trust. She shows me her love and desire without saying a word. Her relaxed state shows both contentment and excitement at the possibilities we have in our future.

She is mine. I am her Dom. And I love it.

Chapter Eleven

Daylight is barely breaking but I'm wide-awake and watching Sophia as she sleeps soundly. Memories from the rest of our day and night are so very fresh in my mind and I'm consciously restraining myself from waking her and making love to her again. Even though we've only experienced the tamest of bedroom antics at this point, I already have an unquenchable thirst and insatiable appetite for her.

She moves and her long hair slowly falls over part of her face and shoulder. If I push it back, it will wake her up and she just looks too content to bother yet. After carefully slipping out of bed, I quickly dress and leave Sophia a note telling her I'm at the gym in case she wakes before I return. Passing the restaurant where we ate last night, I can't help but smile as I recall our conversation.

She had a different glow to her skin and a permanent smile on her face. The way she batted her eyes and looked at me adoringly made me feel like the luckiest man in the room. When the waitress approached our table to ask if we wanted dessert, I couldn't help but smile mischievously at Sophia as I asked the waitress if they had any cupcakes. The light tinge of pink that normally fills her cheeks was replaced with a deep red shade of embarrassment.

When the waitress said they did, in fact, have red velvet cupcakes with cream cheese icing, I thought for a second that Sophia may actually crawl under the table and hide. She was trying to keep from laughing out loud but only succeeded in sounding as if she was choking. The waitress's concern for her was sincere but I could barely contain my mirth over her predicament as the waitress patted her back and asked if she should call an ambulance. When Sophia realized the waitress thought she was really choking, she quickly pulled herself together and assured the poor girl that she was fine.

Back in our cottage after dinner, we reviewed the plan for today's meeting with Rick and decided the best approach to take with him. He's a blowhard type of guy—he likes to think he's in charge but is mostly full of hot air. After looking over his business case, I decided to remain quiet as he presents his case so he can be satisfied with being heard. Then, I will lay down the Powers law and inform him how we will handle this contract or it won't happen at all.

After I finish my workout and my run on the beach, I stroll back across the grounds to our cottage. *My Angel* is still sleeping when I walk in our bedroom and she's snuggled up with my pillow. I stifle a chuckle at her penchant for sleeping with her body permanently attached to something. Last night, it was me that she was glued to—no matter which way I moved, she followed. Apparently, now she is using her 'Dom pillow' to snuggle with in my place.

I crawl across the bed and place soft kisses on her face, moving her beautiful hair out of my way as I move down to her neck. "Wake up, *My Angel.* It's time to get ready for our meeting today," I softly croon to her. She stirs and rolls over to her back as she stretches. The sheet falls away from her breasts and the mark I branded her with yesterday draws my eyes.

I lean over and kiss the red and purple remnants of my love bite and she threads her fingers through my hair, holding my head in place. "Good morning, Dom. Were you looking for something?" she asks coyly.

147

"I think I found something," I retort as I flick my tongue across her skin, across the area where I've claimed her.

"Hmmm...look at that, would you?" she says playfully, her voice still drowsy with sleep. "It seems someone has left me a present."

"There are many more where that came from," I say as I move to her neck. Just as I reach her ear, I murmur seductively, "And I can put them anywhere you'd like." The instant reaction her body has to my voice flashes across her arm and down her leg. I smile against her ear before softly kissing it.

"But not right now. We have to get ready and leave to meet with Rich this morning. Get your fine ass out of the bed, *My Angel*, " I state, ending with a good morning kiss. She stretches her lean body and grumbles in complaint, but she swings her feet over the side and saunters off to the bathroom. I admire the view as she disappears from my sight.

After breakfast, we're being driven to *D-Force Games* headquarters and I look over at Sophia, expecting her to be nervous about the impending negotiations. She's cool and collected with no sign of fretting or anxiety at all. She turns her head toward me and asks sweetly, "What is it, Dom?"

"You just surprise me sometimes. I thought you may be nervous about today but you don't seem nervous at all."

"I'm not. I know this information inside and out. I've been over and over the data until I can recite it in my sleep. I will make you proud," she finishes with a smile.

I have no doubt about that.

The offices of *D-Force Games* are extremely opulent. The marble entrance sets the tone for the rest of the building. With elevators strategically placed in the center of the large, open building, every floor is visible from the first floor to the top. The elevator walls are glass so we can look out over the terrarium-style lobby as we rise to the top floor of the office building.

When the doors open, Rich is waiting to escort us into the executive boardroom. Sophia looks incredible in her black dress suit but she is in all business mode. Rich looks her over appreciatively from head to toe a couple of times, blatantly, and then he gives her his best attempt at a smirk. It takes every ounce of self-control I have to keep from laughing in his face when she levels him with her *don't-fuck-with-me* look in return. His ego immediately deflates and he clears his throat before speaking.

"Good morning. I'm Rich Daltry," he says as he extends his hand to me first and then to Sophia. "Glad you could make it. Follow me and we can get started. We have coffee, juice, and water in the room if you want any," he says to no one in particular as he turns to walk toward the boardroom.

I steal a glance at Sophia and give her an approving smile when she looks up at me. She gives me a half-grin and I can tell she's trying hard to hold in her full smile. Once it gets loose, it's normally out of control and she knows that wouldn't be appropriate after she basically emasculated Rich in front of me. As we walk through the hall, I take note of the many empty offices and cubicles we pass.

Once in the boardroom, the table is full of Rich's department heads, including his finance and human resources officers. Rich makes introductions all around and points to the credenza with the drinks and snacks. Sophia places her belongings in her chair and makes us each a cup of coffee. Once she's seated beside me, Rich narrows his eyes as they quickly shift between the two of us. His sneer tells me everything I need to know about him—he's judging us and thinks this is a simple case of the boss fucking his secretary.

Jumping right in, Rich barely waits for Sophia to take a drink of her coffee before he starts touting all the reasons why DPS should accept a reduced rate of our normal amount for handling their programming needs. He name-drops several other similar companies that he could have called instead of DPS and proceeds to ramble on about how important his company is. Sophia maintains her composure, drinks her coffee, and lets him finish his long-winded rant. I'm starting to think she isn't going to respond at all.

"I believe in being blunt. I think we all know that *D-Force Games* would bring DPS to the forefront of all software programming needs. The exposure from a contract with us would put you on the map more than any other company you could possibly work with and I think everyone at this table knows that," Rich continues, his posture aggressive as he obviously tries to intimidate us. "Now, for that, I am proposing a five-year commitment, with you handling all of our internal programming needs, for an annually contracted rate of nine hundred and fifty thousand dollars."

I sit in stunned silence for a moment, staring at him in disbelief. I expected a lowball amount to start the negotiations with since Rich is known for that, but that amount is *ridiculously* low and he knows it. Had Sophia not been with me, I would have considered this a completely wasted trip and would have already left his contract in shreds on the table. Just as I'm about to speak and tell him where he can stick his contract, Sophia's sweet voice fills the room.

"Mr. Daltry, while we appreciate your interest in DPS handling your programming needs, I think we all know that amount is inappropriately low. For a company the size of DPS, and with the yearly revenue it generates, your research should've shown that every company spends approximately one-percent of its revenue on the IT department alone. Since you're asking us to basically become your IT department, your offer wouldn't *begin* to cover the employee salaries, much less anything else.

"For that reason, our counter-proposal has been drawn up and is our final offer. My own research has shown that *D-Force Games* is on the cusp of signing a thirty million dollar per year contract as a joint venture with another gaming company. On top of your own success, this agreement is expected to *exponentially* increase your profits as well as your IT needs," she concludes her side of the negotiation by sliding our proposal across the table to Rich.

Rich's face turns red with anger and he opens his mouth to protest, but he has nothing to argue with in this case. Sophia has done *more* than her expected homework and came to this meeting more prepared than anyone else at the table, including me. Rich shuts his mouth and looks down at the figure on the contract. His lips form a thin line and he shakes his head in disgust as he reads the stipulations.

"We will supply a team of twenty programmers to remain onsite and handle your internal IT needs. Any large-scale additions to the system and set-up you currently have in place would require the addendum charges, as noted. The total price for a three-year commitment is eighteen million dollars," Sophia further drives the knife in. "You've made some great decisions of late, Mr. Daltry, by sending much of your staff to work at home and reducing your overhead costs. The sale of this building and moving to a smaller building should prove to be very lucrative for you."

All heads at the table snap to Sophia at her final statement. "How did you know about that?" Rich growls at her, causing me to bow up at him to protect her.

"It's her job to know that, Rich. As it's *your* job to know that lowball amount you offered us is an insult. Our final offer is on the table. If you didn't believe my company is the best at this, *you* wouldn't be here at this table right now. If we didn't know that this relationship would be mutually beneficial, *we* wouldn't be here. The terms are reasonable considering what you're asking in return. Now, if we can have your answer, we can conclude this meeting," I growl back at him.

Rich looks at his Chief Financial Officer, who has been reading the contract terms and stipulations during my rant at Rich, for his input. Without uttering a word, the CFO simply nods his head and pushes the contract back to Rich. I can tell that Rich is stalling as he picks it up to read the same words again. He knows he should sign it but he can't stand to feel like he's lost the game. I know the feeling—we're all very competitive.

"I will have my legal team look over this contract and get back with you tomorrow, Powers," Rich finally states.

Sophia and I rise from our chairs and she asks, "Do you still want us to tour your facility, get a feel for the internal requirements?"

"No, no need," Rich says, sounding like a petulant child.

We say our goodbyes to everyone and Rich has his secretary walk us out. Tucker is waiting at the curb with our car as we exit the building and Sophia looks stunned. "How did he know to come get us so soon?" she asks.

"I sent him a text from the elevator," I say with a shrug.

"So, he just waits around for you to need him?"

"Yes, unless I'm sure I won't need him for a considerable time," I explain, confused that she's asking so many questions about my head of security.

"Don't you ever want to drive?"

"I do most of the driving at home. When I travel, I like to have a driver for convenience."

Sophia nods and doesn't question me further, so I guess my answer satisfied her curiosity. She's very different than anyone I've ever dated before. She's not accustomed to money or having the ability to splurge on the luxuries. I find myself getting more and more wrapped up in her and I know she is in me, too. Her eyes tell me without saying a word. Her body tells me without making a sound. Her interactions with other men make it clear that she's not interested or available.

"I predict Rich will call later today and demand another meeting sometime tomorrow. It'll be a time that is most inconvenient for us, so he can punish us in his passive-aggressive way, but he will accept it in the end," I say to her as we get in the backseat. "You did great in there. I'm very impressed, Sophia. You really did your homework."

155

"It's my job," she says and tries to act indifferent, but I can tell she's uncomfortable with praise. "I only did what you pay me to do, Dom. It wasn't anything special."

"It was special," I retort sharply. "Your research and forethought made it much easier for us to have a successful negotiation. Actually, it wasn't a negotiation at all. You pretty much nailed him to the wall and gave him no room to argue. That was awesome to see," I praise her.

"I'm glad I pleased you, Dom," she replies sincerely. Looking at me intently for a moment, she continues, "I know you've been taking it easy on me and I really do appreciate it. I *am* trying and I *do* want to please you."

Leaning over to kiss her, I can't resist, "You *do* please me, Sophia. Enough that I may even indulge and enjoy a cupcake again tonight."

She blushes with embarrassment but can't hide her smile. That word has stuck between us, has a special meaning now, and allows us to share our own private joke. That's the part that makes it more meaningful—it's only between the two of us. It's ours, as a couple, and it creates an intimate bond between us. Sophia leans in closer and lays her head on my shoulder. After kissing the top of her head, I whisper softly to her, "*My Angel*," and she snuggles in even closer.

Tucker drops us off at the hotel and we wind our way through to our private cottage. Once inside, I wrap my arms around Sophia from behind and pull her close to me. "We have plenty of time now, love. What would you like to do while we're here?"

Sophia leans her head back on my chest and wraps her arms around mine. "I don't know. I've never been here before. We could go back to the beach and swim in the ocean."

"Get your bathing suit on this time," I joke. "I'm not swimming in all my clothes again, no matter how much you beg."

She turns quickly in my arms to face me, her mouth gaping open and her eyes narrowed in mock anger. She's trying hard not to laugh, to pull off her mad-at-Dom look, but she just can't bring herself to do it. "*You* are the one who picked *me* up and charged into the water!"

I shake my head in confusion, "I would never do something like that, Sophia. I don't know why you'd want to make up lies about me like that. That hurts." I somehow manage to keep a straight face as she comprehends my words.

"You – you...Dom...that's just mean," she finally says in exasperation but I see a smile playing at the corner of her mouth. "Maybe I should put you on a dessert-free diet now. No cupcake for you!"

"I'm afraid that doesn't work for me, Sophia," I respond, menacing but playful. "You see, you *agreed* to never withhold your body from me, unless I *also* agreed to it. And since I *don't* agree to it, I can have all the cupcake I want!"

"I did, didn't I?" she says with a laugh as she takes a couple of steps back from me. She thinks she's clever and I let her think she has a head start on me. "You'll have to catch me first, though!"

Chapter Twelve

She turns to run and I've already lifted her off the ground and thrown her over my shoulder. After smacking her on the ass a couple of times, I playfully admonish her. "Oh, *My Angel*, you should know better than to run from me. All the rules you're broken in the last few minutes...I'm afraid I have to punish you now."

She's laughing and squealing as she asks, "What kind of punishment do you have in mind?"

"You know, if I didn't know better, I would think that you misbehaved on purpose just to see what your punishment would be. Maybe you're one of those 'don't ask permission, just get spanked' types. Let's find out," I respond as I hurry into the bedroom and drop her on the bed.

She's lying on her back and pulls her elbows up underneath her. As she gives me a sexy, come-get-me look, I walk over to the suitcase that holds the fun devices. She continues to watch with curiosity, showing no fear or apprehension with the threat of punishment from me. Granted, it was a playful threat and I believe she knows I would never really hurt her, but this is a bridge we will have to cross soon. This is a part of her training and she's right, I've been very lenient with her so far.

When I retrieve the paddle from the suitcase, her eyes widen and she watches me approach her. Sitting on the side of the bed, I simply state, "Over my knee, Sophia." I don't look at her and I make damn sure there is no anger in my tone. I'm not angry at all, but I need her to know that, to believe I would never hit her in anger, and to trust that whatever I do is the best for both of us.

I feel the bed shift behind me as she moves and does as she's told. She takes her place across my legs, her ass up in the air and her torso comfortably placed on the bed. I run my hand up her bare leg and push her skirt up around her waist. Then, I smile and my heart swells.

"You remembered," I whisper tenderly to her.

"Of course, Dom," she whispers back in the same tone.

Her bare ass is waiting for me, just as I instructed. It's Tuesday and she's not wearing any panties. She never ceases to amaze me. I rub one perfect, round cheek adoringly and her body relaxes against mine. Moving to the other side, I make sure to give it just as much attention. The paddle I've chosen is actually used more for pleasure than punishment, but it's a step in the trust direction.

It's black with leather on one side and soft, faux rabbit fur on the other. Turning it so that the soft, furry part will strike her smooth skin, I begin talking to her soothingly. *"My Angel*, this may sting for a second. I want to know how you feel, what you're thinking, and if you like it."

"Yes, Dom," she says submissively.

Lifting the paddle up in the air, I swing it down and the fur smacks against her skin, muffling the sound and the sting. Using my hand, I rub the spot I just spanked, and then continue this several more times. In between each time, as I rub her skin, I give her positive reassurances about how beautiful she is to me, how I love seeing her in this position, and how pleased I am with her. She hums softly with each strike and denies feeling too much discomfort.

After ten licks, I rub her reddened skin for the last time and help her up from her prone position. Pulling her down to sit in my lap, I wrap my arms around her, nuzzle her neck, and ask her how she's feeling. Her reaction is very important to me and to our relationship. She needs to feel comforted, protected, and cherished at all times. With this being our first step into the world I'm accustomed to, I need to know that she can handle it. Sometimes, I'm not so sure.

"I feel good, Dom. I feel relaxed and excited at the same time. For the first time in a really long time, I only had one thing on my mind. I just focused on feeling you the whole time. It's so different," her voice trails off, and her wistful tone tells me she's making comparisons. Good or bad, this scene has evoked memories of the other guy, the one who betrayed her trust and made her afraid.

There's a story there, and I know it's one I'm not going to like knowing all the details, but the only way I can help her overcome all this shit someone has put in her head is to get to the bottom of it. Tonight may be a bit rough on both of us, but it'll be better in the long run. For now, she's had enough, even though the "punishment" was anything but punishment. She trusted me, she didn't argue, and she didn't ask me to stop. That's progress enough for now.

Capturing her mouth with mine, I take my time in making love to her mouth. Soft kisses, running my tongue lightly over her lips, pulling her lower lip into my mouth—all of my slow movements and lavishing attention on her are to demonstrate to her that she is adored. Her soft moaning sigh tells me she feels it, she understands my message, and she's in this with me. If we don't quit this now, we will never leave this room today.

Pulling back, she groans in disapproval and I can't help but smile at her. She's a beautiful woman but she can just be so cute at times. I playfully chide her, "Don't groan at me like that. I'll turn you back over my knee. Oh wait—that'll probably make you do it more, won't it?"

She laughs and cuts her eyes seductively at me. "I don't know, Dom. Try it and see," she replies with a purr. Her smile is beaming, completely splitting her face in two, and her eyes are twinkling with playfulness. It almost makes me want to stay here, but she said she's never been to San Diego before and I want to take her out and show her everything.

"Nice try, Sophia," I narrow my eyes at her in mock warning. She knows the difference between the serious Dom and the teasing Dom, so I don't worry that she will misunderstand my meaning. "As much as I would love to stay in this cottage and have my way with you in every room and on every surface possible," I say while wiggling my eyebrows at her, "I really should take you out and show you around San Diego.   What would you like to do first?"

"Is there somewhere we can snorkel?" she asks excitedly.

"Yes, I know just the place to take you—La Jolla.   We can do a snorkel tour and swim with the leopard sharks," I say as we stand and I reach for my phone.

"Seriously?"

"Yeah, let me find their number," I reply distractedly as I look for the tour company.

Sophia starts jumping around in excitement like a little girl. I stop and stare at her for a minute but it doesn't faze her. She's far too excited as she begins rushing around the room to change and pack a beach bag for us. I chuckle, shake my head, and walk into the main room to make our reservations.   Minutes later, I turn around to find her standing in the doorway, the beach bag in one hand and my swimming trunks in the other.

"In a hurry, are we?" I smirk at her.

"We don't want to be late, Dom.   No matter what time it starts," she replies with a serious look. She's not kidding and this makes me laugh harder, which earns me a semi-dirty look.

Actually, I think I just hurt her feelings.

"I'm sorry, baby. You're just so cute and funny. I can't help but laugh sometimes," I explain, still grinning but refraining from laughing out loud again.

"Humph," she replies and looks anywhere but at me.

She remains in the doorway as I walk toward her. I wrap my arms around her waist and pull her to me, but her arms still hang limp at her side. She's petulantly refusing to wrap her arms around me in return. Trying to soften her up, I kiss her softly on her beautiful lips, her cute little button nose, and then on the forehead.

Still nothing.

"I'm sorry, Sophia. I would never make fun of you out of meanness. Forgive me?"

She takes a deep breath and exhales loudly, relaying her inner war to either skewer me or forgive me. Her arms slowly rise to wrap around me, and when she finally makes eye contact with me, I see the glistening of the unshed tears that she's fought back. I don't understand her severe reaction to such a minor situation, but I have to consider that this is a reaction to something that runs deeper than what I see at the surface.

"I have to forgive you. You're my Dom. It would be disrespectful for me not to," she replies sullenly.

"Baby, I'm sorry, okay? Really, I wasn't making fun of you. You are one of a kind. I've never been with anyone like you before. I would never hurt you on purpose," I promise her and myself.

"Do you mean that, Dom?" she asks, searching my eyes with a crestfallen look on her face.

What the hell is going on?

"I always mean what I say, Sophia, and I say what I mean. I won't lie to you and I expect the same from you. You are special—everything about you is different."

"Alright," she replies softly, "I forgive you."

Pulling her closer, I just hold her for several minutes. I really want to get to the bottom of this, but we need to go because traffic in La Jolla can be very congested. I don't want to take any chance that would make us miss this tour. She's far too excited about it and there's no way we're not going now.

A thought suddenly hits me and makes me feel even more like shit. *She's never asked me for anything.* In fact, she's been hesitant to take *anything* from me since the day she started working for me. This one thing that I'm giving her is probably the first thing she's let me do for her without some level of hesitation.

Lowering my arms to rest below her ass, I lift her from the floor and she instinctively wraps her legs around my waist. She lays her head on my shoulder and tightens her arms around my neck. Carrying her, I take a seat on the barstool and tenderly talk to her.

"Sophia, *My Angel*, why do I get the feeling you don't really forgive me?"

She sniffles and I feel like a total asshole. She speaks slowly and her voice is sincere, but strained, as she tries to hide the tears from me. "I *do* forgive you, Dom."

"What's wrong then, baby?"

She hesitates before answering, but I can feel the wheels turning in her mind. She's trying to formulate her answer so I will give her a minute without adding the pressure of reminding her it's also disrespectful to make me wait. Doms, by nature, are demanding and expect things to be a specific way. That's not to say we aren't also lenient when needed and flexible when the situation calls for it. This is one of those times.

"What you said, Dom. I believe *you*, but *that* is just hard for me to believe," she finally answers. I must admit that I am completely baffled.

"What do you mean, love? I don't understand. Explain it to me."

167

"When you said I'm special, one of a kind, and you've never had anyone like me before. No one has *ever* told me that I'm special," she whispers so softly it's hard to hear her. But I know what I heard, and again I have to control my voice so that she doesn't think I'm upset with her.

"You are very special, Sophia. You're beautiful, smart, and loving. You make me *want* to protect and care for you. No one has even come close to that in almost a year and a half, Sophia. So, see, you are *My Angel*."

She squeezes me tighter with both her arms and her legs, as if she can't get close enough to me. Her body shakes as she clutches the back of my shirt in her fists. She's holding back the sobs, and for the life of me, I still don't know exactly what all of this is about. I *do* know she's in no shape to talk right now without getting further upset.

"Sophia, sweetheart," I say as I gently stroke her back, "let's agree to talk about all of this – tonight—after you've calmed down and had a relaxing day. I want to know everything about you, but I don't think now is the best time for you."

Slowly, she releases her grasp on me and puts a little breathing room between us. After quickly wiping the tears from her face, she nods and agrees to talk later tonight. "I'm going to wash my face while you change into your swimming suit,

Dom," she says as she gets up from my lap. "If that's okay," she quickly adds.

"Of course, baby.   Go ahead," I reply thoughtfully.

This snorkeling trip is just what the doctor ordered.   Or, in this case, just what the Dom ordered. Sophia is quiet on the ride over to La Jolla Cove, but she is also much more affectionate. Siting in the backseat on the way to the office this morning, she sat on her side of the car and had her seatbelt on. Now, she's as close to me as she can get without actually being in my lap. Both of her hands are clasped around one of mine, almost as if she's afraid I will get away from her and she's holding on with everything she has.

When I pull my hand free of hers, sadness overcomes her face until she realizes that I'm putting my arm around her to draw her into my side. She willingly comes to me, wraps her arms around my waist, and lays her head in the crook of my shoulder. She has the happiest and most peaceful look about her—just the way she looked on the beach when I snapped the pictures of her.

After listening to all the safety instructions, we finally enter the water. Sophia comes alive again while looking at all the fish, leopard sharks, stingrays, and sea lions. For me, it is equally exciting to see Sophia in a skin-tight wetsuit. It's actually giving me some good ideas for scenes we can play out when we've worked up to that in our relationship. The thing about wetsuits is they seem to enhance all body imperfections. In Sophia's case, she looks like she was airbrushed into it and it only accentuates her beauty. In my case, it does very little to hide the most obvious bulge I get from looking at her.

Good thing the Pacific Ocean is so damn cold.

After the tour concludes, we are able to keep the wetsuits for a while longer to just enjoy the water on our own. Every few minutes, she thanks me again for bringing her snorkeling. After several hours, my rumbling stomach reminds me we haven't eaten since breakfast and I finally convince Sophia it's time to turn our gear back in and head back to dry land. She has been more animated and talkative than I have ever seen her as she describes everything she saw and how incredible it was for her.

We take a short walk to a local restaurant and ask to be seated in one of their sidewalk café seats, since we're not really presentable for a more expensive restaurant at the moment. Sophia is still smiling and glowing with happiness and I'm proud to be the man who gave her that look. Pulling her hand to my mouth, I kiss each knuckle, then turn her hand over and kiss her palm.

"What was that for, Dom?" she asks innocently.

"For being you," I answer truthfully. I have no other reason. The slight pink tinge of embarrassment creeps up her neck and into her cheeks again. "How can you still be embarrassed in front of me?"

She shrugs, as if her answer means nothing, and says, "I'm not used to getting compliments. You always give them and it embarrasses me."

"Well, I will just have to keep complimenting you until you get used to them. Don't you think?"

The waitress arrives with our food, saving Sophia from actually answering that question. My plan is already devised in my mind. It's time to fully initiate Sophia into my world.

Chapter Thirteen

As I suspected, Rich Daltry was just intentionally wasting our time and jerking us around. He had every intention of signing the contract after Sophia backed him into a corner. Instead of just telling us before we left his office, he waited until we left to sign and fax the contract back to my office. After our snorkeling adventure and a late lunch, Sophia wanted to walk and window-shop. While we were strolling down the sidewalk, Dana called to tell me our legal department had approved the contract.

"Looks like we have some time open for a couple of days, Sophia. There's somewhere I want to take you," I intentionally leave the pertinent information out.

"Wherever you want to go is fine with me, Dom," she squeezes my hand as she answers.

An hour later, we've showered, dressed, packed, and the private jet is being readied. Sophia still hasn't asked me where we're going and I'm sensing that she trusts me a little more. My internal smile finds its way to my face and she catches me grinning for no apparent reason.

"What are you smiling about, Dom?" her tone has a teasing admonition in it.

"I was just thinking about you and how you must trust me now," I reply bluntly to gauge her reaction.

"I'm learning to trust you. I do for the most part. I guess I'm just still waiting for the other shoe to drop."

"This is me, Sophia—I'm an open book. I'm not hiding from you."

"I haven't seen you get really mad yet, Dom. I don't know how you'll react when that happens," her eyes are wide and her voice has a twinge of apprehension in it.

"It doesn't matter how mad I get, Sophia. I would never raise my hand to you and hurt you. That is *not* the kind of man I am," I assure her, although I know my words mean little in this case. If I reassure her and show her, she will eventually learn to take me at my word.

"Why are you being so patient with me?"

"I've already told you. I am your Dom. I know what you need, even before you do."

Back on the private jet, Tucker takes his place in the cockpit with the pilot, Steve, while Sophia and I take our seats. Susan is busy making the final preparations before our flight but takes a moment to bring us a drink. Sophia sips on hers and keeps glancing at me every few seconds. It's killing her to not know where we're going, but I have a feeling that knowing would make her even more nervous.

Taking her hand in mine, I simply state, "Calm, *My Angel*. You're with me, you're mine, and I take care of what's mine. Remember?" This tactic works and she obediently complies with my order.

We settle in comfortably on the plush, leather couch and Sophia snuggles up to my side. Within a few minutes, she's fast asleep and using me as her personal Dom pillow. She throws her leg over mine and wraps her arm around me. Even with as uncomfortable as I've become after more than an hour of sitting in this one position, I don't want to wake her, but she just feels too good and my cock is throbbing with need for her. The private bedroom in the back of the jet is calling my name.

"Sophia," I say softly as I rub her back, "wake up, love."

She stirs and lifts her head, looking around in confusion before she realizes where she is.

"We've already taken off?" she asks.

I chuckle, "Yes, love. We've been in the air about an hour now. There's a bedroom in the back of the plane. Why don't you join me?" I intentionally lower the timbre of my voice, leaving no room for misunderstanding.

Sophia reaches up and kisses me intimately before saying, "I'm with you. I'm yours. Take care of me."

Helping her to her feet, I place my hand at the small of her back and guide her to the waiting bedroom. "Stand still for me, love. I want to savor every second of this."

Sophia nods and I begin undressing her. With every piece of clothing that's removed, my hands and mouth worship the skin that's revealed. Her low murmurs of pleasure spur me on, making it more and more difficult for me to wait. As a Dom, I

Her Dom

have trained my body to comply with my will. When I'm with Sophia, the carnal side of me is in a constant war with my controlled side to take over.

Quickly shedding my clothes, my excitement and readiness for her is abundantly clear. Her soft hand grasps my cock and begins to slowly move up and down. Folding her legs, she drops to her knees and wraps her splendid lips around me. Her hand is as the base of my cock and begins working me faster, in tandem with her mouth. My head falls back of its own accord as she takes me deeper and I feel the back of her throat.

"Damn, baby, you're *killing* me," I growl and pull her to her feet. Covering her mouth with mine, I guide her until we're in position on the bed. As I bury myself in her, I pour my feelings into every thrust, every kiss, and every love bite I leave on her beautiful skin. There's something about the sight of my teeth marks on her creamy skin that intensifies my libido.

As we hit our peak together, I fight back the urge to tell her how much she means to me. It's too soon to express the sentiment, to voice the words, or to give life to the thought. Regardless of whether I say it, I've already taken the biggest step and given her the one thing I've never given anyone else. She just doesn't realize the significance of it yet.

Two hours later, we land in Corpus Christi and Tucker secures our car and luggage while Sophia and I freshen up. The Texas heat hits us as soon as we exit the plane and the only consolation is the breeze blowing off the bay. Tucker pulls the S65 AMG Mercedes Sedan around and we climb into the back, instantly feeling the relief of the air conditioning. Opening the compartment between our seats, I retrieve two chilled bottles of water.

"Are you going to tell me where we're going now?" she asks with a sly smile as she sips her water.

Leaning over the center console, I frame her face with my hands and pull her in to thoroughly kiss her. Just as I feel her melting against me again, becoming pliable and willing in my hands, I whisper against her lips, "You're going to meet my parents."

She suddenly freezes—it's like instant suspended animation. Her mouth drops open and she looks at me with both suspicion and disbelief in her eyes. She thinks this is all a practical joke, but she's wrong. It's time for her to meet the family and immerse herself into my life. I've agreed to be her Dom, to take care of her and be responsible for her. To do that fully, she needs to be inducted into the family.

"Tell me you're kidding," she says flatly.

"No, not at all. You will watch your tone and words with me, Sophia," I level her with my Dom look. She immediately assumes the submissive position again. "I think it's time we have that punishment talk."

"Yes, Dom," she replies with her eyes downcast.

"We're going to meet my parents. If you really want to be my sub, you need to meet my family and be part of it. You will not be separate. You're not a dirty little secret. You're an important part of me and this is important to me," I explain with more impatience infused in my voice than I intended.

"I'm sorry I disappointed you. It will be an honor to meet your family," she replies, her voice unpretentious and her shoulders are slumped in resignation.

Tucker pulls up to the front walkway of my parents' palatial home. He gets out to get our luggage and I exit the car and walk around to her side to open the door for her. Taking her hand to help her out, I pull her close to me and give her a chaste kiss on the lips. "Sophia, relax. What have I told you?"

"I'm yours and you take care of what's yours," she recites back to me.

"Have I hurt you yet?" I ask pointedly.

"No, Dom," she shakes her head.

"Then I think I've earned at least some of your trust," I state definitively. "If you want this to work, you have to do your part. If not, tell me now before you meet my parents."

"No, I want this!" she replies emphatically.

"It's time to start showing it, then."

She nods in agreement but doesn't verbally answer. Her bottom lip is quivering as she realizes she was precariously close to losing me. "Let's go. They are waiting for us to arrive. My mother is so excited to meet you."

"She knows about me?"

"Yes, she knows about you. Come on," I turn her to face the house.

Finally really looking at it, she gasps audibly and her hand flies up to cover her mouth. It really is a magnificent home with all the comforts and luxuries money can buy. But my mother has worked very hard to make it a home, not a museum, so it also feels very homey and cozy. Well, to me, at least. Sophia seems to be having other thoughts at the moment.

As we approach the front door, it swings open widely and my mom rushes out to welcome us. She's always so happy to see me and gives me a big hug. I love both of my parents. They've been great and made a wonderful home for my siblings and me. But, being the only son, I've always had a special bond with my mom. She understands me better than anyone.

"My baby boy is home!" she exclaims as she rushes toward me.

"Hi, Mom," I reply warmly as I take her in my arms. She kisses me on the cheek and steps back to look at me, checking to see if I've changed any, even though I'm well past grown.

"Mom, this is Sophia. Sophia, this is my mom, Kayla," I make introductions and the two most important women in my life politely consider each other. My mom grabs Sophia and hugs her like she's known her all her life.

"Sophia, it is so nice to meet you, sweetie," Mom says as she takes Sophia's arm and leads her to the house. "These men can get your things. Let me show you around."

"I can manage the bags, sir. You can go on in and visit with your family," Tucker offers.

"Thank you, Tucker. I appreciate that. Here, I'll take these two with me," I say as I pick up Sophia's personal bag and my special suitcase. As I enter the house, Dad steps out of his study and embraces me.

"Good to have you home, son," he says as we each turn and walk toward the stairs.

"Good to be home, Dad," I reply. "I'm going up to put our things in my room and I'll be right down. Mom took Sophia off on a tour, so if you find them first, don't let them out of your sight or we'll never find them again," I joke and we both laugh as I jog up the stairs.

A few minutes later, I hear voices and laughter coming from the kitchen so I head toward the back of the house. Sophia is sitting at the table with my parents, talking and laughing, and they seem to have bonded. Upon closer inspection, I see that they are actually bonding over the family photo album.

Fucking great.

"Mom," I draw it out in exasperation.

"Sit down, Dominic," she replies in her mom-voice, that tone that says *'don't fuck with your mom'* without actually embarrassing the child because only the family recognizes the inflection.

I do as she says—otherwise she will embarrass me. Mom doesn't tolerate anything that remotely resembles disrespect toward her or Dad. Leaning over the table, I immediately recognize the pictures she's showing Sophia. They're of me, of course, in various activities through high school. There are several different shots of me in football, baseball, proms, homecoming dances, and some just funny shots with my friends.

"Sophia, I see you've met my dad, Rick," I look between them and they both nod.

"This boy here—what was his name, Dominic?" Mom asks as she picks up the picture to show me.

"That's Joey," I respond with a smile. "He was he craziest guy I knew in high school and he always stayed in some kind of trouble with the teachers, but they couldn't resist his personality, so he normally got out of everything."

"What about you, Dom?" Sophia asks and my mom's head jerks up from the pictures. She rapidly looks between Sophia and me as I purposely keep my eyes from meeting hers. Sophia continues, "Did you get in a lot of trouble in school?"

182

"Nah," I say shaking my head. "I rarely got caught." The table erupts into laughter and my mom swats my arm for good measure.

"I know just what this group needs," Dad says as he gets up from the table. Sophia looks up at him, questioning what he meant but not yet comfortable enough to ask him.

"Dad is making a round of his specialty—Piña Coladas. They are the best you will ever have and he won't tell anyone his secret," I explain to Sophia.

"That's right!" Dad exclaims as he gathers his ingredients. "Even your mom can't get that information out of me."

Mom laughs and whispers to Sophia conspiratorially, "I could get it out of him if I wanted to."

Sophia and Mom both laugh and Dad wiggles his eyebrows at Mom suggestively, "I've been telling you for years to just try your best."

Mom gets up and walks over to Dad. Standing on her tiptoes to reach his cheek for a kiss, she replies, "You know I would do anything you want me to—recipe or no recipe."

Sophia smiles, at first, as she watches them, and then her smile fades. The romantic, hopeful look she had just a moment ago has been replaced with sadness. Reaching across the table, I take her hand in mine as I say, "Hey, are you okay?"

"Yes, I'm fine," she says, putting her happy face on again. "I was just thinking about my parents and wishing they could've been like yours. You must've had a great childhood."

I glance over at my parents, who are in a loving embrace in the kitchen, and I have to agree with her. "Our home was full of love. It sounds like yours wasn't and I'm sorry to hear that. But that doesn't mean you can't have a happily ever after."

That longing look is back in Sophia's eyes, but it's not a sexual longing. It's a desire for a real family, to have someone to lean on, and to know that there is someone in her corner who will fight to the end for her. *Unconditionally.* The very thing she's never had but always wanted.

"Okay, everyone, the grill is hot and the steaks are marinated. Kayla, throw the potatoes in the microwave and let's get some food to go with my special *Ricka Co-la-das,*" he finishes with a fake Spanish accent and pitiful attempt at humor. It garners a giggle from Sophia, anyway, and she rises to help my mom with the preparations.

The blender whirs until Dad's concoction is ready and I grab enough glasses for everyone. Dad takes the marinated steaks out of the refrigerator and walks out on the back deck, leaving the door open for me to follow him. Sophia glances up and shrieks, "Oh my god!" Everyone jerks their heads around to see what she's looking at and her eyes are still glued to the door leading outside.

"What is it, love?" I ask.

"Oh, I'm sorry. How embarrassing! I just saw the backyard and I can't believe how beautiful it looks! It rivals even the house!" she gushes.

"I will be glad to show you around as soon as we finish eating," my dad offers, obviously proud of his backyard oasis.

"I would love that, Mr. Powers."

"Rick, please," he says with a smile as he walks back out on the deck.

I join him and leave Sophia with my mom in the kitchen. Dad doesn't even glance over at me as he lifts the lid of the built-in grill of their outdoor kitchen as he says, "Dom, huh?"

Inhaling deeply, I know there's no way out of this conversation, so I answer truthfully, "Yes."

"You've never let any of the others call you that. She's that special to you, son?" Dad's voice is full of concern. He's trying hard not to cross the line of giving unsolicited advice and being a father who cares about his son.

185

"She is, Dad. I can't explain it. I knew she was different from the second I laid eyes on her, and I didn't even know she was already somewhat trained as a submissive then."

"Somewhat trained?" he asks, his brow drawn down and his head titled to the side.

"Yeah, I don't have the full story yet, but he abused his authority and he abused her."

Dad shakes his head in disgust. The look on his face mirrors mine and I know he's thinking the same thing I am—if we could only get our hands on that fucker, he would never abuse anyone again.

"Just be careful, son. Make sure she's the one before you're fully vested in her," he says as he cups his hand on my shoulder.

"What do you think of her so far, Dad?" I ask, genuinely interested in his opinion.

"I think your mom will feel her out and tell us both what she thinks," Dad responds with a smile.

He's right, actually, and that's most likely the very thing that drove me to bring her here so soon. Mom is like a human radar—nothing gets by her. My sisters and I used to joke growing up that no matter how hard we tried to hide something, Mom must really have eyes in the back of her head—and everywhere else—because she always knew the second we looked at her.

Several minutes later, the steaks are ready and Mom and Sophia are setting the outdoor table. Sophia seems to be really enjoying herself with Mom, and Mom loves all the attention that Sophia is lavishing on her. They're chatting about girlie stuff while I help Dad with the grill. Sophia's happiness is radiating from her face and there is an actual glow about her.

We're all enjoying the deck after dinner, sufficiently stuffed, and not eager to start cleaning up yet. Mom, in her usual take-no-prisoners action, breaks the evening pleasantries with a question that has me choking on my drink and Sophie staring at her in stunned silence.

"So, Sophia, tell me, when did you become Dominic's sub?" Mom asks as if she's asking Sophia about the earrings she's wearing instead.

"Mom!"

"Don't raise your voice at your mother, Dominic," Dad chastises me and pins me with his eyes.

"Sorry, Mom," I concede. I was raised to know better. Dad doesn't joke about how Mom is talked to or treated by anyone.

"It's okay, Sophia.   You can tell us," Mom continues, completely ignoring me.

"Officially, just a couple of days now," Sophia finally answers. "But, in some ways, since I started working for him a few weeks ago."

"I see," Mom says without really conveying her thoughts.

"How did you know?" Sophia asks Mom, truly interested.

Mom gives Sophia an understanding smile before she answers.   I cringe, knowing what's coming next.

"Because I'm Rick's sub. I suspected when you first arrived, but I knew when you called him 'Dom'," Mom explains.

Sophia blanches white, staring at Mom, and I know she's trying to ascertain if Mom is telling the truth or if she's just fucking with her mind. What Sophia doesn't realize is, Mom only tells the truth *all* the time, whether it's what you want to hear or not.

"She's telling you the truth, Sophia. This is part of why I wanted you to meet them at this time. This has been their choice my whole life and they're very happy with it," I reassure her.

Turning to Mom, I share some of Sophia's information, "Mom, we're working on building trust now. Sophia had a bad experience where the man responsible for her abused his position and abused her. She's learning that I'm not that man."

Mom's reaction is not unexpected to me, but may be shocking to Sophia. "That bastard needs to have his dick cut off and shoved down his throat then," she says, and then turns to Sophia. "Honey, that is not how we raised Dominic, and while I know he would never do anything like that, *if* he ever did, all you have to do is call me and I will take care of it *immediately.*"

Sophia's eyes are as big as saucers and she stammers for a moment before she can intelligently speak again. "But, I thought you were a submissive?" Sophia questions, clearly confused and trying hard to reconcile all the information she's just been given.

"I am, honey, *to Rick.* I am not submissive to anyone else—ever," Mom declares resolutely. "Just let another man try to dominate me one time. I will put him in his place so quickly he won't know what hit him. *My* man is the only one who has that right."

The wheels are turning in Sophia's head again and confusion has quickly become a resident on her face. Clearly, she has not been instructed this way and she's not sure what she should do. I take her hand in mine, giving her my strength and support as she considers the implications of what all she has just learned. "You can speak candidly here, Sophia. No one will judge you. If you have questions, Mom and Dad will be glad to help."

"You just seem so…loving," Sophia replies as her eyes dart between Mom and Dad.

Dad is thoughtful in his reply, "Sophia, Kayla submits to me because she *wants* to, not because I *demand* it of her. It's a gift that she gives me but I have to earn it. It's my job to create the trusting environment where she feels safe to give me total control. If submission is *taken* from you any other way, it's is abuse, plain and simple. Kayla is free to change her mind at any time, it's not up to me."

"That's right, honey," Mom chimes in. "We are loving, and we always have been, because first and foremost, Rick is my husband. We're in this together as man and wife, equally important and equals period."

"I think, Sophia," Dad says, "that maybe you have been given the wrong impression of a submissive. Being Kayla's Sir means that she is up on a pedestal and I do whatever it takes to keep her happy and meet her needs. That's what she does for me, so why would she get any less from me?"

Chapter Fourteen

"Well, I think Sophia has had enough excitement for one day," I state, saving her from any further parental advice. "Let me show you around the grounds." I help her up from her seat and place my hand on her lower back.

"Thank you so much for dinner," Sophia says to them both. "If you don't mind waiting a few minutes, I'll be glad to do all the cleaning up."

"No, ma'am, you're our guest. Besides, we have a housekeeper and a cook who usually handle all this for us. Rick just likes to fire up the grill himself. It's his man-thing," Mom laughs. "You two go enjoy yourselves and don't worry about a thing."

"Thanks, Mom. Thanks, Dad. No need to wait up," I say with a smile and Dad laughs.

The backyard really is an oasis and is somewhere I could get lost for hours and thoroughly enjoy it. Mom had it professionally developed to provide some shade during the hot Texas summers. Tall palm trees and Saw Palmetto bushes flank the slate rock lined path, with thick Bermuda sod grass and hostas accentuating the lushness of the area. The pathway itself is relaxing and beautiful, but it hides the focal point of the yard until the very last second.

Rounding the bend, Sophia stops suddenly and gushes over the view that is now before us. Tall rocks surround the infinity pool with ledges at multiple heights. Water cascades down the rocks at different places, like multiple waterfalls running at once. The tiki lamps outline the lagoon shape of the pool, and with dusk fading into night, the firelight shimmers off the water. It really is breathtaking and Sophia seems to love it.

The chaise loungers are spread around the perimeter of the pool so I guide Sophia to the closest one. We sit down together on one lounger and I stroke her arm, giving her a moment to take everything in.

"This is so beautiful," she whispers.

"Yes, it is," I reply, not taking my eyes off of her. She feels me looking at her and turns to fully face me. "Talk to me, Sophia. How are you taking all of this?"

"It's a lot to take in, but I'm really glad you brought me here," she says earnestly. "Your parents are wonderful. I wish I could've had such loving parents."

"That doesn't mean that there weren't problems along the way, you know? It just means they worked on them together and stayed together no matter what they faced," I explain. "They've just always loved each other more than anything else."

Sophia stares off into the water and her mind is a million miles away. I kiss her hand and her eyes refocus when she looks up at me. "I do trust you, Dom. I'm sorry for doubting you. I'm really working on putting that behind us," she says as a single tear rolls down her cheek.

"Tell me."

"There are just so many differences in your definition of a submissive and what I've known. I'm having a hard time wrapping my head around it," Sophia admits the very thing I suspected.

"Is my definition so bad?"

"No, it's not bad. It's good—almost too good to be true. I've always been told *'if it's too good to be true, then it probably isn't true.'*"

I nod in understanding. "What does your heart tell you?"

"My heart says to hold on to you and never let go," she replies without hesitation.

"Follow your heart, *My Angel.*"

Sophia's eyes fill with unshed tears and her bottom lip quivers as she vehemently fights against crying. Simultaneously, we reach for each other and our mouths collide in a heated, passionate kiss as I lift her to straddle me. Just the feel of her hands on me is enough to set me on fire. I need to be inside her—*now*—and I don't care that we're in my parents' backyard.

Thankful that she's still wearing her skirt, I push it up around her waist and lift her to sit astride me as I turn to lie back in the lounger. Her upper body is pressed against mine as we continue to caress each other. She moans when she reaches between my legs and feels my cock hard and ready for her. She makes quick work of unfastening my pants and I lift my hips to help her pull them down.

Just when I think she's about to move back to my lap, the wet, warmth of her mouth wraps around me and my head falls back in sheer pleasure. I jerk my head up when my cock hits the back of her throat and she lightly shakes her head before she swallows. As her throat muscles tighten around me, my hands grasp her hair and I tug on it as her head moves up. "Damn, baby, you're killing me," I growl out at her.

Her eyes lift to look at me as she takes me as deep as she can. The sight of her enjoying pleasuring me so much has me about ready to explode. "*My Angel*, I want you on top of me," I instruct. As she takes her place back on top of me, I know the words are on the tip of her tongue. She wants to say them but she won't since I haven't said it first.

Her soft hand draws my attention as she wraps it around my cock and guides me to the ultimate destination. "Fuck, you're already so wet," I grind out as she slides down me. I grab her hips and help set the pace as she rocks back and forth. Lifting my hips as she comes down, I bury myself deeper and deeper inside of her over and over again with each thrust. Then she leans back and puts her hands on my legs as she rides out the waves of her orgasm. Using my thumb, I stroke small circles on her clit as she comes completely unhinged on top of me.

"That's my girl," I praise her, "you're so beautiful. You take my breath away."

She leans forward and I capture her mouth with mine. I wrap my arms around her and hold her tightly to me as I sit up, taking her with me. She readjusts her legs so that her toes are touching the ground on either side of the lounge chair. Using her legs, she moves up and down then circles her hips, repeatedly, and I feel her becoming wetter and wetter. As her inner muscles grip me once again, the sensation is so intense that I can't resist the urge to come with her. The face-to-face experience is powerful—watching her eyes glass over, her face contort in gratification, and holding her body flush against mine.

"Now, *My Angel*, I want to feel you come again *now*. With me," I command and she obeys as she screams out my name.

Lying back with her on my chest and with me still buried deep inside her, this feels incredible. Holding her, making love to her, knowing the feelings I'm experiencing are reciprocated, and never wanting to let her go are all both new and exciting, and familiar and typical. The thought that I've found *the one* keeps running through my mind at various times.

Is she the one? The one I can't live without? The one I spend the rest of my life with? I can't picture my life without her in it now. She's the first thing on my mind when I wake up and the last on my mind before I fall asleep. Even in the time that we were only working together and not lovers, she haunted my thoughts and consumed my dreams.

These are all the things I can't bring myself to tell her yet. We've only started exploring our Dom/submissive relationship, and I'm not convinced that her previous experiences will allow her to fully enjoy what I can offer her. Being honest with myself, I'm not sure I would be fulfilled without being able to fully explore with her, to push us both to our limits and beyond, just to see how much pleasure we can experience. On the other hand, I don't think I would be fulfilled doing those things with anyone else now that we've crossed that line into a relationship.

She lazily lifts her head from my shoulder and places a sweet kiss on my lips. "What was that for?" I ask her.

"For always knowing exactly what I need and what I'm feeling. I've made a decision," she states.

I arch my eyebrow at her dubiously and wait for her epiphany. "And what's that?"

"I'm following my heart, Dom. I'm not strong enough to ever leave you. I'm running to you and I'm never letting you go," she softly declares. "Don't break me. Please don't break me."

Capturing her face in my hands, I pull her mouth back to mine as I pour my feelings into our kiss. I can't say it yet but I can make her feel it, I can show her, and I can do everything in my power to make sure she stays. "You're safe with me, *My Angel*. I would never hurt you—you're part of me now. You're the one I'm falling for and I'm beginning to believe you're the one I've needed all along."

Her tears run unchecked down her cheeks as her eyes shimmer with the love that's bubbling underneath. She snuggles back into her spot and I wrap my arms around her. Like hot magma, just under the earth's surface ready to erupt into a great volcano, her love is waiting for its opportunity to spill over. The way Sophia looks at me, the way the depth of her brown eyes pull me into her soul, and how she tries so hard despite her past are all indications that this is the love I've waited and searched for over the years.

I just can't tell her yet. My own past experiences are still lingering in the dark recesses of my mind—and in my heart. It's like a knife stabbing me every single time she gives more of herself to me. I feel like I'm holding out on her, like I'm keeping a secret that could change everything between us. It's that thought that plagues my mind day and night. It makes me question if I'm good enough for her, if I'm strong enough to carry the load for us both, and if I can be the kind of Dom that she deserves, that she needs, and that will bring out the best in her.

The man I want to be for her and the heartbreak of my past are warring in my mind for the preeminent position. While I know I should tell her and give her the chance to leave now before I'm in over my head, I secretly think it's too late for that. I think I burned that bridge when I allowed her to call me 'Dom,' the name no other has ever been allowed to call me. My mom knew it immediately when Sophia said it, even though I wouldn't look at Mom and verify her unspoken question.

Now, here I am, having brought Sophia home to meet my parents, introducing her to our way of life, and effectively making her a member of the family. Oh, and there's also the fact that, as a grown man who has the utmost control over his emotions, I just made love to her in the backyard of my parents' house. That probably counts for *something* in the way of commitment.

Yet, I can't make the same declaration she just made. I can't tell her I love her and have her say it back to me yet. I can give her anything—I will do everything in my considerable power to protect her, shelter her, and care for her...except for those three little words that would mean so much to her. I feel like such a failure and a hypocrite in that area.

I don't know how long I've sat here and mused over our fate, but the skies are very dark now and most of the lights coming from the area of the house have faded to near black. "Sophia, *My Angel*, we need to go in and get some sleep. It's been a long day, love," I coax her awake.

She stands and straightens her skirt as I adjust my pants. Walking back to the house, Sophia shuffles her feet in exhaustion and leans into me for support. I quickly hook one arm under her knees and one at the small of her back to carry her the rest of the way. Wrapping her arms around my neck, she's sound asleep in my arms within a minute. Her sweet breath is warm against my neck and her hair tickles my face, but I still nuzzle as close to her as I can get. I think she's under my skin now—there's no turning back. I may not say it, but it's there.

Like any other secret, it can only stay hidden for so long before it comes out for all to see. That knowledge is the only thing that scares me. Secrets, truths, lies, and regrets—there are just so many. Hindsight provides too much clarity, points out too many things I should've handled differently, and reveals too many missed opportunities that I didn't see at the time. I'm smart enough to know that hindsight doesn't guarantee a better outcome—maybe not even a different one. The thing is, I will never know.

Carrying her to our bedroom, Sophia barely notices when I remove her clothes and get in the bed beside her. She turns on her side and I spoon her from behind, pulling her close to me and noticing the way her body molds perfectly into mine. Nuzzling my face into her hair, I kiss her head goodnight and wish I could say it, even now while she's asleep. The last thing I remember is falling asleep to the rhythm of her breathing.

"Dominic! Dominic! Wake up!" I hear the sweet, feminine voice calling to me. I see her face in my dreams and I rush to her. She's just out of my reach, no matter how hard I try or how fast I run to her. I can't reach her and the foreboding feeling of impending doom is heavy, like a wet blanket covering me and suffocating me. But I can't give up because she needs me. She's still calling me.

"Dominic, please! Can you hear me?" my siren calls again.

Yes, baby, I can hear you and I'm trying desperately to reach you. Wait for me this time. Give me a chance to help you.

"Dom!" she screams and shakes me. My eyes fly open at the name she used, and for a few seconds, I look around the room, completely disoriented and unsure of where I am. "Oh my god, Dom! You scared me! Are you okay?" Sophia's face comes into focus and I realize I've been dreaming. Only this time, I mixed some of my real life with my dream life, and the realization that I must be all kinds of fucked up hits me like a ton of lead.

"I'm okay, baby. I'm sorry I scared you. What happened?" I ask, hiding the fact that I'm cringing inside because I don't know what I said in my sleep. I won't lie to her to try to explain it away. If I have to, I will have to tell her now, at a time when I'm certainly not ready to tell her. It's definitely not my first choice, but I've learned the hard way that sometimes there are no choices.

"You were thrashing around," her voice still holds the panic I awoke to, "and you kept mumbling something. I couldn't understand what you were saying, but you sounded so...sad...so distraught. Do you want to talk about your dream?"

"No, baby, I'm okay. I don't need to talk about it. I'm not sure I could even describe it," I state calmly. She cocks her head to the side and narrows her eyes at me in disbelief. "Don't worry about me. Really. I'm fine. Let's go back to sleep," I cajole her and she snuggles against me again.

Soon, her breathing evens out and she's fallen back into a deep slumber. I lie awake and run one scenario after another through my mind. *How should I tell her? What is the best way to approach the topic? How would I even start that conversation?* Once I envision the scenario I think

202

would work best for us both, my racing mind slows to a snail's pace. Once I commit to telling her soon, the dread and doom dissipates and I soon join her in sleep.

Chapter Fifteen

Waking early, I watch Sophia sleep for a few minutes. She's resting peacefully, so I decide to let her sleep as I ease out of bed and slip into my pajama pants. Taking my time going down the stairs, my mind is on the dreams I had last night and how whatever I was doing in my sleep scared Sophia. As I turn the corner toward the kitchen, I know my mom is already in there. The smell of coffee wafts down the hall along with the soft clinking noises from the dishes.

"Morning, Mom. What are you doing up so early?" I ask as I walk straight to the coffee cups and pour a cup.

"Morning, son. I just couldn't sleep," she replies and I can see the weight of the world on her shoulders. I've always been close to my mom and I know when she's stressed.

"What's wrong, Mom? What are you stressing over?" I get straight to the point. I guess I get trait that from her.

She sips her coffee and looks over the rim of the cup at me. She's deciding what she should and shouldn't say. I can read her as well as she can read me. I'm man enough to say I love my mom with everything I am. We have always been very close and she knows everything about me. I trust her and value her opinion. Taking my seat across from her at the table, I patiently wait for her to answer my question.

"You've taken a big step by letting her call you *'Dom,'* son," she finally says. No beating around the bush, no hinting or working up to whatever is weighing on her mind. Not for my mom—she goes right to the heart of the matter and puts it out on the table for all to see. "It's only been a couple of days. I think it's too soon."

"Mom," I reply, drawing out the one-syllable word into at least three syllables, just like when I was a teenager and she called me out on my bullshit. And much like back then, I have no other response in my arsenal.

"Don't *'Mom'* me, Dominic. That is part of your name and part of you. We've stressed how important it is that *'Dom'* would be reserved for the one you would spend the rest of your life with,"

205

Mom admonishes me. "This is a big deal, son. If it doesn't work with Sophia, that title will still be linked with her. It can never fully belong to anyone else."

She's right—it *is* a big deal and it *is* very soon. I've never let anyone call me that name, even as a nickname in school. If anyone even tried, I shut it down immediately. Soon, no one even attempted it and my employees would definitely never be so informal with me. Sophia is different and I knew it as soon as she stepped into my office.

"It's alright, Mom. It *is* very soon, I will give you that, but she's so unlike anyone I've dated before. I can't even explain it to you adequately. She's naïve, inexperienced, and insecure—but at the same time, she's bold, she's smart, and she's brave. There's something in her that drives her to try the things that scare her the most. Her courage amazes me." I try to articulate all the things that make me crave Sophia more and more every moment, but I'm only scratching the tip of the iceberg with a fork.

The dubious look Mom gives me in return doesn't help matters. The dream is still at the forefront of my thoughts and sometimes I would swear my mom is a mind reader. She stares me down as she takes another sip of her coffee and part of me wants to laugh at her attempt to intimidate me. But she knows me better than anyone—she knows all of my deepest secrets and fears—so her concern is valid. She arches an eyebrow at me and no words are needed.

"It's too late, Mom," I confess. "Don't worry. I'm fine."

She sighs heavily and slowly nods her head as if she already knew and was just waiting for me to confirm it. "You know, Dominic, it really doesn't matter how old you are. A mother never stops worrying about her children."

Mom gets up from the table and begins taking ingredients out of the refrigerator to make our breakfast. For as long as I can remember, Dad has offered to have our cook come early in the morning so Mom wouldn't have to cook but she would never agree. There were very few things that she solidly put her foot down over, and this was one of those things, so Dad always indulged her. She wanted us to start every day as just a normal family. Breakfasts with my family are some of my favorite memories from my childhood.

As I enter the bedroom, I faintly hear the water running in the bathroom and then a moment later, Sophia comes sweeping into the room. The aroma of jasmine, rose, and orchid drifts into the room in her wake. She's dressed and ready for the day, looking beautiful as always, when she sees me staring. She stops walking and stares back at me for a second before her smile lights up her face.

"Good morning, Dom," she says sweetly as she walks to me and kisses me. "I missed you this morning. I hope I didn't sleep too long."

"No, baby, you're good. Dad hasn't made it downstairs yet. Mom and I just had a cup of coffee together and she's cooking breakfast now," I say as I pull her into my arms.

"How rude of me! I should go down and help her!" she exclaims as she frantically searches for her shoes.

I calmly grasp her by the shoulders to get her attention, "No, baby, breakfast is her *thing*. She won't let you—she *likes* doing this for us."

After I take a quick shower and get dressed, I join everyone downstairs in the kitchen. As I approach, I hear Mom, Dad, and Sophia talking and laughing together like old friends. Mom is putting the last of the breakfast foods on the table as I walk in the room.

"Just in time," Mom smiles at me.

After a way too big breakfast, we spend the majority of the day with my parents, doing nothing and everything together. Sophia seems so much more at ease now and she's enjoying this close family time. I notice, at times, she has a forlorn look on her face but she quickly rejoins us in the moment. I suspect she's making comparisons again and feeling regrets of how her life could have been had circumstances been different. In the late afternoon, Sophia and I say our goodbyes and Tucker drives us back to the airport.

"You look happy," I comment to her as we ride in the backseat.

"I *am* happy, Dom," she replies. "Why wouldn't I be?"

"You seem happier now than when we first arrived."

"I feel closer to you now, after meeting your parents. I felt like I fit in with them, like they accepted me," she says as her eyes drift off to gaze out the window past me.

Taking her chin in my hand, I capture her attention and hold her gaze steady as I assure her. "They *do* accept you and you *do* fit in with my family. My parents understand how important you are to me. You don't ever have to worry about that," I state with finality.

Her eyes dart from side to side as she gazes deeply into my eyes. She looks like she wants to say something that's hard for her to express, but she withdraws into herself again. I keep reminding

209

myself that I have to take baby steps with her, but the Dom in me is ready to start demanding all of her. He thinks maybe it's time to remind her of the dynamics of our relationship and I'm inclined to agree with him.

"Sophia," I deepen my voice and steel my expression, "you are *mine*. I shouldn't have to remind you of that again. Being mine means you don't withhold from me when something is on your mind. If it's important to you, then it's important to me and I need to know what it is."

She swallows hard and nods her head in agreement. "It really isn't anything—just the old insecurities I'm fighting. My mother always told me I was worthless and would never amount to anything. She said I didn't fit in with anyone and I never would. I love my younger brother, but she's tried to turn him against me, too. I don't even know if he will speak to me now.

"And then, there's *your* family. Your parents just took me in and made me feel welcome, like I belonged there, and not like some outcast. Your mom let me set the table for breakfast and made me feel like I had a family. Your dad is just great— he's so funny and thoughtful. I was also thinking about you, Dom. You've done more for me in the short time I've known you than everyone else in my life combined. I don't deserve you," she finishes on a whisper.

"No one talks about *My Angel* like that," I gently scold her. "I won't let anyone disparage you. Not even *you*."

Tears escape her eyes and roll down her beautiful cheeks. I gently wipe the tears away and replace them with tender kisses. "You will have so much more love, *My Angel*," I whisper, "than you've ever known. You'll never question how much you mean to me. You'll never doubt your worth again— I will remind you every day. I promise you this, you will *never* be sorry that you're mine."

The sobs wrack her body as she climbs into my lap. I hold her in my arms, her body glued to mine with her fists holding on to my button-down shirt as she finally lets go of everything that's been holding her back from giving herself to me. Every fear that's reared its ugly head in her mind, telling her she's not good enough for me, and reminding her of past failures, is fading away. Her sobs gradually diminish until she's lying limp in my arms, cried out and ready to surrender all to me.

"I want that so much, Dom. So much," she whispers into my neck. "I want that with you."

"It's yours, *My Angel*. It's all yours," I pledge. "No more hiding from me."

"No more, Dom. I'm yours and I want you to have all of me."

Tucker stops at the steps leading up to the plane. "Give us a minute, Tucker," I instruct and he gives a single nod in response.

I help Sophia collect herself as much as she can. Before we exit the car, I have an idea. "Sophia, once we take off, you and I are going to spend the rest of the flight in the bedroom. You need some time to regroup and we just need to spend some time alone."

"That sounds perfect, Dom," she sighs in relief.

Tucker has already loaded our luggage and taken his place on the plane when Sophia and I board. I lead her to a plush loveseat near the back of the plane, closest to the bedroom. Once we're able to move around the cabin, we retreat behind closed doors. After helping her disrobe, we climb into bed and I take her in my arms as she lays her head on my chest. I love how it feels to be skin to skin with her.

"I've waited so long for someone like you, Dom," she says in her small, watery voice. "Why couldn't I have met you *first*? Before anyone else put these wrong ideas in my head?"

"Don't worry, *My Angel*. No one else matters now. You're connected to *me* now. Feel *me*. Hear *my* voice. I get all of you, all the time, in every way."

"My Dom," she sighs with contentment as she snuggles in closer to me. Inhaling deeply, she says, "You always smell so good. I would say I should bottle your scent and sell it, but I don't want anyone else to have you."

"I'm a one-woman man, love," I kiss the top of her head. "You can rest now. You've had a busy week."

After another hour of flying, we're in the backseat of the car with Tucker taking us back to Sophia's apartment. She looks concerned but she hasn't voiced anything. I watch her every move and wait patiently for her to confide in me. She feels me staring, knows she's being watched, and like my good girl should, she turns her body toward me and prepares to speak.

"Dom," she says tentatively, "a lot has happened over just a couple of days. It wasn't just...what I mean is...it was more than just a...one-night stand. Wasn't it?"

I give her a reassuring smile and take her hand in mine. Some asshole has really done a number on her. "Sophia, I don't take one-night stands home to meet my parents. I don't take them as subs. And I sure as hell don't let them call me

'Dom.' So, no, *My Angel*, this is far from a one-night stand. You are mine regardless of where we are or what we're doing. Coming home doesn't change that—it confirms it."

When we reach her condo, Tucker gets her luggage out of the trunk and I open her car door to help her out. She looks at her suitcase and then up at me. Her surprise is evident when she asks, "You're not staying?"

"No, love, not tonight. I have some things at home I need to see to before work tomorrow," I explain as I take her suitcase from Tucker and guide her to the elevators.

She nods slowly. She's not happy, but not upset, either, "Alright. I understand."

"Hey," I say as I gently take her chin in my hand. "We will spend nights together, days together, weekends altogether—all kinds of time together. Being apart sometimes doesn't change how important you are to me."

"You're right. I'm sorry, I'm not usually this clingy," she laughs. Shaking her head, she asks rhetorically, "What is wrong with me?"

"Not a thing," I reply genially as we exit the elevator. Opening her door, I enter first and check her apartment before leaving her alone.

"I'll see you in the morning, *My Angel*," I murmur against her lips before kissing her good night. "Dream of me."

"I definitely will, Dom."

"Don't forget tomorrow is Thursday."

She smiles seductively, "How could I forget that?"

"There's my girl," I praise her. "Goodnight, love."

I'm in my office early in the morning, pouring over the top-secret contract again. Line by line, I've been reading this for hours and my eyes are starting to cross. Sitting back, I rub my eyes and lean my head back against my chair. My office door opens, and without opening my eyes, I know that it's Sophia. My body comes alive, humming with electricity that involuntarily jolts my eyes open.

As our eyes clash and I take in her choice of attire for the day, the bulge in my pants quickly becomes uncomfortable. The hunger in my eyes must be palpable because she stops, leans against the door, and quietly locks it. *My Angel* immediately knows what I want from just a look. She's learning me quickly and her response tells me she feels the same.

I sit motionless as she slinks across the office toward me and drops her purse in the chair across from me. She's wearing a short, flowing skirt with a tastefully tight, dressy shirt. Her heels are just shy of being considered stilettos, and her long, reddish brown hair is styled with an intentionally sexy, wind-blown look. When she reaches my chair, she turns it so that I'm facing her.

"What can I do for you today, Mr. Powers?" she asks coyly as she moves to stand between my legs, waiting for me to state my wishes.

I give her my cocky half-smile as I run my fingers up and down her smooth, bare legs. Looking up at her, I move one hand higher up her inner thigh while the other grips her ass, holding her close to me. Her breathing increases, the rise and fall of her chest quickens, and her skin flushes from my touch. Higher still, my fingers slowly roam as she waits for them to find their mark. She grips my shoulders, anticipating what she knows is coming at any moment. I intentionally take my time, first circling around behind her and lightly stroking the back of her thigh.

Withholding my chuckle at her groan of frustration, I suddenly slip my other hand under her skirt and directly into her wetness. "Fuck, I love a moist cupcake. Nothing better for breakfast," I say as I swing her around and she sits on the edge of my desk in front of me.

Pushing her skirt up, I pierce her with my hungry gaze and commend her, "My good girl, you remembered no panties on Thursdays."

She nods and smiles knowingly as she grips the edge of my desk until her knuckles turn white. I spread her legs wider as I lean in, lightly licking and teasing her when I barely graze her clit with my tongue. It's driving her wild and I know she's about to lose control. She lifts her hand and starts to extend it toward me, but I pull back and slowly shake my head back and forth at her.

Understanding her place, she puts her hand back on the desk and waits for me to continue. After several more seconds of making her wait for her pleasure, I decide she's been good enough. Once more, I lean in, take her clit in my mouth, and nimbly suck it through my teeth, letting them gently graze her and enhance the feeling. My tongue delves deep into her wetness and she can't contain her sexy moans.

Gripping her hips, I hold her tightly to my mouth and devour her, stopping only to say, "I'm

217

ready for my icing now, *My Angel*. If I have to wait for it, you will be waiting all day to finish this." Taking my position between her legs again, I eagerly lick, suck, and nip at her before inserting my finger and sending her over the edge. After finishing her off, I sit up and she watches me intently as I lick her essence off my finger.

"Best icing ever," I declare. "I could bottle it and sell it, but *no one* else gets to taste what's mine. Ever."

"I take it you're pleased with me then?" she asks genuinely as she stands and adjusts her skirt.

"I'm *very* pleased with you. Instead of 'Casual Friday,' we should promote 'Titillating Thursday.' Or, on second thought, maybe that would be 'Clitillating Thursday' instead," I quip and we both laugh at my stupid attempt at a joke. "Next time, I think I'll just bend you over my desk and have my wicked way with you."

The real world calls and the rest of our plans will have to wait until later. Sophia kisses me goodbye before she goes to her office and I sit back down to review this infuriating contract once again. At least my mood has improved since Sophia walked in. She is *My Angel*.

Chapter Sixteen

Reflecting back over the past month, I'm pleased with how Sophia and I have grown so much closer. We're more comfortable in our relationship, and the trust between us has strengthened over this time. Others in the office have seen us standing closer than normal co-workers would. We're not trying to hide our relationship, but we're not flaunting it in front of others, either. We both have jobs to do and it's still important for us to be professional.

"Dana, have you made arrangements for my trip yet?" I ask as she enters my office, bearing coffee.

"I have, Mr. Powers. You'll arrive in Knoxville, Tennessee, and then it's just a short drive to Oak Ridge. Will Miss Vasco be joining you?" Dana asks in her usual business tone.

"No, not this time."

"Is there anything else you need, Mr. Powers?"

"No. Thank you, Dana," I reply as she takes her leave.

A nagging apprehension plays in the back of my mind at the thought of being away from Sophia for any length of time. When I think back to the week I introduced her to my parents, I realize there has been a pattern with her moodiness. The night I dropped her off at her condo, she wasn't entirely happy that I didn't stay with her, but she said she understood. We talked more about it the following day, after our first sexual encounter in the office. On my desk.

"I missed you last night, Dom," she admitted. "I'm surprised how quickly I've gotten used to having you with me at night."

"You did use my pillow as my substitute one time, as I recall," I teased and she laughed.

"You've spoiled me! It's your fault!" she played back with me.

"I didn't want to leave you, Sophia. I hope you know that," I tried to calm her fears. "It's early for us and we're not ready to just move in together yet. That doesn't mean we can't spend nights together, though."

"I know. I thought about it after you left and you're right. For now, I'd like to ask to have Sunday nights at my condo," she stated cautiously, eying me for any indication that I disapproved.

"Why Sunday nights?" I asked. My curiosity was piqued at her very specific request.

She looked away when she answered, "It just gives me some time to adjust for the work week. Time to get prepared, get my things ready, and unwind for a little bit...just a little time to myself."

"Alright, Sophia," I replied, intentionally using her name, "I will agree to that for now."

She looked relieved that I agreed to her request. I've noticed that every Monday morning after that discussion, she is moody and distant. It takes a little while each time for her to readjust to our relationship and our arrangement. While I watch her, study her reactions, and consider all the possibilities, I still give her the benefit of the doubt that she is simply passively-aggressively acting out at me for insisting on keeping separate places.

Today, travel plans have been made that will take me away for a week and Sophia won't be joining me. There will be more of these trips as I finalize the confidential contract with the Oak Ridge National Laboratory. The plant is highly classified, highly protected, and a limited number of people are allowed in or around the facility. I've already been through extensive background checks and given temporary security clearance that has been months in the making just to be able to conduct business onsite. There's no way Sophia would have time to meet all the security requirements to attend it with me.

My concern is centered more on what her behavior will be after being away from me for that long. I have three weeks to introduce my more formal method of behavior modification, show her what I expect, and watch her willingly submit to my requests. It's time for Sophia to spend the night at my house for the first time. I haven't brought her over because I know that before I do, our relationship must be in the right place.

It's time for the next phase of our relationship and I feel my spirits lifting just thinking about it. Perhaps her petulance has been because I've given her *too much* leniency. The submissive in her craves the structure a Dom provides. The knowledge that there are consequences for her actions is often an aphrodisiac, especially if she intentionally breaks the rules just so she can be punished. It's not that I enjoy inflicting pain—I don't at all. I enjoy the trust that's instilled in me, how she willingly submits to me, and the sexual thrill of using punishment devices for pleasure.

She will see tonight, for herself, that pain can also be pleasurable. Performed in the right way, it will enhance the intensity. In the right hands, she'll love the feel of the flogger as it sensitizes her perfect skin. Floggers, paddles, and wrist restraints are definitely in order tonight. She'll have nowhere to hide once I take her to my playroom.

As if she read my mind or heard my inner thoughts call her, Sophia taps on my office door before walking in. Another Monday morning and I can see the same look on her face as the past few weeks. Her mood is a mixture of both sadness and anger. It's been taking several hours to get her past this mood and back to her normal self. Today, I'm not waiting.

"Good morning, Sophia. How was your night?" I ask, intentionally poking her with the proverbial stick.

A disgusted look flies across her face before she quickly masks it. "It was fine. How was yours?" she asks stiffly.

"It's never quite as much fun without you there," I quip. Sophia takes a deep breath, straightens her back, and exhales slowly. She's calming herself before she responds and I can't help but watch, bemused.

"I'm here now, so what do you need from me today?"

I smile wickedly, knowing that she's unwittingly walked right into my trap. She eyes me suspiciously but it only fuels my fire, my desire to see her in restraints with light red whip marks across her beautiful skin.

"Today, I need your submission, Sophia," I say pointedly and with total domination in my tone. "Tonight, I need you at my house. You're spending the night with me and we're moving to the next stage of our relationship."

"What stage?" she asks, narrowing her eyes at me.

Narrowing mine in response, "Punishment, Sophia." Emphasizing her name so that she understands I don't appreciate the lack of respect in her tone and her demeanor, she quickly amends her posture and facial expression. "It's also time for you to trust me, so we will move on to bondage tonight, too," I state resolutely. It's not a request.

Sophia nods her head in agreement, knowing it's pointless to argue and that there is nothing to argue over anyway. "You're right, Dom. What time do you want me to come over?" she asks contritely.

Something is still off. I feel it, I sense it, and I know it deep in my bones. She's still holding back for some reason but why is not clear to me yet. Tonight will be telling. The cushioned handcuffs are waiting for her in the playroom. My hand craves the feel of the leather flogger and its soft leather tails. Under my persuasive techniques, she will not be able to keep her thoughts to herself any longer.

"You will ride home with me after work. We will go out to eat first and then once we're behind closed doors, you are all mine," I firmly command.

"Yes, Dom. Is there anything else you need from me before I get started this morning?" she asks sincerely.

"Yes, there is," I say. I wait, watching her for any hint of rebellion, but I don't see it now. She waits patiently for my command. "I've missed you. I haven't had a good morning kiss yet."

She smiles and walks across my office toward me. I stand and meet her in the middle. She splays her hands out on my chest, under my jacket, and slowly runs them up and around my neck. She presses her body up against me as my arms wrap around her waist and pull her closer into me. Tilting her head back, she reaches her mouth up to meet mine.

Our kiss is hot and consuming. It's becoming a living entity that has suddenly taken on a life of its

225

own. Her taste is exquisite and unique. Her smell is inviting and intoxicating. I crave the feel of her soft, supple body in my hands. Her submission is only hers to give and she freely chooses to give it to me. She gives me strength and she is my undoing.

Running my hand along the smooth skin of her upper thigh, I move upward under her skirt. It's Monday, but she's still not wearing any panties. Groaning into her mouth and punishing her lips with my kiss, my fingers find her wet core and I thrust two into her. She welcomes the sudden intrusion as her knees bend and her hips involuntary jerk as she reaches her climax. Increasing my tempo and pressure, she moves faster and faster until she can no longer contain her orgasm as her body shudders with wave after wave of pleasure.

"Damn, Sophia, watching you makes me want to fuck you right here on my desk," I growl out at her. "In fact, I think I will."

Her whimpering response says she's submitted to me once again. Whatever was on her mind when she entered my office has dissolved into pure satisfaction and willingness to obey. As I devour her neck, my stubble marks her skin, leaving evidence of my claim.

"Go lock the door, *My Angel*," I command with a whisper and intently watch her as she sashays back to me. She stops immediately in front of me, and without warning, I thread my fingers through the hair at the base of her neck with one hand while pulling her skirt up to her hips with the other.

Whirling her around, I push her face down toward the desk and use my foot to spread her legs farther apart. "This will be quick, but you will not come before I tell you to. Do you understand, Sophia?"

"Yes, Dom" she murmurs in response.

After dropping my pants to the floor, I grab her hips with both hands. "Hold on to something," I suggest, but I don't really give her time to respond. Thrusting forward, my cock finds her already wet entrance and I slide in to the hilt. She cries out and quickly bites her hand to muffle the sound. I continue plunging into her repeatedly as her muffled moans increase in tempo and volume. I feel her body gripping me, squeezing me, and she tenses to try to stave off her impending orgasm.

Leaning over, I wrap my hand around her neck and pull her up to meet me. Grinding into her for the final time, I roar into her ear, "Now, *My Angel*, come for me now." Her body can't hold out any longer and I feel the warmth of her orgasm flow over me as I empty myself into her.

227

Sophia folds over, limp, onto my desk, as I lovingly stroke her back and tell her how wonderful she is. Gently pulling back, I move quickly to the restroom in my office and return with a wet washcloth to clean her up. She hums and a sweet smile is fixed on her face.

It's been a long damn day when Sophia and I finally leave work and head for my car. She looks perplexed as we approach it but she's not questioning me. "What's on your mind, Sophia?"

"I was just wondering if I should drive my car or not."

"No. Tucker will send someone to pick it up," I explain as I open the door and she gets in the passenger seat.

"Where you would like to go eat, Sophia? Your choice tonight."

"It's been a really long day, Dom. Would you rather just eat something at your house?"

"Not a chance, love. I'm showing my girl off tonight. You are too beautiful to keep hidden away."

Her beautiful blush flashes across her face and she lowers her eyes. I chuckle to myself, close her door, and jog around to the driver side. Climbing in, I'm still smiling wide at her embarrassment. "You really still get embarrassed around me, love? After all the time we've spent together and all the intimate things we've done to each other?"

The blush deepens to red as she laughs heartily. Her mood is much better now and my assessment that she's been holding on to some perceived hurt becomes more viable. It's taken her most of the day to finally return to *my* Sophia, just as it has the past several Mondays.

"It's just that you've always stayed at my condo. I've never even been to your house before. I was beginning to feel like you were ashamed of me or something," she replies.

The thought has crossed my mind before that she would think that, but nothing could be further from the truth. "No, *My Angel*, I'm not ashamed of you at all. There's only one reason why you haven't been to my house yet." I inform her.

"Why is that?" she inquires.

Taking her hands in mine, I bring them up to my lips and gently kiss them one at a time. Choosing my words carefully, I explain, "Because you weren't ready for this yet. Your past experience with punishment scarred you and I won't add to that. Sophia, I had to make sure that you're in this for the long haul. That you won't run the first time you feel scared. That you know I would *never* hurt you like he did."

"I know," she whispers and her bottom lip quivers.

"Why do you still cry when I bring him up?" I suddenly have to know if there's something about me that makes her think of him. There's a burning need to know if, in her mind, he still owns her or if there's something else that makes her tear up with a simple mention of him. The fucker whose name I don't even know, and at this point don't want to know, for my own sanity. I may very well hunt him down and beat the shit out of him if I found out.

"It still hurts, Dom. It bothers me that I'm so weak," her eyelashes flutter, fighting back tears as she speaks.

"You're not weak. You're a survivor. What did I say about disparaging yourself?" I ask, not in a domineering way, but a gentle reminder to help her state of mind. A good Dom, a good *man*, knows when to push and when to soothe.

230

"No one gets to talk about me like that—not even me," she recites back to me.

"That's my girl," I say before leaning over to give her a chaste, but lingering, kiss.

"Don't take this the wrong way, I'm not disparaging myself," she starts to speak, then waits for my nod of affirmation before continuing. "This is a compliment for you. You are too good to me. I've done nothing to deserve you."

"No, *My Angel*, you only deserve the best of everything. Let me give it to you. Lifting you up to the highest pedestal gives me pleasure and it's exactly where you deserve to be."

Shaking her head in obvious disbelief, Sophia leans over toward me. Just as I think she's about to kiss me again, she wraps her little arms around my neck and clings tightly to me, squeezing me as hard as she's able. In our embrace, I feel the remaining walls she's built around her heart begin to crumble. It's an amazing feeling to know that this incredible woman is all mine.

I murmur into her hair, "Let me feed you, love. You'll need your energy tonight." The promise is there, hanging in the air and waiting for her to take it, accept it, and surrender to it.

"Then I guess it's a good time to tell you that I'm starving, huh?" she murmurs back. "Just not so much for food."

I chuckle at her response and she coos, "Dom, I love the feel of your laugh as it rumbles through your chest. It's so sexy."

"After we eat, I will show you all the sexy you can take, *My Angel*." My solemn vow to her, no matter how lightly or how seriously it's stated.

"I'm ready, Dom."

With that, I take her back to my favorite restaurant at the Four Seasons Hotel. As we approach the valet stand, I glance over at her and say, "You know, you really do need to tell me what your favorite restaurant is so I can take you there."

"I go where you go, Dom. That's all I really want."

Dinner cannot come and go fast enough for me tonight. I usually prefer an unrushed, relaxing dinner after a long day at work, but tonight, all I can think about is getting Sophia home. *Home*—that word just popped into my head. Not to my *house*, but home. Depending on how tonight goes in the playroom, I've considered having her stay a few nights a week with me. Perhaps on our agreed play days—Tuesday, Thursday, and Saturday. We can discuss it if she still wants Sunday to herself. For now, anyway.

Just as we are finishing our main course, a voice from my past interrupts the pleasant evening I was having. The very sound of it is worse than a thousand fingernails scraping across chalkboards. He's yelling across the room, calling out to me, and acting like we're long lost best friends. I know him all too well, however, and can hear the disdain for me permeating his voice.

"Dominic Powers? Is that really you?" he yells in mock surprise. "Well. Fuck. Me," he rudely roars, drawing out '*fuck*' in his Southern accent for as long as his breath allows. Every eye in the restaurant turns to my table, disgusted with the inappropriateness of his comments. "Never thought I'd see *you* again."

Looking around him, I signal our waiter for the check and then look up at Harrison Dictman, who does *not* understand the concept of personal space and is standing entirely too close to me. Stretching my elbows out, I intentional hit him and force him to take a step back. He's lucky that's the worst he got from me.

"Harry Dick-man," I purposely mispronounce his name just as I did in the past. My intense dislike of him has only deepened over time. "Never

233

thought I'd see *you* in a place like this. I thought you preferred the seedy strip clubs."

Hell yes, that's conceited of me, but this guy deserves so much worse.

"Aw, you know me," he continues, unaware that he's just been insulted, "I have to get out with the high-falutin' crowd every now and then. Show them what a *real* man looks like. They forget with all these sissy boys hangin' around."

The waiter brings the check, and without looking at it, I hand him my card and tell him we're in a hurry. He takes the hint and sprints off to settle the bill. Harrison continues his tirade, insisting that any man who has money can't have a shred of manliness about him. The waiter appears just as I start to rise from my seat and prove him wrong beyond a shadow of a doubt.

I quickly sign the receipt and help Sophia out of her chair. Turning to Harrison, I quickly dismiss him, "We were just leaving. So, Harry Dick-man, we will let you get back to your dinner."

Sophia and I turn to leave and she doesn't question me, sensing that I'm on edge and about to lose my composure at any minute. Not at her, of course—I know she doesn't want to add fuel to the already blazing inferno inside of me. As we approach the front doors of the hotel, several couples are quickly making their way inside. The wind has picked up and lightning flashes across the sky in the distance, forcing the others inside to await their valeted cars.

"Sophia, love, why don't you wait here while I get the car?"

"Dominic Powers!" that same, irritating voice roars from behind me. "Don't you fuckin' walk away from me like that! Just who the fuck do you think you are, anyway?"

All heads turn to look at Harrison and several move out of the way, appropriately sensing this will not end well from his tone and words. I glare at him intently and grind my teeth. As much as I don't want to get into a knockdown, drag-out fight here in the lobby of the hotel, he will not get away with disrespecting me like that.

"Why don't you show at least a *little* decorum, Harry Dick-man? You may need a dictionary to look that word up later. But for now, why don't you and I just step outside and we'll finish this discussion?" I growl back at him.

Storming out the front door, pushing the door open wide enough that it slams against the building, my stride is determined and confident. If he steps outside, his ass is mine and I will fucking pound him into the ground. As my feet hit the first step, I hear his loud taunts coming from directly behind me.

"What's the matter, *Mr. I'm-So-Fuckin'-Perfect-I-Shit-Gold-Bricks Powers*? Don't want all these fancy people to know that YOU KILLED MY SISTER?"

The next thing I know, five very large security men are pulling me off of Harrison's bloodied face. He's lying on his back on the ground, yelling obscenities and swearing his retribution on his life. The valet has pulled my car around and is standing inside the car door, staring at the commotion with his jaw on the ground. A couple of other security men are helping Harrison up off the ground.

"This type of behavior is not acceptable here," the manager hisses. "This is the Four Seasons and we have an *immaculate* reputation. I will *not* have it tarnished by allowing this sort of behavior."

"Do you want to press charges against this man?" the manager asks Harrison, gesturing toward me.

"No, I don't wanna press no charges," he drawls. "I don't want him in no jail where I can't get to him."

I roll my eyes in disgust and say, "Bring it on, Harry Dick-man. I'll fuck up your face again for you."

236

"Sir!" the manager yells this time. "Do you wish to press charges against this man?" he asks, gesturing toward Harrison this time.

"No. No charges," I smirk at Harrison. I'm ready for round two.

"You both need to vacate the premises immediately. If either of you return, I will press charges for trespassing," the manager informs us.

At some point during this whole exchange, Sophia moved to my side. As Harrison starts to leave, he stops and rakes his eyes over Sophia while licking his lips. Pushing her behind me to protect her, I reach to grab him again just as the security team pulls me back and another set of men grabs Harrison's arms and forcibly walks him away from us.

Flexing and relaxing my fingers, I inhale deeply and blow my out breath, trying to let go of the intense anger that is still welled up inside of me. If they hadn't stopped me, I might have beaten that bastard to death. Sophia's hand softly lands on my arm and slides down to take my hand in hers. She's silently giving me her support, so I meet her expressive eyes with my own. Moving in closer, she wraps her other arm around mine, pulling her body as close to me as she can.

Pulling my arm free from her grip, I wrap my arms around her and kiss her gently. "Let's go home before they call the police on me," I whisper to her. She nods and we walk to my car just as we are now—our bodies are as close as we can get, our arms are wrapped around each other, and we lean in to keep our faces close.

The thought on repeat in my mind is, *When do I tell her*?

Chapter Seventeen

We're both quiet as I drive us to my house that is as far away from the crowded Dallas suburbs as I could find but still within a reasonable distance to my office. Sophia picks up my free hand and examines my knuckles. They're an angry shade of red and slightly swollen from pounding Harrison into the ground. She gently strokes my hand with hers, careful to not further aggravate the slight injuries I sustained from his face repeatedly slamming into my fist.

She examines my hand thoroughly, moving it gingerly as if she thinks she can hurt me. I can't help but smile at her as she bites her lip at the corner of her mouth, furrows her brow, and genuinely looks concerned for my wellbeing.

"Does it hurt?" her small voice breaks the silence.

"No, just a little sore but nothing major," I reply and wrap my hand around hers to show her that I'm fine.

"You were so fast. One second, you were walking off to get the car and the next second you had him on the ground. I don't even know how you moved that fast," the awe and shock is thick in her voice.

"To tell you the truth, I don't remember how that happened, either. I guess the old adage of 'seeing red' and not remembering anything after that is true," I shrug with my reply. I don't want to get into the details of this in the car. There's no good place to do it, but there are bad places to discuss it. In the car, while I'm driving at night, is one of those bad places.

"Have you ever done that before?" she asks, and I hear the trepidation in her voice. I know now where her mind automatically went.

"No, Sophia, I haven't. You never have to worry about that with me. Ever," I promise her again. Seeing me in that fit of rage must have scared her and brought back that seed of doubt. That actually makes my plan for tonight even more important to carry out. I have to prove to her that she can trust me, regardless of the circumstances.

240

Harrison deserved what he got and more. I would still be there pounding the shit out of his face if they hadn't stopped me.

Sophia is quiet—*too* quiet. She's now gnawing on her thumbnail and staring out the side window. In deep thought, she has mentally left me here in the car while she's off reliving some terrible situation. I gently squeeze her hand and bring it over to my lap, resting it on my leg. This gets her attention and her eyes drift to meet mine. She stops chewing on her nail, finally conscious of her nervousness, and drops her hand.

"Do you trust me, Sophia?" I say, knowing that we're now within a couple of minutes of my house. "Or did my outburst back there make you doubt me again?"

Her eyes soften as she tilts her head, "I don't doubt you, Dom. Of course I still trust you."

"Good. We're about to pull into my driveway. This is another big step for us, Sophia. You're ready for this and I'm ready for this, but we have to be together in your mind, too," I begin.

"Together?" she asks for clarification.

"On the same page, love. You need to *know* that there is nothing I will do to you that you won't enjoy or that you don't want me to do," I explain. "You can't doubt that."

She nods and shifts in her seat to face me just as I turn onto my street. My house is at the end of a cul-de-sac, set on a sprawling estate with no close neighbors. "I don't doubt anything about you, Dom. I promise," she replies so sweetly.

We approach the gated entrance to my driveway and she glances over her shoulder when she feels the car slowing. Seeing the wide, brick gates on either side of my driveway, coupled with the tall brick fence and lantern posts that line my yard along the front, her jaw drops open and her eyes fly open wide. "Where are we?" she gasps.

"Home," I reply nonchalantly.

"This is where you live?" she asks, looking around even though there's really nothing to see here except the landscaping beds my gardener created.

Continuing slowly down my driveway, she's still trying hard to see even though it's pitch black outside. My headlights are the only illumination until we round the curve and my house comes into view. The landscaping spotlights are lit up, showcasing various aspects the house. It's a fairly large house, considering only my house staff and I live here, but it gives me the space I need for the playroom, my office, overnight guests, parties, and anything else I could possibly need.

Stopping in the circular drive in the front of the house, one of my staff, Lewis, meets us at the car to open the door for Sophia. Lewis then takes the car to park it in the garage as I escort Sophia inside. She's awestruck as we enter the front door. Walking slowly, she's trying to absorb every detail. Instantly remembering the apartment she lived in when I first met her, I feel a twinge of humility at how blatantly I've taken this house and its luxuries for granted.

"*This* is your house?" she asks disbelievingly.

At first, I'm almost embarrassed at her reaction, but I know how hard I've worked at building my company. Just getting it off the ground was a major ordeal in itself. I've worked long, hard hours to achieve my success and I'm not ashamed of that at all. There were days, and long nights, that I questioned whether this was the right business for me to go into. The software giants just kept growing exponentially while I struggled to make ends meet. When I developed my current bestselling software, then customized it for commercial use, I knew I'd found my niche. It took a lot of my own blood, sweat, and tears to get here, but I'm here and I'm damn proud of the company I've built from nothing.

"This is home," I reply and look at our surroundings, trying to see it through her eyes.

The mixture of light and dark wood in the flooring gives it a warm ambiance as we enter the wide, open foyer. Rather than take her on a tour, like a tour guide, I decide to tell her where everything is located. Then, she can take her time exploring and getting used to where everything is so that she won't feel as much like a guest when she's here. I want her to be comfortable and love it here as much as I do.

"Directly ahead to the left are the stairs that lead upstairs to all of the bedrooms. The first floor has a media room, a formal living room, a formal dining room, a library, my office, and the kitchen. Off the back of the kitchen is the patio area with a full outdoor kitchen and lighted, heated pool and hot tub combination. Just before you reach the kitchen, there's a door that leads downstairs to Tucker's apartment.

"The upstairs bedrooms are all master bedroom suites. Each bedroom has its own separate sitting area and full bath, complete with a garden tub and walk-in tiled shower. The upstairs patio extends the full length of the house and every bedroom has double French doors to access it. They all overlook the pool area that is lit up at night and the fountains jet streams of water in a choreographed pattern.

"The room at the end of the hall is the playroom. I designed the layout and have everything in there that we could possibly need."

Taking a step closer to her, I thread my fingers through her hair and lightly tug from behind, pulling her head back and exposing her neck to me. Leaning down, I lick and nip on the sensitive area below her ear. She plays with my hair at the base of my neck, lightly stroking as she purrs with pleasure. As I reach her ear, I take her earlobe between my teeth and cold chills flash down her arm.

I murmur in her ear, "Take some time, look around the house, and make yourself at home. There's nothing I have that is off limits to you—feel free to look in every crack and crevice. The staff quarters are not in the main house and they're all finished for the evening. Some of your clothes have already been brought over, along with your car."

She smiles like I've just given her the keys to the kingdom and excitedly hurries off to explore. Funny, I feel much the same way since I know what tonight holds for us. I'm anxious to get started but I won't rush her. Once she's finished her exploration of the house, she will find her way to the playroom when she's ready. That's the room I will be waiting in, with the scene set up with nothing but her pleasure in mind.

As I climb the stairs, I hear her on the first floor opening and closing doors, pulling open drawers, and making little squealing sounds as she finds something she likes. It makes me smile and makes me want to give her so much more. She never asks for anything, tries to avoid taking anything, and profusely thanks me for anything I do for her. Tonight, she will beg me to do more, but for very different reasons.

The playroom is the same size as the rest of the bedrooms, but its contents are much different. I tend to go for originality rather than conformity, so the theme of my room is not like a basement dungeon at all. I prefer the finer things, and even though the *whish* of a flogger or the *crack* of a bullwhip against my lover's skin excites me, I don't want anything overly abrasive on her, either.

Walking contradiction, that's me.

All the furniture in this room has been custom made per my specifications. The bed is centered on the back wall with the restraints connected to the wall and the footboard. The mattresses are extra firm—too firm for me to sleep on—but their purpose isn't for sleeping. There's a custom designed padded cross that locks into place in three different positions, a spanking horse, and a four-point sling stand. One wall is lined with an assortment of paddles, floggers, handcuffs, ropes, and several other necessities. The walls are painted a warm shade of amber and the lighting gives a sensual glow to the room.

After preparing the spanking horse, I choose the flogger with the multiple suede tails. I turn the sheets on the bed down and arrange the handcuffs for easy access. I'm waiting for *My Angel* to join me so we can get started with the part of this relationship that scares her. This will help to seal her trust in me, and it's safe to say, it will also bring us even closer.

I hear the click of the doorknob as it turns and she walks in, cautiously peering around the door as her eyes search for me. Once our eyes lock, she unconsciously licks her lips and I feel my cock twitch. While arranging the furniture, I unbuttoned my shirt and took my shoes off. The heat from her eyes is searing my skin as she drinks in my bared chest.

"Close the door, Sophia," I direct as I keep my eyes locked on hers. She does as she's told and then steps fully into the room. "Do you know what that is?" I ask as I incline my head toward the spanking horse.

"I think so. I've been strapped to one before, but it didn't look exactly like this one," she says as

247

she runs her hands over the soft, padded leather. "It was scratchy wood and it gave me splinters. I didn't like it," she says ruefully.

"You won't get any splinters from this one, love. It's very soft and very comfortable. Your hands and feet will be bound, but if it becomes too overwhelming for you, just use the safe word and I will stop immediately.

"Your safe word that tells me to stop is 'heartbeat.' Use it, and I will stop in a heartbeat. I will also use a different type of binding this time so we can untie it quickly, if needed. Trust me." It's both a command and a request that Sophia seems to instantly understand.

Speaking of heartbeats, I can see her pulse increasing rapidly as the vein in her neck jumps in anticipation. She's still rooted to the same spot as when she first came into the room. I'm patient to a fault. It's an inherent part of me, much like being a Dom is. She needs a moment to process everything in front of her and what she knows is coming with the spanking horse. Part of her is excited to experience it with me and part of her is terrified to experience it at all.

"It's time, Sophia," I command. "Show me what's mine."

She nods and begins to undress. I watch as she removes her shirt and her bra. She hesitates for a few seconds before reaching behind her and unzipping her skirt. Her hesitation is only meant to heighten the anticipation, make me want her more, and to an extent, delay my gratification as long as possible. She's not doing this in a rebellious way— she just wants to extend the time for my viewing pleasure as a gift to me. It's one of the ways she gives all of herself to me.

She deliberately takes her time pushing her skirt over her hips and down her legs. Remaining as still as a statue, with my arms crossed across my chest and my feet hips-width apart, I relish in the show she's putting on for me. She intentionally left her G-string on so that she could take more time to languidly roll it down her legs. When she finishes, she stands up straight and waits for her next command.

I smirk at her, one corner of my mouth quirking up in a half-smile as I take in her beauty. Uncrossing my arms, I stride closer to her and stop at the halfway mark. "Come to me, *My Angel.*"

Quickly walking to me, she lowers her eyes when she reaches me and then seems to remember because she immediately looks back up at me. "Relax, love. You can look down when you need to. Your eyes belong to me any time I'm pleasuring you in any way. Other than those times, you can look wherever you're most comfortable."

"Thank you, Dom, for explaining what you want me to do," her tone holds both admiration and relief in it. The memories of the abuse from her former partner still have a hold on her.

Stroking her cheek with the back of my hand, I lean in and kiss her gently. "Always, love," I promise her. "Do you trust me?"

"Yes, Dom," she responds without hesitation.

"That's my girl." Taking her hand, I lead her to the spanking horse. "Get into position," I gently command and wait.

Sophia moves into position, putting her knees on the padded step and stretching her arms over the top to the other side of the bench where I've attached the wrist restraints. I watch her carefully to see whether she will put her wrists in the restraints. Without being told, she slips her hands in up to her wrists and waits for me to tighten them.

Pulling the strap, I tighten the padded wrist restraints and check to make sure they're not too tight on her. "I'm not restraining your feet this time, *My Angel*. Unless you give me reason to, that is. Keep still for me."

"Yes, Dom."

Her bottom lip is quivering and her eyes are squeezed shut. Her first lesson is coming up as I select the black ping-pong paddle from its place on the wall. It's wider than most, so it covers more area. One side is covered with leather and the other side with fleece. Pain and pleasure is wrapped up in one package.

She doesn't realize it yet, but one of her fears is about to be annihilated. She is about to see that I can give her what no other man can. I can take her to heights so high, she will never come down again. She will beg me, and I will give her what she needs every time.

"*My Angel*, we are starting with this because you need to know that you can trust me with every little thing that concerns you. This is about pleasure, trust, and need—*yours*. My job is to make sure that you are pleasured beyond the limits that you can stand," I lower my voice an octave and let my words settle into her mind. "Pleasure through pain at times, but pleasure nonetheless. Are you ready?"

Sophia nods.

"I need an answer, Sophia," my voice is authoritative and unyielding.

"Yes, Dom, I am ready."

Using the leather side, I raise my arm and swing, swatting one side of her ass. Her smooth skin immediately reddens in the shape of the paddle. I rub the spot with the fleece side of the paddle to soothe it as I speak softly, murmuring soothing words to her. While doing this, my fingers lightly stroke her skin until I reach her core.

Running one finger between her legs, I suck in a breath and hiss, "Fuck, baby, you're already soaked for me. Did you like that?" I ask as I push my finger in and out of her until she's on the edge, her body involuntarily writhing and her hips bucking as much as they can in her current position. Simultaneously inserting a second finger and swatting her other cheek with the paddle, she cries out in ecstasy as she comes.

"Tsk, tsk," I admonish her. "I didn't give you permission for that one, *My Angel*. You know what that means." Quickly, I give her two more swats, one on each side, as my fingers continue their work at making her come apart in front of me. The fleece side of the paddle is soft and plush against her skin, lessening the sting. The mixture of sensual pain and erotic pleasure is reconditioning her mind to make her body crave it.

"Have you learned your lesson?" I ask her, my voice low and sensual.

"Yes, Dom," she breathes out.

252

"Good girl," I say as I move to release her hands. She actually looks disappointed for a moment. "Don't worry, love, we're just getting started." I help her to stand and motion toward the bed. She waits for me to move and follows one step behind me.

I stop suddenly and turn to face her. Looking down at my still fully clothed self, I draw my brows down and scratch my chin like I'm in deep thought.

"Something's off here. Something just isn't right," I start. Although I'm not looking directly at her, I can see and feel the tension rising in her. "Hmmm, how about that? I'm still dressed. I really shouldn't be dressed at this point, should I?"

"Would you like for me to undress you, Dom?" she asks hopefully.

I nod and she puts her hands on my chest. Taking her time to caress my skin, she runs her hands underneath my shirt and pushes it off of my shoulders without taking her hands off of me. As my shirt falls away, her fingers trace the tattoos on my chest, shoulder, and arm again. She's fascinated with them and takes every opportunity to intimately study them.

She raises her eyes to meet mine and I see panic flash across them, as if she's done something wrong. I smile lovingly at her and nod, wordlessly

253

giving her permission to take her time. I have all night if she needs it. This is about her, all about her, and not me. This is about her pleasure, her trust, and her peace of mind. Unshed tears glisten in her eyes as she shakes her head to clear them away.

"Tell me," I state.

"I'm so lucky to have you," she says. "I just get overwhelmed with gratitude sometimes. They're not sad tears, Dom, but I know you don't like them."

"I don't like you hiding your feelings from me, Sophia," I clarify. "If you have happy or sad thoughts—or tears—I want them. I want you, all of you, and if they're ever sad tears, I want to be the one to make them go away."

She nods and swallows hard, pushing her feelings down her throat again. "You have all of me, Dom. Forever. You have all of me," she vows. She lowers her hands to my pants and eases them off of me.

Leading her to the bed, I shower her with kisses all over her body as I tighten the restraints on her wrists and ankles. Her arms and legs are secured to the bed and she's in a comfortable, but spread eagle, position. "Do you know why we use restraints, love?" I ask as I double-check her comfort.

"No, Dom. Why?" she asks, cocking her head to the side and looking genuinely interested in the answer.

"When you move, it subconsciously takes your mind off the pleasure you're feeling. It makes your mind and your body focus elsewhere so you don't get the full effect," I state and she bites the corner of her mouth as she considers my words. "The restraints keep you from squirming as much, as well as showing your submission and trust. They're just as much for your pleasure as for mine, just in a somewhat different way."

Crawling up her body, starting at her feet, I take my time to make love to her entire body—not just the act of sex but also the demonstration of total love. My mouth and my hands properly worship every inch of her. As much as she wants to move, to squirm, my words return to her and she relaxes to accept the full effect of our union.

When I finally enter her, my dick is throbbing beyond belief, but I move slowly and purposefully, bringing her to orgasm time and time again while I maintain control over my body. She pulls against the restraints and cries out again, asking me to join her.

"Please, Dom, now," she begs reverently.

I can't refuse her, especially when she asks like this, or when my body physically can't hold back another second. Thrusting into her harder and faster, she reaches her peak again just in time for me to join her. Lying on top of her, my body covering hers, and I reach up and release the restraints from her wrists. I gently massage each one to relieve any numbness and help completely restore the blood flow.

Sniffling catches my attention and I look at her to find tears streaming down her face. "Are you alright, *My Angel*? Tell me what's on your mind."

Her words shock me as she speaks her mind between tears and sobs. "I love you, Dom. You're everything no one has ever been to me. You're good, kind, loving, and honest. You take care of me, and I may get in trouble for this, but I just don't deserve you. I can't let you go, though. No matter how undeserving I am, I can't let you go."

Cocooning her with my body, I shield her from the outside world so that all she can see and feel is *me*. There is nothing else in the room. There is nothing else in the house. There is nothing else in the world. There is only she and I, and every day I will make sure that she knows she is my world. She is on my pedestal and she is my queen. I am her Dom but she is my heart.

Chapter Eighteen

Hours later, Sophia and I are in my comfortable bed and she's lying on her side, snuggled up facing me. Her hand is tracing small circles on my chest, straying over to my tattoos again. We've napped on and off for a few minutes at a time but we can't seem to get enough of each other tonight. The experience in the playroom has solidified my feelings for her. She gave me all of her—no holding back and no fear. Her full submission was willingly handed over to me and I treated it with the utmost respect and care.

"Dominic?" she asks quietly. Using my full name now instantly alerts me. I don't think I'm going to like what she says next.

"Yes, love," I reply, stroking her back.

She continues absently tracing her fingers over my skin while she works up the nerve to say what's on her mind. Finally, after a couple minutes of me waiting patiently, she asks, "Why did he say you killed his sister?"

I knew this conversation would eventually surface and I've dreaded having it. My only solace is in knowing that our mutual trust has just multiplied several times over tonight. I consciously make my arm keep moving, skimming across her smooth skin, and focus on the wonderful lady lying in my arms. Taking a deep breath that I know I will need to get through this conversation, I dive in headfirst.

"His sister, Carol Ann, was my last submissive. She—died," I stumble over the words, "and he blames me."

Her hand stops, she inhales sharply, and every muscle in her body tenses simultaneously. Not changing my rhythm, I continue to slowly caress up and down her spine, feeling every bump and dip along the way. She's grasping to process the bomb I just dropped on her.

"What happened?" she whispers. "How did she die?"

I've relived this so many times in my mind, it's almost like I'm right there with her every time. "It was our one-year anniversary of being together and I had a special night planned for us. Carol Ann didn't like crowds, so I had hidden surprises for her to find throughout the day while she was at home and I was at work.

"When she got up that morning, she found a basket of new bath supplies—bubble bath, shower gel, all that stuff women love. It was sitting on the side of our garden tub, all wrapped up with a big bow. She always dressed in the walk-in closet, so I hung her new silk lingerie and matching robe up just inside, right where she would see it first. There were other things hidden all through our condo— earrings, necklaces, bracelets, shoes—just in random places, but she loved the scavenger hunt," I smile but my heart clenches, remembering these little details of her.

"I had planned an elaborate dinner for us at home, knowing she would be wearing her new lingerie and waiting for me to arrive. Her fear of going out around people had increased over the time we were together. She didn't even want to be around her family—especially her brother. I'm sure you can see why from our brief encounter with him. But her phobia had become worse, and in hindsight, I did worry about her becoming depressed with staying home so much. She assured me over and over that she was happy— that she couldn't ask for more. I believed her and trusted her to tell me when she was overwhelmed.

"Our favorite restaurant made us special plates to go and delivered them to the condo, along with a cake and special vintage bottle of champagne. The champagne I had picked out was special in many ways, actually, and I had to order it months ahead of time. There were very few bottles available so I was fortunate to even get one. The bottle design itself was very unique since the 1998 version was the only vintage in a plated, white gold bottle. It was Dom Perignon White Gold Jeroboam champagne.

"Anyway, I had a courier deliver the champagne to the restaurant and then they delivered it all together to our condo. As usual, I had meetings that ran over and I was late leaving from work. Carol Ann called just as I was walking out of the building to ask where I was. I apologized profusely for being late for our anniversary celebration and she laughed. She said, 'Dominic, you know you don't have to apologize to me. I'm not going anywhere.' We both laughed at that double entendre joke and I assured her I would be home soon.

"She told me the food and champagne had already been delivered and she couldn't wait to get into that bottle. I told her she could have *one glass* without me but no more than that. I decided at the last minute to stop and get her a bouquet of flowers on my way home. Carol Ann always loved flowers.

When she would become sad over her family drama, I would give her flowers and her face would glow from excitement. It was always the little things that she loved the most," I reminisced.

What I'm about to say is the part I don't want to talk about. The next scene changed me forever. Even though I've taken another sub, the memories of the past haunt me. I can't get it out of my mind. The lingering doubts are still there. *Should I even be allowed to be a Dom? Am I worthy of such a title? Am I deserving of the complete trust and total submission given to me?* These are the questions that have plagued me relentlessly for the last sixteen months. Every fucking day.

Sophia lifts her chin to look up at me, waiting for me to finish the story. I know I can't leave it here and the least I can do is man-up and just tell her what happened. Scraping my hand down my face, I blow out a forceful breath and unconsciously ball up my fist.

"When I turned into our condo drive, the first thing I saw was red and blue flashing lights everywhere. It was obvious there was an emergency, with the fire trucks, an ambulance, and several police cars parked haphazardly. Of course, I was concerned with what was happening, but I really just wanted to get to Carol Ann. I was already so late," my voice trails off and I feel Sophia grip me tighter as she tries to give me her strength.

"Grabbing the flowers from the front seat, I hopped out and quickly strolled toward the entrance. A cop was stationed at front of the door, checking everyone's identification before he let anyone pass—coming *and* going. He saw my name, and even though I saw the flash of recognition across his face, I chose not to see it. I don't know if that makes any sense to you or not," I wait for Sophia to catch up with me.

"Yes, I think I know what you mean," she says quietly.

I nod once and continue, "I reached to take my license back from him and he said, 'Mr. Powers, we need to speak to you somewhere private, sir.' Those are not the words I wanted to hear at all. It suddenly became very important for me to just get to the condo and see Carol Ann. I told him that I had dinner plans, I was already late, and I needed to go.

"A detective came up behind me and told me that I had to go with him, and even though I was severely fucking pissed off, I went into the complex manager's office with him. It was then that he told me that everything was still being investigated, but it appeared that Carol Ann had killed herself by jumping from our twenty-third floor balcony," I recite like I'm a fucking robot.

Sophia gasps loudly and instantly covers her mouth with her hand. When I glance down at her, I see her eyes well up with tears and she shakes her head from side to side, as if she's saying 'no.' I know the feeling—I did the same thing every day for months after it happened. I ran through every scenario, I recounted every word, but I always came back to the end conclusion—Carol Ann is no longer with me. She's dead and I didn't protect her.

"The detective asked if we had any trouble in our relationship, had she been depressed, and if she had any other mental problems. You know, all those really intimate, intrusive questions feel so very impersonal when the other person is taking copious notes as he asks you about the death of someone you love. I was questioned for a while longer, but they wouldn't let me see her no matter how much I threatened. It was an ongoing investigation and any suicide is treated as a crime until the medical examiner rules on it.

"Her brother, Harrison, has always blamed me for her death. He accused me of making her agoraphobic—said I *forced* her to stay hidden away in the house all the time with 'our lifestyle.' He knew she was my submissive and he always accused me of taking advantage of her. Said I brainwashed her, that I was abusing her, stupid shit like that. That's why he says I killed her—she wouldn't have been depressed or afraid to leave the house if I hadn't controlled her so much," I finish, drained of all energy now, but I know it will be a sleepless night.

"Is that why you have nightmares?"

"You think I have nightmares?" I ask, not to dodge the question but to find out why she thinks that.

"You talk in your sleep pretty frequently. Most of the time, I can't understand what you're saying, but you always sound so...sad. So desperate. I've wondered why that was."

"Yes, that's why I have nightmares. As her Dom, her wellbeing was my responsibility. If she was depressed, sad, hurt, sick, or whatever—it was *my* job to make sure she was taken care of and I let her down. In a way, Harrison is right—I *did* kill her."

"Did she leave a note?" Sophia asks, opening another wound.

I sigh, "Yes, the police found a note. It wasn't out in the open, but it was somewhere I would've found it."

"What did it say?"

"It's late, Sophia. I think you should get some sleep," I try to steer her away from this.

"Please, Dom," she asks.

Rolling over to my side, I open the top drawer of my nightstand and retrieve the folded note that Carol Ann left behind that fateful day. Holding it for a few seconds, I can almost feel her with me again. It's the most painful, familiar feeling I've ever felt. Without looking at her, I reach behind me to hand Sophia the note to read on her own.

I don't expect her to read it aloud, but it's not like I haven't already memorized every syllable of that handwritten note over the last sixteen months. It's the only time I've ever had photographic memory in my life, and it just happened to be the worst fucking thing that's happened in my life.

Sir,

I can't believe we have been together for a whole year. So much has happened in our short time together. I often feel that I've brought more sadness than happiness to your life. You have brought me nothing but happiness and I want you to always remember that. No matter what storms have hit, you have been my steadfast rock in the turbulent seas.

Never doubt the good you've done for me. Never doubt my appreciation for you. And never doubt my love for you. I'm paralyzed at the thought of losing you and I know I could never live without you. Through all of my problems, it's been your love that has pulled me through. I love you, My Sir, and there's nothing about our life together that I regret. I'm sorry for the trouble I've caused for you.

Sophia finishes reading and turns the paper over to the other side. Not finding anything else, she asks, "She didn't sign it?"

"No," I shake my head and stare at the ceiling.

"I don't understand. Why wouldn't she sign it?"

"I don't know, Sophia. I tore our condo apart looking for else—*anything* else—but there was nothing. Only that incomplete note that doesn't even really tell me goodbye," I reply solemnly. "I understand if you don't trust me to be your Dom, or if you don't want me to be any longer."

Sophia launches herself off the bed and directly on top of me. The look of horror on her face speaks volumes and makes me feel a little better about our commitment. Placing her hands on my face, she leans over close to my face and speaks softly, "I trust you with all of me and there will never be a time that I don't want you to be my Dom. Don't even joke about that."

The pain etched in her beautiful eyes gets to me. Just the thought of losing me bothers her tremendously. She lies on my chest, wrapping her lean body around me as if she's trying to shield me from the world like I did her. I feel the other half of my soul in her. Like a jigsaw puzzle that has been missing a piece, I haven't felt whole in a very long time. Sophia is the piece of the puzzle that perfects the picture, and as if it was always meant to be, the picture in my mind is the two of us—Sophia and me.

Over the last six weeks, Sophia and I have become closer than I ever imagined. She spends most of her time at my house now, except Sunday nights, as she still insists on staying alone at her condo. While I do miss her, the time alone gives me a chance to handle other matters without any interruptions. Not that she's hard to have around— on the contrary. But I can't do much else, besides her, when she's here.

We've moved way out of the plain vanilla sex realm into truly experimenting with limits and new techniques. Although, as far as vanilla goes, I have had plenty of my favorite kind of cupcake and icing over these past many weeks. I can hardly bear to think about the first time I used the flogger on her without then taking her back to the playroom to have another go at it.

She walked to the padded cross, spread her arms and legs to the restraints, and quietly waited for me to secure her to the furniture. Once she was bound, she had a look of pure satisfaction on her face that must have completely mirrored my own. When I picked up the flogger from its place on the wall, she let out a small gasp and tried to hide the smile playing at the corner of her lips.

I walked to her, leaned in, and bit her lip, not too hard but not too soft. She just needed a reminder of who was in charge. She had to remember that she didn't tell me what was in store for her. So, I turned and put it up and picked up the bullwhip instead. Flicking my wrist and curving the whip to make an "S" shape, the clacker popped loudly as it struck her thighs. I aimed perfectly, after years and years of practice, so that it didn't wrap around her and cause damage, but gave just enough of a sting to be sensual, too.

Once she was sufficiently submissive again, I approached her with the multiple stranded flogger and proceeded to whip her breasts until they were red and swollen with desire. The flogger isn't intended for stinging pain like the whip, but it does sweetly sensitize the skin, making the sensation of skin-to-skin contact more heightened. Twirling it in my hand, rolling my wrist, and watching the strands as they smacked against her skin was pure bliss.

These thoughts are continuously running through my mind as I climb into my car this dark Monday morning before work. Tucker has the day off but I don't mind since I really enjoy driving my car. The rumble of the engine, the feel of the leather covered steering wheel gliding through my hands, and the power of the horses under the hood when my foot hits the gas are all there for my pleasure and control. On days when I just need to think, driving is my refuge.

As I make my way from my house to the office, my mind is elsewhere as I drive on autopilot. It's the same drive every day, and at this time of morning, it's normally fairly isolated. My need for privacy dictates that I live well outside the suburban area, resulting in a longer drive than most. The eerie silence in the car brings me out of my daze and I realize the radio isn't on. Just as I move my hand, the headlights of a car coming up behind me catch my eye. The driver is flying up on my ass at an incredible speed, so much so that I brace for impact.

I hear a popping noise and then my car makes a sudden, violent jerk to the left, then the right, and back left again. The dark images along both sides of the road come into view as my headlights sweep back and forth with my out of control car. As much as I try, I can't regain control of it—everything is suddenly gone. The steering feels like it is nonexistent, the brakes aren't working, and the throttle seems to be accelerating on its own. My mind is flooded with thoughts and questions as to what the fuck is going on.

Did that car hit me? Is that what the popping noise was?

No, no way. That wouldn't explain losing complete control of all drive systems.

Is there a mechanical failure?

Of every major system? Try again.

How do I stop, or even intentionally crash into the ditch, before something really bad happens?

Without steering, brakes, or control of your acceleration, you're shit out of luck, buddy.

This entire conversation with myself lasts about three seconds and then, regardless of my attempts to change the course of my car, my headlights illuminate the rapidly approaching drainage ditch. The one I didn't want to crash into, since it's at the bottom of steep drop off, but I have no say in the matter. I consider jumping from the car and taking my chances, but the steering is so erratic, I'm pretty certain I would end up being run over by my own car. Taking my chances with the safety systems inside the car, I decide to remain inside and literally ride it out.

Chapter Nineteen

I absolutely love the feeling of flying. It's so liberating and thrilling to soar through the air, feel absolutely weightless, and climb higher and higher. It's the hurdling back to earth that breaks the magical spell. The knowledge that, at any moment, I will hit the ground and my heart will stop beating fills me with a panicky feeling.

Then, I see her and the panic completely disappears. She is all that matters in my world. My feet carry me toward her—she's waiting for me in the den. Wearing the new lingerie I bought her, she is the most beautiful sight I've ever seen. It's pure white with lace in the most suggestive places. Her matching silk robe is untied and hanging open to show off all her assets. I ache to put my hands on her, to feel her, and to taste her.

She points to the balcony to show me what's waiting for us. The table is set with lit candles, our dinners plated, and the champagne has been chilled and poured. Her glass is empty and mine is more than half empty. She's grinning mischievously because she's had more than one glass of the champagne, even though she knows it wasn't allowed.

"You know you'll have to be punished for that," I warn her with a playful grin. "In fact, I think you did it just so you can be punished."

I'm still trying to walk to her but I'm not getting any closer. It's like I'm walking on a conveyor belt—I'm not making any ground and she still beckons to me.

"You can spank me all you want, if you can catch me," she challenges me. It's our game and it's all in fun. She would never disrespect me like that. It's simply playful foreplay that we both enjoy.

"Oh, I will catch you, don't you doubt that, little one. And when I do, your ass will be red for a week," I issue a mock threat while arching one eyebrow at her.

She laughs and turns to run from me. Breaking out in a fast sprint, I run as hard as I can but I can't catch her. She runs to the balcony, and just as she reaches the rail, she turns and smiles at me. Without warning, she jumps over the rail and her robe catches on one of the spindles, tearing it as she falls the twenty-three stories to her death. It's then that I'm instantly standing on the balcony, the torn piece of fabric in my hand as I lean over, screaming her name with all my might.

"Carol Ann!" I exclaim.

I blink and suddenly my eyes hurt from the flashing, bright blue and red lights that seem to come from every direction. Unfamiliar voices come from all around me, shouting orders and commanding more people to gather around. I try to move—I need to get away from all these strangers. I want to get away from all of these eyes that are peering into me, into my life, and judging me. Judging us.

But I can't move. I'm immobilized and I can't break free.

"Relax, sir," the soothing female voice says. "Don't try to move."

Nothing makes sense. In my haze, a preposterous thought enters my mind as I momentarily question if the roles have been reversed and I'm now the one who has been bound with ropes in the playroom. The thought is so insane, I laugh out loud and then quickly grimace in pain.

"I'm glad to see that you find something funny," the female voice says again, "but I really need you to remain still. We'll have you out of here in just a minute."

There's no point in arguing and I don't feel up to it, anyway. The muddled voices around me adopt an urgent pitch and I'm suddenly hoisted up in the air. This doesn't feel like I'm flying, though. Pain shoots through my body, causing me to mumble curses under my breath. Being unable to move and jostled around like a child's plaything is not my idea of fun.

"Sir, what's your name?" the female voice asks, her tone louder and more authoritative this time.

"Powers," I reply.

"Try to stay awake, Mr. Powers," she says.

I think I'm being carried somewhere but I can't see where or how. Everything is so confusing and I don't have the faculties to try to figure it out right now. I decide to accept what's going on—even if I don't know exactly what's happening at the moment. Suddenly, there's a sharp pain to the middle of my chest.

"Mr. Powers!" she screams at me. "Move faster, people! Mr. Powers, you have to stay awake. Do you understand? I need you to stay awake!"

Yeah, right, lady. The overwhelming urge to sleep is taking over me and I don't really want to fight it. It feels so warm and inviting, enclosing around me and shielding me from the harshness of the outside world. It's peaceful and inviting as it pulls me under a black blanket of nothingness.

My damn head is fucking killing me and my body feels like it weighs a ton. Struggling to open my eyes, the bright light above my head is blinding and doesn't help my headache. Something is attached to my arm when I lift it to rub my eyes and it takes me a second to make my eyes focus. There's an IV sticking in my arm and I follow the tubing up to the bag hanging on a pole. That's when I notice the heart monitor and the blips jumping across the screen.

Slowly turning my head to the other side, I see a blood pressure cuff on my arm and a pulse oximeter on my finger. I'm definitely in a hospital, and from the looks of my surroundings, I'm in some kind of intensive care unit. A nurse approaches my side and presses the call button. Another voice comes across the speaker and the nurse at my side speaks, "Can you ask Dr. Cole to come in Mr. Powers' room?"

Addressing me, she says, "Mr. Powers, I'm your nurse, Jennifer. Do you know where you are?"

"I'm in a hospital but I don't know which one," I reply.

"You're in Baylor Medical Center," she says and watches my reaction, I presume for recognition, so I nod. "Do you remember what happened?"

I scrunch my brow as I try to recall the events that brought me here. I get short snippets of scenes but they're jumbled and don't make a lot of sense. "I think it was a car wreck. I don't remember everything."

"That's right, it was a car wreck. It's normal to not remember all the details right now," she explains compassionately. "The doctor will be in to see you and explain everything in just a minute."

Jennifer stays with me, monitoring my vital signs and all the machines that surround me as we wait for the doctor. "Can I have some water?" I croak out, my throat feels like it's lined with cotton.

She looks at me sympathetically, "Not until the doctor approves it." She turns her head toward the door and says, "Speak of the devil."

A tall, older man with white hair walks in. His stride is confident and hurried. He's on rounds, no doubt, and trying to make it through his day. "Mr. Powers," he says as he approaches my bed. "I'm Dr. Cole, your neurologist. I've been in charge of your case since you came in through the emergency room," he explains. "Has Jennifer told you anything yet?"

"I'm in Baylor Medical Center and I had a wreck," I respond and he nods.

"Do you remember anything about it?" he asks.

"Just bits and pieces. Brief glimpses," I respond, trying to speak as little as possible. "Can I have water?"

Dr. Cole steps closer and takes out his pen flashlight. After he's checked my eyes, my coordination skills, and my vital signs, he tells Jennifer to get me some water. "What year is it, Mr. Powers?" he asks as he scribbles in my chart.

"2014. But I don't know how long I've been here."

"What city is Baylor Medical Center in?" he probes.

"Dallas. The state is Texas."

"Good. You're oriented to person, place and time—meaning, you know who you are, you know what year it is, and you know where you are. Your CT scan showed no brain bleed and we've been monitoring you for any swelling.

"You've been here with us for a few hours. When you didn't show up for work, you had a lot of people worried. Your car had veered off the road and into a culvert. You're very lucky they found you when they did.

"As far as other injuries, you have some significant bruising but nothing major. Our main concern has been your head. The paramedic said there was an indention inside the car where your head hit. You'll be sore and may have headaches, so you'll have to take it easy for a week or so. We'll keep you here overnight to continue to monitor for swelling in your brain, but I don't expect any complications."

Jennifer returns with my water and the doctor says his goodbyes with a promise to return to check on me again later. Jennifer reviews the chart he left with her and says, "Dr. Cole has put you on a clear liquid diet for the rest of today. I can get you some broth or Jell-O. What would you like?"

I give her my most practiced disgusted look and answer, "So hard to choose between those fine menu choices. Why am I on clear liquids?"

"It's standard protocol, Mr. Powers. Solid foods are unsafe if you should require emergency surgery," Jennifer says with finality.

"Fine. Jell-O," I concede.

Jennifer smiles knowingly and starts to leave but suddenly turns around. "There are a couple of people here to see you in the waiting room. Neither of them is family so we couldn't let them in before. Would you like me to bring them in now?"

"Yes, please. Thank you, Jennifer," I say, knowing exactly who's waiting to see me.

Minutes later, Sophia rushes into the room with Tucker fast on her heels. Her eyes are red and puffy, and her beautiful cheeks are stained with tear streaks. When she sees me, her unshed tears pour down her face and she runs to my side. She's suddenly unsure of what to do with all the tubes, wires, and gadgets everywhere.

"Where are you hurt?" she asks, her voice watery and she's barely holding back the barrage of sobs that lie just under the surface.

"The doctor said I used my head to break my car," I try to joke with her.

"Dominic, this isn't funny! You were missing for hours!" she cries.

Jennifer comes back in with more water and my Jell-O with a plastic spoon. *Dinner of kings*, I think to myself.

Once Jennifer leaves the room, I put the bed rail down and pull Sophia into the hospital bed with me. She tries to resist but I just hold her tighter.

"Dominic, you're hurt! And you have an IV stuck in your arm!"

"Then quit squirming and just lie here with me," I reason. She relaxes and gingerly moves the IV tubing out of the way. "That's much better. See, I'm healing already."

She shakes her head and I hear her sniffle. She's crying again but trying to hide it for my sake. "Hey, shhh, I'm okay, baby. Just a little bump on the head. The doctor says I may have headaches and need to take it easy, but that's it. Other than a few bumps and bruises, I'm fine."

This actually causes her to cry harder and confuses me even more. Before I have a chance to ask her what she's thinking, Tucker pipes in.

"Sir, do you remember anything about the accident? Anything unusual?" he asks in his usual, straight to the point manner.

I shake my head slightly since any sudden movement makes me dizzy. "Not really, Tucker. I get quick flashes of it but nothing I can piece together yet. They said it was normal to not remember everything."

"Do you mind if I ask you some questions to try to jog your memory? It's important," he states.

"If you say it's important, I believe you. Go ahead," I say, curious to see where he's going with this.

"Was there another car that seemed to come out of nowhere?"

I try to focus on the events of the early morning, "I think I remember seeing headlights coming up behind me."

"Did your car seem to have a mind of its own after that?" he asks, but it almost sounds more like a statement than a question.

Images of swerving but not being able to steer flash through my mind. "Yes, but how could you know that?"

"Just a hunch, sir," Tucker responds ambiguously. "Let us do some digging and I will get back with you. I've already called in a favor and have another man who will be with us at all times. You may not always see him, but he'll be there."

"Who is it?"

Tucker walks over to the door and motions for someone to enter. The biggest man I've ever seen walks in. He's tall, with bulging muscles everywhere, black hair, and blue eyes. His gait is confident and everything about him screams don't-even-try-to-fuck-with-me. Tucker is a big man, but this guy dwarfs him in size.

"Mr. Powers, this is Shadow, with Steele Security. He flew in from Miami as soon as you didn't make it to work this morning. Shadow, this is Mr. Dominic Powers," Tucker makes our formal introductions and Shadow walks over to shake my hand.

"Is that your real name?" I ask the mountain standing beside me.

"As real as it gets," he replies amiably and with a smile.

"Fair enough," I chuckle. "I know Tucker wouldn't call you unless he trusts you."

"With my life, sir. Shadow has had my back more times than I can count. He won't let us down," Tucker confides.

"I have a few things I need to check out, but I will be back to help Tucker with your security detail.

I'll be around, Mr. Powers. I'm not always visible, but I'll never be too far away," Shadow says.

"How in the world can a man as big as you be invisible?" I ask incredulously.

Shadow and Tucker both smile, and I think it may be the first time I've seen Tucker smile like that. It's the smile that says they know something I don't know. They have an inside secret that I'm not privy to know, and they're also not going to let me in on it.

"There are ways, Mr. Powers. Leave that to me," Shadow says as he moves toward the door. The way he silently moves, especially with as big as he is, must be an indication of his skills. "I'll be back as soon as I can. Time is of the essence if this is what I think it is."

"I'll be right outside the door if you need anything, Mr. Powers," Tucker says as he walks out the door.

Sophia's head is on my shoulder with her face close to my neck. The warmth of her breath fans across my throat and I feel her tears dropping on my skin. "Talk to me, baby. What are you thinking?"

She laughs but it's a humorless chuckle, "You shouldn't be consoling me right now, Dom. You're the one in the hospital."

"Don't worry about me, love. I'm fine, really. Now, tell me what's on your mind," I say into her hair.

"It's been a really emotional day. When you didn't show up at work, I knew something was wrong. I immediately called Tucker and we both left to search for you and met in the middle. He noticed the tracks in the grass where your car went off the road, so we doubled back to search the area. He sent me off to call for help when he saw your car because our cells weren't picking up service for some reason.

"I rushed back and Tucker was down in the ditch with you. He wouldn't let me go down there with you, saying it wasn't safe and that you would be mad if I went down there anyway. I felt so helpless. I couldn't do anything but watch when the ambulance, the rescue trucks, and the police showed up.

"They had to extricate you from the car and they put you on a backboard. Then several of them carried you out of the ditch. The paramedic was yelling for you to stay awake. You weren't responding so she had to stop and rub her knuckles in the center of your chest to try to get you to respond.

"You had been awake for a few seconds before that, just when they were getting you out of the car. That's when you..." her voice fades away and her hand flies to her mouth to hold back a sob.

"That's when I what?" I ask, but she can't seem to answer me. "I'm here now, baby, and I'm not going anywhere. You can tell me what happened. Maybe it'll help jog my full memory."

She nods and wipes her face. Pushing up to a sideways sitting position, she looks me in the eye and says, "When they pulled you out, you yelled out for Carol Ann."

Oh, fuck!

"That really hurt because I was afraid I was about to lose you and you were calling for someone you lost. It made me think two things. First, I thought that you were seeing her, like you really were dying, and that just about killed me," she confesses.

"And? The second?" I press.

"That she's the one you still want and I will never mean as much to you as she does," she says sadly and hangs her head.

There is a good explanation for this, but I have to be careful with my words so that she doesn't take them in the wrong context. She's every emotional right now and she feels like she's competing with a ghost. In a way, I guess she actually is, but not in the way she thinks.

"Sophia, sweetheart, I need you to listen to me. This is important and I know it's emotional. You need to hear every word I say, though, so that you fully understand," I instruct her in my dominant tone.

She nods, "Okay, Dom."

"I dream of Carol Ann frequently, but it's always the same theme. The details may vary but the meaning is still there. It was my responsibility to make sure she was safe, healthy, and well cared for. I failed her and I failed myself in the worst possible way.

"Those dreams have haunted me for a year and a half now. If I called out her name, it's because I saw her falling to her death again. Not because of any other reason. I don't compare you to her," I explain and wipe away the tears escaping from her eyes.

"Don't cry over that, My Angel. No one else has ever called me 'Dom' before and no one else ever will in the future. You're the first and will be the only one. My parents always stressed that if I lived this lifestyle, 'Dom' must be reserved for the one I intended to keep. I've known that was you from the start. You are second to no one," I promise her.

Sophia tries to hold it back, but like water building up behind a cracked dam, I know the sobs will burst forward any second now. As if on cue, her face contorts and she wails with sobs she tries to muffle with her hand. She falls forward and clings to me, her body convulsing as the sobs take over. Long hours of pent up emotions and uncertain outcomes release at once, overwhelming her.

Waiting patiently, I let her cry until she gets it all out of her system. Once the sobs slow, I push her hair back from her face and gently stroke it. "Feel better now, love?"

She nods her head but remains still, holding me and trying to overcome the destructive attack of emotions. "Dom, I need to tell you something," she says, her voice laced with fear.

"You can tell me anything, Sophia," I try to comfort her.

"I'm afraid my family will try to hurt you to hurt me. That keeps running through my mind. They don't approve of this life or my choice to live it. They think it's a form of abuse. I couldn't stand it if they hurt you because of me."

"I'm not afraid of your family, Sophia. I'll be glad to meet them and show them that there's no abuse if you'd like," I offer.

"No, Dom! If they don't already know about you, I want to keep it that way," she says adamantly and squeezes me tighter. "Please, no," she whispers, more to herself than to me.

"If it means that much to you, Sophia, we won't go around them," I pacify her, but decide to have Tucker check more into them discreetly.

"Thank you, Dom," she says sleepily.

We rearrange our positions so that I can hold her from behind as we sleep. My stomach rumbles from lack of food, but the Jell-O cup still isn't the least bit appetizing. I just close my eyes and let sleep overcome me. At some point in the night, I'm roused from my sleep for a second while the nightshift nurse refills my water and checks my vital signs. The diligent man in the doorway stands watch and I know I'm well protected.

The nurse stops and looks at Sophia lying in the bed with me. She starts to object, but the daunting figure in the doorway clears his throat in warning. The night shift nurse quickly closes her mouth, her lips pursed in disapproval, but she says nothing. I think to myself, as I drift off to sleep once

again that Tucker is a very handy man to have
around.

Chapter Twenty

"I've been out of the hospital for more than two weeks. I'm fine, Sophia," I say for the fifth and final time. She's not happy that I will soon leave for my trip to Tennessee and has been showing her ass more and more these last few days. Some of it has been intentional, I think, but most of it is because of genuine concern for me.

"Why can't I go with you then? I don't like you going alone so soon after a head injury."

"It's hardly a head injury when I just got my bell rung, Sophia. All the tests are clear and I haven't had any headaches or dizziness. I'm fine. And you know you can't go with me because you have to stay and oversee the daily operations," I reply. "Plus, you don't have the security clearances to go with me."

"What if your wreck was *because* of your involvement with this top-secret place?"

Honestly, the thought has crossed my mind. When Tucker returned to pick us up from the hospital the day after my wreck, he had a concerned look on his face. I've never seen Tucker with such a look before. He's always been the epitome of cool, calm, and collected. For Tucker to be concerned meant he knew something very disturbing.

He wouldn't discuss it with anyone else around, but Shadow had obviously briefed Tucker on what he'd found since both men stayed glued to my side. Shadow even refused to let the nurse push my wheelchair out to the waiting car, but the nurse wasn't the least bit offended since Shadow turned on the charm to get his way.

When we arrived back home, Tucker asked to speak to me alone in my home office. After excusing ourselves from Sophia, Shadow, Tucker, and I met behind closed doors as they explained the situation. Since Tucker had also initiated background checks on Sophia's family, he wanted to convey that information in private as well.

"What do you have?" I asked Tucker and Shadow.

"Have you ever heard of a 'Boston Brake Job,' Mr. Powers?" Shadow asked in response.

"Can't say I have. What is it?"

"It's a pretty effective assassination technique originally developed by the CIA. It's been adopted by some drug cartels and other generally bad guys," Shadow explained. "Unfortunately, the technology in your car made it a perfect fit for this type of accident. No one would ever find it if they didn't know what they were looking for."

"What technique? How does it work?"

"The drive-by-wire technology in your car allows the computer to control most everything—brakes, steering, accelerating, etc. Instead of the brake pedal actually controlling the brakes, it sends a signal to the car's computer to apply the brakes. In this case, someone put a small chip on your car, sped up close to you with the remote and activated it, frying the car's computer that controls everything.

"I checked your car out myself. I don't think it's related to your government contract negotiations. Had it been a sanctioned hit, someone would've gone back to retrieve the chip from your car and erased any proof. It would be deemed a freak accident and nothing would ever be questioned.

"This may have been an experienced hit man, but he didn't get back to your car in time to retrieve the chip, so he's not a pro. However, there's no doubt it was an attempt on your life," Shadow explained.

Tucker took over the next part of the conversation, "Sophia's parents and brother all have ties to the Mexican drug cartel. That cartel has been well known in deploying these types of devices against their enemies."

"I haven't had any dealings with anyone in a drug cartel!" I exclaimed.

"No, but they may be trying to get to Sophia, and her family, through you. The condo she lives in isn't in her name, so they wouldn't be able to trace her to it. If they know she's with you that may be our link. Her brother has been in some trouble with possession with intent to distribute charges lately. Somehow, they've 'lost' the evidence and his case is pending. Has Sophia told you any of this?" Tucker asked.

"She did say that she was afraid her family would try to hurt me in order to hurt her," I said. "She has no interaction with her family, though. She wouldn't even let me talk to them to try to smooth things over between them. There's something missing with this—it just doesn't add up to me. What would they get from killing me?"

"Would your company go to Sophia?" Shadow asked pointedly.

"No, everything is left to my parents in my will."

"They may not know that. While I don't believe in coincidences, the drug cartel angle may be a false lead. I'm still on the case, but this was a definite attempt on your life. We will take additional precautions until this is resolved," Tucker said.

"Thank you—both of you—for everything. It's disconcerting, to say the least, but I'm grateful to have you two in my corner," I said sincerely while inwardly reeling from being told someone had just tried to kill me. "What are their names—her family?"

"Her father is Manuel, her mother is Sarah, and her brother is Shawn but goes by Smoke," Tucker replied.

Sophia eyed us suspiciously when we left my office, tightlipped and somber. At that point, without further evidence, I didn't think it was a good idea to tell her what Shadow and Tucker had found and I advised them both of that before we left my office.

We did have to sit down and discuss the amped up security measures for both of us with Sophia. She wasn't happy and asked more than once, "If everything is fine, why do we need increased security?"

Shadow answered, "Standard protocol for any of our high-profile customers, Miss Vasco. Mr. Powers is well known, wealthy, and in contract negotiations with a top-secret facility. It's prudent to be safe than sorry. In this case, we will be safer than sorry." His emphasis on the '-er' in 'safer' didn't go unnoticed.

Today, Sophia and I are discussing my upcoming trip to Tennessee and her insecurities are showing again. Someone tried to fucking kill me two weeks ago, but I have to keep my concerns to myself until we know more—like who is after me and why. Part of me is concerned to leave her here and part of me is concerned to take her with me. If they make another attempt on me, I don't want Sophia anywhere around the danger.

My nightmares have also increased in frequency and intensity since this happened. The most disturbing part of them now is that Sophia's face has replaced Carol Ann's. The balcony has been replaced with a mixture of exploding cars, car wrecks, or her falling down a long flight of stairs. The end result is always the same, though. I'm standing over Sophia's dead body, once again feeling inept at protecting her.

Not knowing who is after me, and why, is really weighing on my shoulders. Leaving Sophia at this time feels much like I'm abandoning her to fend for herself, even though I know either Tucker or Shadow will stay with her at all times. They are both masters at their jobs and I know I can trust them both. Keeping this from her seems wrong at times, but then when I see her so worried over my bump on the head, I know she would have a much worse time with handling the current situation.

"Little girl," I respond to her latest tantrum, "if you argue with me one more time, I *will* spank you, and it will *not* be pleasant like last night's spanking was."

"You said you wouldn't ever hit me in anger," she rebuts.

"Do I sound angry?"

"No."

"It won't be in anger. It *is* part of your training as my sub, though. Punishment is not abuse, love, but it's necessary when you get out of line, as you are now."

"I don't think I'm out of line," she challenges.

And I answer her challenge. Walking to the dresser, I remove the long, rectangular paddle from the top drawer. I take a seat on the bed and instruct her to pull her skirt up. She does, tentatively, and reveals that she isn't wearing any panties. Fuck, how I love that sight.

"Across my knees, Sophia," I demand.

She moves to me swiftly and positions herself across my legs, forcing her ass to rise higher in the air. After ten licks to each cheek, her beautiful skin is bright red and stinging. Picking up the lotion on the nightstand beside me, I rub some into her skin to help soothe it.

"Don't argue with me, Sophia. Once we've discussed it and I've given my final answer, that's the end of the discussion. It's for the best for both of us," I explain as I continue to rub. "This trip is important and I can't and won't change it now. I am going—alone—and that is the end of the discussion."

Helping her to stand again, she keeps her eyes dropped to the ground as she stands before me. "I'm sorry, Dom," she says contritely. "I just worry about you being away from me."

"My sub wants to protect her Dom?" I ask, half-teasingly as I stand and wrap my arms around her waist.

She chuckles a little, "Always, Dom. Always."

Leaning my face down to hers, I capture her mouth and kiss her deeply. My feelings for her are deeper than I've admitted to her. She's proven herself and her love to me. Even though I gave her the name that is reserved only for my soul mate, I still haven't said those three little words yet. With everything that's happened and with my upcoming trip, a sense of urgency wells up inside me, urging me to tell her.

Breaking the kiss, I withdraw and stroke her lip with the pad of my thumb as I look at her lovingly. "Sophia, *My Angel*," my voice lowers, "there's something I want to tell you. These words bind you to me and can't be broken."

"What is it?" she searches my eyes as my hands frame her face.

"I love you," I tell her. "You are mine and I won't let you go now. I am your Dom, *only* yours. You are *My Angel,* for all time."

She opens her mouth but speaks no words as she's stunned silent and continues to search my eyes for confirmation of what she just heard. "Yes, I love you, *My Angel.*"

She leaps into my arms and wraps her legs around my waist as my hands slide under her to hold her up. She kisses me passionately, pouring herself into her kiss and taking everything I give her. Stopping to breathe, our foreheads touching, she whispers, "You really love me, Dom?"

"I really love you, Sophia," I say. "I have something for you."

"For me?"

I place her on the bed, "Stay right here." Walking away to retrieve it, I come back to face her. "This is very special, Sophia. In other Dom/sub relationships, the sub sometimes wears a true collar around her neck or her ankle to show she belongs to someone. When you wear this, everyone will say, '*She belongs to her Dom.*' I want you to wear this to show that you belong to me."

Opening the box, I remove the white gold band engraved with an inscription that reads, "*My Dom's Angel.*" She inspects it closely, staring at the engraving for several minutes before she starts to slip the ring on her finger. I stop her just before she does.

"This is my promise ring to you, Sophia. I want to shout it out to the world—*I am her Dom and she is My Angel!* But know that once you put this ring on, it doesn't come off for any reason. This is your collar, the symbol that you are mine, and there is no going back," I explain sternly.

She pushes the ring onto her finger, "I never want to go back. I want you, my Dom, for the rest of my life."

Staring at the ring, her fingers lightly brush over it again before holding her hand out in front of her to examine it. She looks so happy now and pride swells in my chest knowing I'm the man who put that beautiful smile on her face.

"You've really only said that to one other?" she asks.

"Yes, but you're the only one I've ever collared, *My Angel*," I confess. "I don't say it just to say it. I certainly don't collar someone I don't intend to stay with. It's not marriage yet, but it's a step toward it."

Through her smile, she wipes away tears from her beautiful face. "Tears of happiness, Dom," she says when she sees me looking at them. "You've made me so happy. I love you—with all my heart I love you!"

After thoroughly going through every detail of my accident, Shadow is convinced that I am indeed the target and he will accompany me to Tennessee. As a former CIA agent, and a member of the elite Delta Force special operations team, he still has the security clearance needed to enter the facility in Oak Ridge. Tucker is still with Sophia, and while I trust both men with my life, I am the only man I completely trust with Sophia's life. It's killing me to leave her in Dallas. Shadow senses my discomfort and again reassures me that Sophia is fine and in good hands. He's been in constant contact with Tucker and they have coordinated all of our activities.

After landing in Knoxville, Shadow and I make the short drive to the facility in Oak Ridge. This facility is the storage place for the weapons-grade enriched uranium and home to one of the few supercomputers in the world. Gaining this contract is significant to DPS. Our software development will revolutionize their security systems in several different areas of their operations. The hardest part of this entire deal will be over the next few days. Once the contract provisions are approved, the 'easier' work of changing their systems over can begin.

Pulling up to the expansive facility, Shadow and I are checked out thoroughly before granted access to the grounds. Because of his past, Shadow's credentials were a little easier to verify than mine. The guard double-checked every signed paper and every bit of my personal identification to ensure it exactly matched the information they had in their systems. I am excited to think about how my company's software engineers can change this process, making it more streamlined and more secure.

At the end of the day, I'm mentally exhausted. We were given an extensive tour of every division within the top-secret compound. At various stations, multiple people quizzed me on my ideas to change, upgrade, or enhance their current operations. It was all a test—some of the processes didn't need upgrades and some did. They wanted to know that I had done my homework before wasting their time with the contract provisions.

That was actually the more grueling part of the day since their policies required that we review every single line of the contract. We talked and negotiated through multiple pages, the administrative assistant would make the required changes, and then we would start the next section. This will be the sum of my week here and I have to keep reminding myself of how the benefits outweigh how mundane this week will be.

Shadow and I are on our way back to the hotel where I will experience the highlight of my day—the distinct pleasure of calling Sophia via Face Time.

Checking the time, I realize that since Dallas is an hour behind Oak Ridge, Sophia is likely still at the office.

"Not that I haven't enjoyed your company today, but I think I will just have room service and relax in my room tonight," I say to Shadow.

He nods, "Sounds good to me. That was boring as shit."

I throw my head back in laughter at his candor. "Hell yeah, it was! And this is my business!"

"I don't know how you do that every day. I've had to do a lot of different jobs as an undercover agent, but thankfully it was never anything like that. That was just pure torture," Shadow laughs.

"Only four more days of that," I quip and he groans in frustration.

We check into our hotel and Shadow checks my room first. Before leaving, he gives me strict instructions.

"Don't leave this room for any reason. When room service comes up, I will check it out and deliver it. If it's not me at the door, don't open it."

"Got it. Thanks, Shadow." He gives a single nod in response and walks off to his room next door.

304

Grabbing my cell, I immediately call Tucker. "How's Sophia? Any problems today?"

"She's fine. No problems. She's still working and I'm sitting outside her office waiting for her. It's been a normal workday—nothing exciting and nothing suspicious," Tucker advises.

I'm instantly relieved at the good news. "Thanks, Tucker. Glad to hear it. I'll give her a call and tell her it's time to go home."

"Sounds good, boss," Tucker says and we disconnect.

I call Sophia's work number and wait for her to answer, "DPS. This is Sophia Vasco. How can I help you?"

"You can go home, take off all your clothes, and Face Time me," I respond using my bedroom voice.

"That is actually the best offer I've heard all day. I just may have to take you up on that."

"Then, do it. Get out of there. You've been working long enough. You need to eat and get ready for my call. I'm going to order room service and I'd like to have my cupcake for dessert."

"You are quite the tease, Mr. Powers. You know you're not here to have dessert," she says with her embarrassed laugh.

305

"Surely you don't still get embarrassed with me, Sophia."

"No. It's just that I've never done this. I'm a little nervous about it."

"Neither have I, but it'll be great. It's with you, so there's no other choice but great."

"I'm closing up shop now and heading home, Dom. I'll talk to you soon," she says seductively.

"There's my girl," I say. "Be careful, love."

We say our goodbyes and I order my food from room service. What I really want is not on the menu. But it *is* on the agenda for tonight.

Chapter Twenty-One

Two more long days of line-by-line contract analysis has my eyes crossed but my nights are filled with Face Time talks with Sophia. We've found new, inventive ways of passing the time and dealing with the forced abstinence. Last night, she put on a full strip tease for me, complete with music. She wore a provocative bustier that boosted her cleavage, thigh-high stockings trimmed with scalloped lace at the top, and my favorite stiletto heels. Watching her is a total turn-on for me and makes me want her so much more I can barely stand it.

After the last two nights of watching her but not being able to have her, I've decided that phone sex, even *visual* phone sex, is just not enough. My craving and desire for her is much more than just physical attraction. She fulfills all of my senses—touching, smelling, tasting, seeing, and hearing—

but I need them fulfilled in person. Otherwise, it just falls flat.

It's Wednesday evening and I call Tucker first, as usual, just to check on the events of the day. He answers on the first ring, "Tucker."

"How's everything today, Tucker?" I ask, expecting to hear that everything is status quo.

"Today has been interesting, Mr. Powers," he answers matter-of-factly.

On instant alert, I sit up straight as I grind out, "Interesting *how*?"

"There was a break-in attempt earlier. The man entered the lobby and said he was a courier. He was carrying a package and signed in, so the guard allowed him up. Once he entered our floor, he attempted to enter your office when Dana and another employee happened to walk up on him. He took off down the back stairwell and out the back door. The police have scoured the security video and he obviously knew exactly where the cameras were because he kept his face hidden," Tucker reports.

"Why the hell did the guard just let him up without calling to confirm someone was there to meet him at the elevator?" My blood pressure is sky high, I'm sure, at just the thought of Sophia being there in the same building with whoever is after me.

"He's a new guy—just started today. The guy he was working with had gone to take a piss. He chewed the poor newbie out pretty badly when he came back. We think the intruder must have been watching and waiting for the right moment. He also made the new kid believe this was an urgent delivery for you and that you would fire him if you didn't get it on time. He dropped the box when he ran off but it was empty. There are no prints on it since he was wearing gloves," Tucker informs me.

"Is Sophia okay?" I quickly ask.

"She's fine. She wasn't anywhere near him when all this happened. Did you talk to her earlier today, boss?" Tucker asks, although I can tell he already knows the answer.

"No, I haven't. I've been stuck inside a military-guarded compound all day and they take my cell phone on the way in every morning," I answer dryly. "Why do you ask?"

"She went out for lunch today and, of course, I tailed her. She received a phone call that very obviously upset her on the way to the restaurant. At first, she was talking while walking, but then came to an abrupt stop with a shocked and pissed off look on her face. She didn't talk long, and never mentioned it to me, but I thought you'd want to know," Tucker says.

"Yeah, I'll wait and see if she says anything about it. I know her mother and her brother give her a hard time on the rare occasions when she talks to them." In my mind, I'm thinking that if they *are* trying to cause trouble for my Sophia, I will have their asses in a sling.

"Family can definitely suck the life out of you," Tucker sympathizes. "Right now, everything is calm and she's still working. The police have canvassed the area and are looking into pulling traffic camera data to review, maybe see which way he went or if he showed his face anywhere."

"I know I don't have to tell you to thoroughly check everything—the garage, the car, the house. Make sure nothing happens to her," I demand.

"On it, boss. I won't let you down," Tucker responds confidently.

"Thanks, Tucker. I don't say it enough, but I *do* appreciate everything you do for me." He has been such a loyal employee and friend, conveying my gratitude is the least I can do.

"It's my pleasure, Mr. Powers. Working for you is not a hardship at all."

We hang up and I dial Sophia's office number. She answers with her standard greeting and I try to make small talk even though the events Tucker described are looming in the forefront of my mind.

"How's my girl?"

"Better now that I hear your voice. I miss you during the day, especially since I can't even talk to you at all."

"Same here, love. Not much longer now and I'll be home," I say. "Anything exciting happen today?"

"Let's see. I finalized the deal to completely refurbish the operating systems at TexCare Health Insurance. The terms are great and we will really reap some benefits from this one. I also have an appointment with another major insurance company," she replies excitedly.

"That's great, babe. You're really doing very well at negotiating these contracts," I compliment her. "What else?"

"Hmm...that's about it. Nothing else really exciting," she claims. "Oh, unless you think that someone getting in illegally and then trying to break into your office is exciting."

"Oh, you think you're cute, don't you?"

She laughs, "Come on, Dominic. I know Tucker already told you. You don't need to hear it from me again."

"Fair enough. I just want to know that you're okay, love. Anything else that I should know?"

She sighs deeply and says, "My mom called me today. She said she wants to meet you but I told her no. It's a really, *really* bad idea, Dom." Her tone tells me she knows the final decision is mine, but she's trying to dissuade me without going overboard.

"We'll talk about it when I get home, love," I tell her, glad that she confided in me. "Are you almost finished working for today?"

"Yes, I'm closing up shop now. Call you when I get home?"

"Definitely, love. I love you."

Her voice becomes lower, more sensual, and loving at the same time, "I love you, too, Dom. I miss you. Hurry back home."

"Believe me, I'm going as fast as I can with this contract. Be safe and I'll talk to you soon," I tell her and we hang up.

While waiting for my room service to be delivered, I can't help but consider that Sophia's mother called her so soon after an attempt was made on my life. Since I don't believe in coincidences, I'm immediately suspicious of her family's intentions. Was she calling to see if the attempt succeeded? Did she want to see if we suspected them?

Shadow and Tucker are both running their checks on Sophia's family members and exactly how they're tied in with anything illegal. I cringe at what the implications of my relationship with Sophia could have on this contract with the Department of Energy if her family is involved with a criminal organization. It's my job to make sure everything is secure in this venture, and even though I love her, I need a plan of action in the event this all blows up in my face.

The knock on my door tells me Shadow is outside with my food. He hasn't let one hotel employee in my room with me unless he is also here. It's a little comical to me that, with his size and demeanor, no one has been brave enough to argue with him over it. When I open the door, he brings the tray in and I prepare myself for what I have to ask him to do next.

"Shadow, I need you to look into someone else while you're at it with Sophia's family," I reluctantly tell him.

"Sure thing. Who?" Shadow casually responds.

"Sophia," comes my somber reply.

"Already working on that, Mr. Powers," Shadow says with a smirk. "I wouldn't be much of a security asset if I didn't validate *everyone* that has access to you, now would I?"

"When did you start researching her?"

"As soon as I was contacted by Tucker. I have plenty of sources, Mr. Powers. We're gathering intelligence on everyone associated with you— known acquaintances, family members, and any suspicious ties. If anyone is hiding something, we *will* find it," Shadow says assuredly. "You should also know that I'm looking into *your* background. It could be someone with an old vendetta just now making their move."

Hold the fuck up. I'm being investigated, too?

"What. Did. You. Just. Say?" I punctuate each word, emphasizing my annoyance with the intrusion into my life, especially without being told. Something in the back of my conscience points out that I just asked him to do the same thing to Sophia, but I quickly squash it to make it shut the hell up.

Shadow's steely glare is the only visible sign that he's less than pleased with me. His voice is even and controlled as he speaks, "Mr. Powers, you hired me to do a job and I don't do anything half-ass. I don't care what you've done in the past. I will look at every angle to identify anything that may bite us in the ass. If you can't handle that, I will pack my stuff and leave now."

He's right and I know it. I'm just on edge and irritated with the whole situation. I'm mad at myself for even questioning Sophia but simultaneously feel foolish for not doing it when I hired her.

"You're right, you're right," I concede. "I shouldn't have questioned your techniques. I hired your firm because you're the best in the industry. Do what you need to do."

Shadow nods, "Ten-four." Leaving me to eat alone, I decide to call Sophia earlier than usual. When she answers her Face Time video call, she's just taken a bite of her food and mumbles her greeting, "You're early, Dom."

"I thought we'd have dinner together tonight," I say as I remove the lid from my plate.

"What a great idea!" she says more clearly. "I'm so glad you thought of this! I've missed having meals with you."

"I've missed having *you*," I reply suggestively.

"Keep talking like that and neither of us will be able to finish our dinner," she playfully chides. "When will you be home?"

"Still looks like it'll be Friday. We should finish the word-by-word contract review tomorrow. Friday morning, we are scheduled to run a test simulation with one of our programs. It's their version of a pop quiz," I deadpan.

"Well, I have no doubt in your capabilities, Mr. Powers," Sophia coos. "You'll knock them dead!"

"Don't say that around weapons-grade enriched uranium storage," I joke and Sophia throws her head back in laughter.

"Fine! You'll knock their socks off! Better?" she asks while still laughing.

"Much," I smile in return.

We finish our dinner, and as much as I hate to have this conversation via video chat, I have no other choice under the circumstances.

"Sophia, I need to ask you some questions about your family. You have to be completely honest with me," I warn with my stern tone.

She nods and swallows hard. Scrunching her face up like she just bit into something sour, she's obviously dreading this conversation, but reluctantly nods in agreement. "What do you need to know?"

"What happened to cause your separation from them?"

She pulls her bottom lip between her teeth and looks away as she prepares to answer. Sighing she says, "It wasn't just one thing—it was a culmination of many things over the years. When my dad lost his job, he became a completely different man. My mother was depressed and my brother was hanging around some bad people and started getting into trouble. I hated what our family had become and I just wanted to get out and away from them."

"Tell me what happened, Sophia." There's no need for me to elaborate. She knows exactly what I mean. She knows both sides of her Dom—the loving, affectionate man, and the relentless, unyielding disciplinarian man. She lowers her eyes in submission and nods.

"I was really young, so I don't know all the details of what happened with my dad, but I know somehow he lost his job. They were both very stressed, especially since my mom didn't work, so money was more than tight. One day, my dad just started bringing home large bundles of cash.

"My parents fought all the time at first, but they tried to keep it from us kids. I overheard my mom telling my dad that it was wrong and it would come back on all of us one day. I never knew what 'it' was, but my dad had changed so much I didn't even recognize him as the man I'd known all my life. He started staying gone for long periods of time and was mean when he did come home, so we all just tried to avoid him.

"This went on for several years. At first, I thought my mom just cried at the drop of a hat, but one day I noticed a pattern. Every time the news reported about an assassination-style murder, she would cry and wring her hands. Then she would go into a deep depression for several days, never getting out of bed. I had to feed and take care of my little brother and get us both to school. It's like she forgot us both when my dad disappeared.

"Then, one day, he just came home. He just walked in like he hadn't been gone forever...like we'd never gone hungry because he forgot to send money or bring us groceries. Mom just took him back with no questions asked, no demands, and no expectations. It was hard to deal with, honestly. I spent so much time wishing he would come back and make everything go back to the way it was. When he came back, I was so resentful of everything that I couldn't stand being around him.

"So, I ran away. I left them all behind and that's when I met...m-my Sir," she stutters as she's unsure of what to call him.

"You can call him your 'ex' now, Sophia. I don't like hearing you refer to another man with that title," I reply dryly.

"Yes, Dom. That's when I met my ex. I was hungry, dirty, and sleeping in an abandoned building. He saw me on the street, begging for change, and took me in. I thought he was my savior, but he turned out to be so much worse than what I'd run from at home," she says sorrowfully.

"We can finish talking about him later. Tell me how he plays into your family issues," I say. This is bad enough without having to picture that fucker hurting her.

"I had secretly kept in touch with my brother because I was worried about him. I love him so much and felt so bad leaving him behind. Then, my ex and I ran into my family out at the farmer's market one day. When I introduced them, he insisted that I tell them what he was to me, so I did. My family looked absolutely horrified. My father started a fight with him and the police had to separate them. One of the policemen recognized my father and instantly let him go and gave my ex a warning not to mess with my father again.

"When the police left, my ex and I were walking away when my father approached us from behind. He said I had embarrassed and dishonored him and to never come around them again. I tried to call my brother again after that, but he told me the same thing. I've tried to talk to him a few times since then, but he would just hang up on me. He knew I was the one calling him. He answered just so he could hang up in my face.

"I haven't heard a word from any of them since then until my mother called today, wanting to meet *you*. I don't even know how she knows about you, Dom. Is this causing trouble for you? Is that why you asked about my family?" she asks remorsefully.

"I just need to know what could come up, Sophia, especially with this government contract on thin ice. If you had to guess, how do you think they would know about me?"

"I honestly have no idea, Dom. I wish I did."

We talk for a while longer about everything and nothing, just catching up and spending time together as long as we can. After we disconnect, I lie in the bed and stare at the ceiling. I'm usually pretty good at puzzles, being a software engineer by trade, but this one has me completely stumped. I can't see the connection between her parents and me, or why they would want to kill me. That is *if* they are even the guilty party behind it.

The next thing I know, my eyes fly open with the shrill ring of my six o'clock wake-up call. I'm no closer to unraveling this mystery than I was last night and I have another long day ahead of me. Pulling my thoughts together, I put on my game face as Shadow and I head back to the facility to complete the contract negotiations and move on to the next phase of this project.

Then I can get back to my life before someone makes another move.

Chapter Twenty-Two

Friday evening, I'm finally on my way home on my private jet. Darren Hardy, my CFO, and I are going through the financial data from the government contract. He's more excited and animated than I've ever seen him. The contract has to be approved by the governance committee, but the director at the facility was confident there would be no problems. Especially since my proprietary software was ingeniously compatible with their current operating systems but made their security protocols infinitely more secure.

I was in such a hurry to get out of that place and on the plane back home, I didn't take time to stop and call Sophia. Deciding it will be best to surprise her when I get home, Shadow calls Tucker to ask if Sophia is at my house or her condo tonight. Knowing I'm due back at any time, she had

Tucker take her to my house where she's currently impatiently waiting for me to arrive.

I have so many plans for her this weekend and not a single one of them involves leaving the house. Her Sunday rule will have to take a backseat this time. I've had to go without touching, feeling, smelling, tasting, and seeing her all week. We have a lot of missed time to make up for and I'm not letting her out of my arms for more than a few minutes at a time.

If *that* long.

Thirty minutes after we land, Shadow has thoroughly checked every square inch of the car and we're finally on our way back to my house. It's a forty-five minute drive from the private airstrip and I curse myself again for not having one made on my other property. The thought occurs to me that I haven't taken Sophia there or even told her about it yet.

It's a lake house about an hour south of Dallas. It's not as isolated as my main house, but it's still secure and it's beautiful there this time of year. Maybe next week I will take her there so we can just get away from all this for a while. Just not this weekend since I'm not leaving the house for any reason at all. We pull into my driveway and I feel a rush of excitement and relief hit me. I'm home.

As we reach the front door, Tucker steps outside and Sophia rushes around him and flies into my arms. I lift her off the ground and carry her into the house. In between urgent kisses, I call over my shoulder, "Tucker, you can just leave the bags in the car until morning. I won't need them tonight."

Tucker and Shadow both chuckle. "You got it, boss," Tucker replies.

With Sophia plastered to my body, and her hands working feverishly to unbutton my shirt, we finally make it upstairs to my bedroom. No playroom antics tonight. I just need to immerse all of my senses in everything that is Sophia. She pushes my shirt off my shoulder and then grips my hair in between her fingers. Walking her backward until we reach the bed, I unzip her skirt and let it drop to the floor. Breaking our kiss only long enough to quickly remove her shirt, I deftly remove her bra before gently guiding her to sit on the bed.

"Leave the shoes on, *My Angel*," I take a moment to admire how sexy her legs look in those heels.

After quickly shedding the rest of my clothes, Sophia moves backward on the bed and I crawl up her body. Leaving wet kisses in my wake, I stop and peer into her eyes. "I love you, Sophia," I fervently tell her.

Her Dom

Reaching between us, I glide my finger across her entrance, spreading the wetness and preparing her for my intrusion. I can't hold back my groan of satisfaction as my finger slides deep inside her. Her resulting moan intensifies and her fingernails grip my back as I add a second finger. "*Fuck, baby*, you feel so good," I growl out.

She lifts her hips, taking everything I offer and asking for more. Sliding down her body, I stop when I reach the sweet spot. "You know, I haven't had desert *all week.* A whole week with no cupcake or icing makes Dom a very grumpy man, so I'd better fix that first," I utter with my lips against her, causing my voice to reverberate through her core.

In a slow, controlled approach, my tongue delves into her most sensitive area and she cries out. Her fingernails dig into my scalp as I become more and more vigorous with my performance. Looking up at her, but not moving away, I command her, "Be still, Sophia. No squirming allowed."

She breathes heavily, her chest rising and falling in rapid succession as she tries to calm her overheated body. Positioning her legs so that her knees are bent, I slide my hands under her hips and lift them in the air. She knows what's next and

325

she grips the sheet with her fists to try to keep from moving again.

"Don't make me have to stop what I'm doing, Sophia. My cupcake *needs* icing. I've been deprived of it all week," I warn her with my domineering tone. "Don't deprive me again tonight."

With that, I dive back in full force and Sophia's fingers are the only part of her that dares to move. They dig into the sheet and mattress, fisting the material and pulling as hard as she is able. When I add fingers to the mix, she completely comes undone in my hands and I lap up her essence like a starved man.

"That's more like it," I praise her. "Are you ready for me?"

"Yes, Dom," she simultaneously pants and pleads.

Gripping her lithe body in my hands, I flip her body over, face down on the bed. Knowing exactly what I want, she keeps her head down and raises her hips into the air. The ultimate submissive pose in my opinion, she's offering her body to me freely. Gripping her hips from behind, I position my cock at her entrance and slam into her. Her body lurches forward and I pull her back with my hands while surging my hips forward into her over and over again. Her face is buried in the pillow to muffle her repeated screams.

"Move that pillow and let me hear you, *My Angel*," I demand and she complies. The sweet pitch of her voice climbs higher and higher as she reaches her peak yet again. Leaning over her, I grasp a handful of her hair and twist it around my hand. With the next forward thrust, I pull her hair and her upper body rises to meet me. The additional sensation is exactly what she needed to bolster her orgasm and her inner muscles clench around my cock, milking me until it's impossible for me to withhold any longer.

We both collapse exhausted on the bed and I pull her into my arms, facing me. Kissing her eyes, her nose, her cheeks, and finally her lips, I shower her with love and attention. "You are so beautiful, love. I could stay awake all night and just stare at you."

She strokes my face, my manicured scruff, and my hair as she looks at me adoringly. "I've missed you so much this week. I'm so glad you're finally home. I was starting to think they were going to keep you another week."

"Not a chance," I smile.

"Will you have to go back again?"

"Yes, in a few weeks. We passed the test with flying colors, so I will go back with the first set of our engineers to start implementing the system upgrades. The good news is I won't have to stay the whole time, but I *do* have to be there to kick it off."

"Then, I hope you plan to make up for lost time before you leave me again," she purrs.

"*Absofuckinglutely*," I reply before covering her body with mine again. The morning light begins to dawn before we're both finally sated and totally dehydrated. I fall asleep with Sophia tucked safely in my arms and sleep better than I have in the past week since I've been away.

We start to stir around noon and somehow shuffle into the shower. The warm water seems to revitalize us both, along with our appetites. "I'm starving, love. Are you?"

"You shouldn't be. All the cupcakes you had last night should have filled you up," she flirts.

"You're just asking for more, aren't you?" I say as I reach for her.

She laughs and jumps back from me, "No, Dom! Please—can we wait?"

Smiling warmly at her, I respond, "Are you sore?" She nods her head eagerly and I stifle my laugh behind my smile. "Then, of course, *My Angel*. But know that you *will* be punished for telling me no. You agreed to the '*no withholding your body from me*' rule."

Sophia nods slowly, "Alright then, I'll take my licks from the paddle like a woman because I'm too sore for anything else right now."

Laughing richly, I pull her under the hot water spray with me and wash her from head to toe. She's relishing the attention, and for once, isn't insisting that she doesn't deserve it. My young sub is learning to let her Dom take care of her, do things for her, and cherish her in every way possible. She just doesn't fully realize the value of what she gives me in return.

After we've showered, dressed, and had a big lunch, I take her out for a walk around my property. After being cooped up in the hospital, then the hotel room and the top-secret compound, I've stared at enough walls and need some time outdoors. Telling Tucker and Shadow to hang back at the house, Sophia and I venture out on our own. The warm afternoon temperatures make for perfect weather to swim in the small spring-fed lake on the distant part of my acreage.

After convincing her no one will see us, we jump in for a little skinny-dipping fun. The temperature of the spring water is still very cool, even in the hottest part of the summer, and takes some adjusting to stay in for very long. After our swim, we allow the late afternoon sun dry our wet skin while we stretch out on a blanket. Out here I feel like I don't have a care in the world.

"Today has been wonderful, Dom. I'm so glad we came out here," Sophia gushes.

"I'll have to take you to my lake house, then. You would *really* love it out there."

"You own a lake house?" she asks, surprise lacing her tone.

"Yes, it's about an hour south of Dallas. I don't get down there nearly enough. Maybe we should change that," I say as I roll over to my side and prop up on my arm to look at her.

"Let's do that," she says excitedly. Her face falls as she notices the sun dropping in the sky. "I just got you back. I hate that I have to leave you so soon," she says distractedly.

"What do you mean—leave me so soon? You're not going anywhere."

"Tomorrow is Sunday. I only have tonight with you."

"No, I've been gone all week. You don't have to leave on Sundays. You're staying with me," I insist.

330

Panic controls her features for a few seconds as she stares at me, wide-eyed and slack-jawed, until she realizes I've sat up and my arms are folded across my chest. I'm waiting for an acceptable explanation of why she can't be with *me* all weekend. She twists her lips up as if she's deep in thought and replies, "Fine. Have it your way. I'll give up my night of watching soap operas on my DVR."

"Soap operas?" I ask disbelievingly.

"Okay, fine. It's *The Walking Dead!* I'm addicted to that show and it comes on every Sunday night. Happy now?"

"That's better than soap operas. But you just broke another term of our agreement, so that means more punishment for you, I'm afraid."

"What term?" she asks, alarmed.

"The one when you agreed there would be no deception at all. You just lied to me and said you were watching soap operas."

"It's a *nighttime* soap opera!" she defends.

"I guess I'll see for myself tomorrow night. Won't I, Sophia?"

"Yes, Dom, you will," she replies confidently.

"Fine. I'll give you that one. No punishment for watching *The Walking Dead*, but you can watch it here, too. You don't have to go back to the condo *every* Sunday night," I try to compromise with her.

"It's also for a little time alone for myself, too, Dom," she says. "It doesn't mean I don't want to be with you."

"We'll just have to work out a compromise that better suits both of us," I counter.

"I'm open to suggestions," Sophia smiles.

"You just like Daryl," I accuse.

"Who doesn't?" she exclaims and I answer with a sigh and a shake of my head.

During the commercial, I decide to make some popcorn and grab some drinks for us. As I enter the den, Sophia's phone rings and she quickly grabs it to look at the screen. Hitting decline, the call is sent to voicemail and she quickly turns it off. I watch with suspicion that I've never felt toward her before.

What is going on?

"Who was that?" I ask as I sit down and share the popcorn bowl.

"My mother, *again*," she says flatly. "I can't deal with that tonight."

"Maybe we should just go talk to them," I offer.

She shakes her head and vehemently responds with, "No, Dom. I'm serious—I don't trust them. She wants something—probably your money. That's the only reason she ever calls me."

"You don't have to face this alone anymore, Sophia. I'm here with you and I will take the heavy burdens off your shoulders," I assure her.

Sophia moves the popcorn bowl to the other side of her and swiftly swings her body around until she's in my lap, straddling me. She caresses my face with her delicate hands before kissing me softly on the lips. When she pulls back to speak, her voice is soft and low, but full of so much emotion.

"I never really believed there were men like you. I always thought they only existed fairy tales and romance novels that have happily ever after endings. I've done nothing to deserve how well you treat me. There's not much you wouldn't do for me, is there?"

"No," I answer plainly. There's nothing I wouldn't do for her. There's nothing I would deny her. There's nothing I wouldn't do to see her happy. "This is how it works, *My Angel.* Taking care of you is not only my responsibility. It is *my honor.* I'm proud to do it, but I am also humbled by it."

She nods her head and I know that she is seriously contemplating my words this time. They finally click with her and she understands this is not about control. It's not about having the final word or being in charge of everything. "It's a deep-rooted need in you that needs to be fulfilled for you to be truly happy, isn't it?" she asks to clarify.

"Yes, but it's also more than that. Letting me care for you and do only what's good for you is a sign that you trust me. Your submission with your body is one thing, but submission with your mind and your free will is another. When you depend on me, it gives me another purpose in life. When your heart, your mind, and your body all belong to me, no one can ever break that bond," I explain.

Sliding off the couch and onto her knees on the floor between my legs, she leans into me and lays her head on my chest. Her arms are wrapped around me and she squeezes me as hard as her arms will allow. I stroke her face and head, pushing her hair behind her ear and watching her lovingly.

"I give you all of me, Dom. My mind, my heart, and my body are yours. You're in my thoughts nonstop, my heart is overflowing with love for you, and my body craves your touch. If anything had happened to you in that wreck, no other man would ever have me. No one else could ever take your place," her words are steeped with emotion.

"If you say we should go talk to my family, I will do as you say. It would be wrong for me to not warn you, though. I can't just let you walk into that viper's nest without knowing how they are. Just consider that when I push back on anything regarding them," her voice pleads.

"Sophia, part of taking care of you is listening to your needs and your fears. If being around your family bothers you so much, I won't force it. Just know that when you *do* go around them, you won't be alone," I promise her. "Now, my love, it's been a long week and I'm ready for bed."

Once we're settled in bed for the night, I can't contain my desire to have her just one more time. Rolling over on top of her, I use my knee to part her legs and make room for me to ease in between them. What starts out as a slow sensual kiss quickly turns heated and animalistic. Our tongues

Her Dom

dance and caress, fueling our desires past the boiling point.

Reaching down and placing my hands behind her knees, I pull her legs up and slowly push into her. She moans in pleasure into my mouth and then tries to increase my pace. "Easy, baby," I murmur against her lips, "Just relax and let me do all the work. I don't want to hurt you."

When she relaxes her body, I feel all of her muscles become lax at once and I slowly push fully into her. Withdrawing, I repeat my slow, sensual movements over and over again until our bodies are covered with beads of sweat. She wraps her arms under mine and curls her hands around to grip my shoulders. With each thrust, her fingernails dig deeper into my skin.

When she seductively whispers, "I'm ready for you, Dom," I take my cue and put all of my might into the finale. She screams out my name and I growl into her ear, "You have me."

Chapter Twenty-Three

I'm startled awake at 2:03 in the morning. Having no idea what roused me from my sleep, I listen for a moment, but hear nothing moving in the house. It's pitch black outside with the clouds covering the moon. The weatherman said we can expect bad storms to move through the area today and it seems they're coming in early. Sophia is still sound asleep, but for some reason I'm wide-awake. Easing out of bed, being careful not to wake her, I slip on my lounging pants and head to my study.

The whole ordeal with my wreck, the hospitalization, and the knowledge that someone intentionally planted that device to make me wreck has kept me on edge. I haven't admitted this to anyone—including Tucker and Shadow—but I can't shake the foreboding feeling I've had since then. I've tried to dismiss it as an after-effect of all these traumatic events, but the fact is, whoever is responsible is still out there.

Keeping my movements as light and quiet as possible, I pace back and forth, trying to make square pegs fit into round holes. The gaps in my memory the wreck are becoming narrower as bits and pieces of that morning come back to me. Leaning my head back in frustration, I look up at the ceiling and focus on the recessed lighting directly above me.

Headlights. I remember headlights approaching way too fast and from out of nowhere that morning. Whoever was in that car must've been waiting for me to pass them and then they pulled out and floored it to catch up with me. The way Shadow described that device indicated they had to be close to use the remote control.

Strolling over to my desk, I grab a pen and pad to make notes about everything before I forget a single detail. Maybe seeing it in writing will jog more details that could be useful. I scribble my questions on the paper. *What kind of car was it? What color? How long were they close to me? What happened to them when I lost control?* They sure didn't call for help, so I have no doubt that was their sole purpose.

Not that I had any doubt that my life was in danger, but the memory of this car speeding up

338

from nowhere both infuriates and alarms me. If it was so easy to get to my car, they could do it to Sophia's just as easily. I'm leaning over the front of my desk with my back to the door, busily making notes and writing more questions, when I feel a presence behind me. I quickly straighten my back to turn and face them, but before I can move, there's a sharp pinch in the back of my neck and my vision instantly starts fading.

"Dominic! Dominic!"

I can hear Sophia frantically calling my name but I can't respond. She sounds terrified and I struggle to fight against the heaviness that has engulfed my entire body. I'm having a difficult time moving my arms and my eyelids feel like they've been weighed down with cinder blocks. My mind is reeling, knowing something bad has happened, but I can't make my body cooperate to help her, shelter her, and protect her.

"Dominic! Open your eyes!" she cries. "Please, Dom, please open your eyes!"

Despite being more than groggy, I finally win the battle and force my eyes to open. Everything is blurry, but there's a bright light over my head, and those damn flashing blue and red lights everywhere. Shaking my head, I sit up more and put my head in my hands. Rubbing my eyes in an attempt to make them cooperate, I look at my surroundings again.

Sophia, Tucker, and Shadow are all standing in the doorway, looking at me. I look down and see that I'm on a gurney. In the back of an ambulance. *What the fuck is going on?*

As I start to get up off the gurney, the paramedic tries to stop me, "Whoa! Whoa! Where do you think you're going?"

"I've had about enough of this shit," I say, madder than hell now. "What the hell is going on?"

When I climb out of the back, it's then that I realize Sophia is covered in soot and another medic has an oxygen mask on her face. She keeps taking it off to try to talk to me and he keeps putting it back up to cover her nose and mouth. "Ma'am, if you don't wear this and get your oxygen saturation level back up, I will have to transport you the hospital," he says decisively.

"Keep it on, Sophia," I agree with the medic. Tucker has his oxygen mask on and is also covered in black soot. "Shadow, what the hell is going on?"

Shadow walks me around the side of the ambulance and I get a good look at my house. There are fire trucks all over the front yard. Hoses are stretched out across the lawn from the tanker and several men are holding the hose as they put out the last of the fire. There's definitely no way the house is livable with all this damage.

"What do you remember last?" Shadow asks.

Taking my eyes off the disastrous scene in front of me, I focus instead on my last memories. "I couldn't sleep so I got up and went to my study. I started writing down the events I was remembering from just before my wreck. I felt someone in the room with me, but before I could turn around, I felt a pinch in the back of my neck. That's the last thing I remember," I tell Shadow.

He walks me back over to the ambulance and motions for me to get in. He climbs in behind me, effectively taking up all the space left in the back, and meticulously examines my neck. "Here," he says to the medic when he puts his finger on a specific spot. "Make sure to note this in your trip report. Mr. Powers was injected with a drug, most likely a benzo since it was so fast acting."

Sophia is listening to the conversation and quickly removes her oxygen mask, "*Someone drugged you?* You need to go to the hospital!"

"I'm fine, Sophia. There are other things I need to take care of right now," I say distractedly as I climb out of the ambulance again. Sitting down beside her, I take her hand in mine and kiss the back of it. "Are you okay, love? Are you hurt?"

"No, Dom, I'm not hurt," she replies, "just coughing a little, but they said that's normal."

Lacing our fingers together, feeling so grateful she wasn't hurt, I ask Tucker the same thing. He waves me off as if this was an everyday, run of the mill occurrence. Typical Tucker. "Someone fill me in on what happened after I was knocked out," I state to my motley crew.

Tucker's eyes cut to Sophia and she immediately lowers her eyes to stare at her lap. Tucker won't look at me and Shadow has the biggest shit-eating grin on his face I've ever seen. "Someone better start talking."

"Well, Mr. Powers, while you were napping in the study, someone set fire to the house. Since your fire alarms are all wired together as one unit, when the first one goes off, it sets the rest of them off, too. Tucker ran upstairs and bypassed the first floor, thinking you and Miss Vasco were both in your bedroom. The alarm woke her up and she ran into the hall just as Tucker arrived at your room.

"Tucker got her outside and met me here in the front yard. It was then that Miss Vasco realized you weren't already out here. Tucker confirmed he hadn't seen or heard from you, so Miss Vasco ran *back* into the burning house to find you," Shadow paused for effect and let his words sink in.

"YOU. DID. WHAT?" I bellow. Sophia shrinks away and doesn't dare to look at me. I immediately remember to watch my temper, especially given her past. I'm still beyond pissed off, but I lower my voice and try again. "You ran back in the burning house, Sophia?"

Huge tears well up in her eyes and she swallows hard. "I couldn't leave you in there!" she points at the house that's now in shambles. "How could I not go back for you, Dom?"

Tucker speaks up, "She found you, Mr. Powers. I grabbed a fire extinguisher and Shadow and I ran inside right behind her. We picked you up while Miss Vasco used the extinguisher to make a path for us to escape."

I know that Tucker is purposely only giving me the bare minimum details. He knows that I know, too, since he's using his stoic face with me right now. Shadow is the only one of us who looks even the least bit amused about how this is all playing out. There is so much more to this rescue story that they're not telling me.

"I see," I purposely hide behind my cool façade. "So, let me get this straight. Sophia just strolled back in the front door of a burning house, and somehow she walked straight to me in the midst of all the thick, black smoke. Then, Tucker, you and Shadow came in immediately behind her, picked me up and we all just miraculously escaped unscathed? Did I miss anything?"

Sophia and Tucker quickly look away, avoiding looking at each other and at me. Shadow quickly puts his hand over his mouth. But even as big as his hand is, it can't hide the huge smile that's still on his face. I'm impressed that he has actually kept from laughing out loud at this point.

"That's about it, Mr. Powers," Tucker responds cryptically. And then Shadow does laugh, turns his back, and tries to cover it up with a fake cough. Tucker glares at the back of Shadow's head, throwing daggers with his eyes, before meeting my gaze again.

"Well. That's just fucking amazing. Why do we even need the fire department then?" I ask sardonically.

"They have the big water trucks," Sophia replies and Shadow completely loses his cool composure. He walks off, his laughter echoing across the still dark morning, even over the noise of all the emergency personnel. I look at Sophia, momentarily at a loss for words, as she sulks, "Well, they do."

"Try again," I state.

Shadow walks back over to us, and while his eyes still hold laughter, he has controlled his outburst. "Tucker tried to stop Sophia, but there was no way in hell she would have left you in that house, Mr. Powers. She jerked out of his grasp and took off running into the house. We both tried to catch her, but I have to admit, she's *fast*," Shadow looks at Sophia with well-founded admiration.

"Tucker ran to the garage to get the fire extinguisher and we both rushed in to find Sophia and you. She had already found you and was dragging you out as best she could. She's the reason you don't have more smoke inhalation than you do. She kept you low to the ground, but she was breathing in and out heavily from the exertion, so that's why she had to keep the oxygen on longer.

"Tucker and I grabbed you from her and carried you the rest of the way out as she sprayed

345

the extinguisher to help clear a path. We barely make it out the front door before the top floor caved in over where she found you," Shadow finished.

Like an idiot, I stand motionless and gape at all of them. Once again, I've found myself searching for what to say and do next. Should I be mad that Sophia put herself in danger? If she hadn't, would I even be alive? Should I be mad at Tucker for covering for Sophia? They all three saved my life, but Sophia led the charge.

As if she can read my thoughts, Sophia puts herself on the line again. "Please don't be mad at Tucker, Dom. He was only trying to help me. This was all my fault. If you're mad at anyone, be mad at me. If you want me to leave, I will go," she sounds so sorrowful and despondent.

Her bottom lip is quivering and she's fighting hard to hold back the tears. Somewhere in her mind, she believes this will make me send her away from me. She should know this only makes me love her more. I pull her up from her sitting position and wrap my arms around her. Lovingly whispering into her ear, I reassure her, "I love you, Sophia. You're not going anywhere without me."

"I thought I had lost you," her voice cracks and her arms tighten around me.

"Never," I promise. "You'll never lose me, baby." While holding her and looking at what remains of my house, something occurs to me. "You know what?"

"What?"

"You are *My Angel*—my guardian angel, in fact," I smile against her hair. Tilting her chin up with my thumb and index finger, I hold her eyes captive with mine as I reiterate, "I love you, *My Angel*."

Looking at Tucker, I mumble, "You're forgiven, too."

Tucker smiles and chuckles at my sarcastic humor. "I'm so glad. I was so worried about that," he deadpans.

Somberly, I look at my three saviors and tell them, "Thank you. Every one of you—I owe you my life. I mean that."

"Can we have the day off?" Tucker responds, breaking the serious moment with his brand of levity.

"Someone just tried to kill me again. Sure, why not let my security have the day off? Sounds reasonable to me," I reply in my own sardonic tone.

"Damn. The man has a point," Shadow chimes in, teasing. "I guess we better get to back to work."

347

Somewhere in all the commotion, the Fire Chief, Greg Floyd, arrived on the scene and started gathering information for his investigation. He makes his way over to our group and questions each of us about the details of the fire. He's a short, stocky man with white hair, a thick, white mustache, and a keen eye.

"Mr. Powers, I can't tell you anything official until I can conduct a full investigation, but just from how hot and fast the fire burned, I do highly suspect arson. It usually takes a well-placed accelerant to make a house blaze like yours did. I'm sure the police and my department will have questions for you once this has cooled off enough for us to conduct the tests we need to make a final determination," Chief Floyd advises.

Tucker, Shadow, Sophia, and I give him all the information we have about the fire itself. For some reason, Shadow keeps the information about the wreck out of the conversation. I follow his lead, knowing with his background and expertise, he has a good reason for it. Floyd makes his rounds to every firefighter and policeman before he leaves the scene.

The police are instructed to not let anyone in until Floyd comes back to investigate. Since the house is considered structurally unsound, we're not allowed to go back in to get our personal belongings that don't have fire, water, or smoke damage. Currently, we are all in our pajamas and only Shadow has access to his clothes since he's been staying in the guesthouse.

"Looks like Christine gets to have some fun shopping and spending my money again," I quip.

"I have most of my clothes at the condo, Dom. We can go by there and get my things," Sophia reminds me. "You're welcome to stay there with me."

"We should all go stay at the lake house. It's a little farther out from work for us, but it has plenty of space and is in a more secure location. Plus, not many people know about it," I decide.

Shadow and Tucker agree while Sophia looks concerned. "What is it, Sophia?" I ask.

"That house is in a more remote location if it's that far out from Dallas. Won't that be more dangerous?"

"Not necessarily," Shadow says. "There's an advantage to it being a little known asset of Mr. Powers'. We will drive the two of you back and forth to work and can spot a tail in a second. It may actually draw this person out and make them more desperate to find Mr. Powers. When he gets desperate, he'll get sloppy."

Tucker agrees with Shadow and that solidifies my resolve. Once Shadow has collected his belongings, we all congregate at Sophia's condo until Christine can get clothes for Tucker and me. Sophia is in her bedroom, packing all her belongings, when I walk in to check on her.

"The lake house has cable, too, so you won't miss *The Walking Dead*," I tease her.

"I'm glad. I was worried about that for a minute there," she laughs.

"Are you really okay? All of this is really a lot of stress on you."

She suddenly stops folding clothes and looks at me like I've lost my mind. It's entirely possible, but not about this. "Dom, this is incredibly stressful on *you*. I'm fine, physically, but I am so worried about *you*."

"You did an incredible thing this morning, rushing back into a burning building, Sophia. What if you'd been hurt? The smoke could've overcome you—*should've* overcome you, really." I still can't believe she did that—she put herself in danger but she saved me. As her Dom, I'm really having a hard time with this one.

"I covered my nose and mouth with my shirt, so that filtered some of the smoke out. Plus, I was bent over, so it wasn't like I was standing straight up where the hottest air was. I never had a second thought, Dom. When I realized you were still in there, my only instinct was to get to you."

Two hours later, our new clothes have been delivered, we've all showered and dressed, and we're now on our way to the lake house. Dana had our cell phones replaced and delivered first thing this morning and she is sending all my urgent work calls directly to me. She's handling the ones that she's able to and Sophia is busy on her phone, conducting her scheduled conference calls.

Another normal day on the job.

Chapter Twenty-Four

Settled in at the lake house, it's obvious that the four of us living together will take some getting used to. It's a necessity, however, so I will just have to deal with it for now. It's already been such a long day that I decide Sophia and I will not go into the office at all. It would be a wasted trip for the small amount of time that we would actually be there.

"Tucker will drive you to work tomorrow," Shadow informs us. "One of my guys thinks he has hit some solid leads, so I'm joining him tomorrow to gather more information. Apparently, one of his informants needs more motivation to talk and I'll be glad to oblige him."

"That's great news," I reply. "Maybe this will all be over soon."

"Don't get your hopes up. This guy is a low-level informant, but every little bit helps and brings us one step closer to the truth," Shadow replies.

We are all beyond tired, stressed, and frazzled after whoever this bastard is tried to kill every one of us this morning. Food preparation is just too much to ask of us at this point, so I call the local pizza place and have several large pizzas delivered. The poor kid just trying to earn a few bucks was scared to death by Tucker and Shadow's inquisition and inspection of every box before they would accept the food.

After our stomachs are full and we've all crashed from the emotional and physical drain of the day, I announce that Sophia and I are going to bed. This time, it's really to sleep since we have to get up even earlier in the morning to get to work. The executive condos would have been much more convenient for work, but they would also be much too convenient for whoever is doing all this. The DPS executive perk package is well known and I'm not inviting any psychopaths to dinner tonight.

Sophia and I settle into bed and I pull her close to me. Nuzzling into her hair, I whisper softly to her, "Don't ever put yourself in danger like that again. You are far too important to me, love."

"I won't, Dom," she whispers back, "unless *you're* in danger. I'm not making any promises if that's the case."

"Sophia," I warn in hushed tones.

"Dom," her tone warns back.

We're back in the swing of things at work today. It's already past lunchtime and I haven't stopped since I walked in the door this morning. Everything that wasn't handled yesterday has piled on top of what must be finalized today, so I'm working double time to get through all the documents and emails that require my final signoff.

When my stomach growls, I decide it's time to grab Sophia and have lunch together. As I approach her office, I see her on the phone. Her gestures are very animated and it's clear she's giving someone an earful. Just before I start to open her door, Shadow and Tucker approach me.

"We need to talk, Mr. Powers," Shadow says in a very serious tone. "In private."

"Sure, let's go in my office," I say as I turn and walk back down the hall to my office. As I pass Dana, I instruct her to hold all my calls and keep anyone from interrupting us. This can only mean that Shadow has been successful in getting the information he needed to start unraveling what the hell has been going on.

Shadow and Tucker follow me into my office and both men take a seat in front of my desk. As I sit, I draw in a deep breath and say, "Let's have it. You must have something pretty good to tell me."

Tucker's eyes cut to Shadow but he doesn't return the look. Shadow is in all business mode and there's no hint of the jokester that I know him to be in the man sitting across from me. The pit of my stomach drops and I instantly sense that whatever he is about to tell me will change my life.

"Do you know a Harrison Dictman?" Shadow asks.

"Yes, I know him. Why? You think *he's* behind this?" I ask disbelievingly. Harrison is a dick, but I've never pegged him for someone who would be smart enough to pull all this off.

"Does he have any grudges against you?" Shadow asks, ignoring my question.

"Yes, he hates me and the feeling is mutual. He thinks I'm the cause of his sister's death," I state flatly.

"*Are* you the cause?" Shadow asks.

"No," I don't elaborate.

"He has a serious vendetta against you, Mr. Powers. He's been trying to recruit some real low-life thugs to manhandle you. The most concerning thing I've found about this Harrison Dictman, however, is that he has very strong ties to Sophia," Shadow drops an atomic bomb on me.

"What the fuck do you mean, '*strong ties to Sophia*,' Shadow? Spell it out," I growl.

"Did Sophia tell you she had previously been trained as a sub?" Shadow asks.

"Yes, she told me. Wait a fucking minute, you're not saying that *Harrison* was her Sir, are you?" My blood pressure is about to make my head pop off my shoulders.

"That's exactly what I'm saying," Shadow replies, still in his business tone. "I've pulled all her phone records. Every Sunday night, without fail, Sophia and Harrison have had lengthy conversations. The only exception is this past Sunday night, when you almost died in a house fire."

356

Shadow hands me the phone records and I pour over the numbers listed. Every Sunday night, when she was at her condo, she was on the phone with *Harry Dick-man*.

"They've been plotting together? All of this was a setup? For what?" My tongue trips over all these questions as they pour out of my head, unfiltered, unbidden, and without a plausible answer. This isn't happening. "He showed up at the restaurant one night when Sophia and I went out. We got into a fight. She never acted like she knew him."

"She wouldn't, Mr. Powers, if she's in on this. It all looks very suspicious. There may be a plausible reason, though I can't think of one right now. Until we know exactly what the end game is, you need to continue on as usual. Don't tip her off and reveal our hand. If they think we're still in the dark about them, it gives us a tactical advantage to trip them up."

"Exactly how in the *fucking hell* am I supposed to pretend I don't know any of this? How am I supposed to pretend I believe in something I know isn't true? The woman I fell in love with, and who *supposedly* loves me, has been conspiring with *Harry Dick-man* against me!" I roar.

"Dominic," Tucker interjects, "trust us. We are doing everything we can to make this move as quickly as possible." Tucker's use of my first name is intentional. It reiterates the brotherly bond of trust we've developed over the last several years.

I quickly stand, sending my office chair rolling backward and crashing into the credenza. I don't even care. I just want to break every fucking thing in my office right now. Pacing back and forth like a caged animal, it occurs to me that phrase accurately describes my circumstances. I feel caged and backed into a corner, unable to do anything else but pretend that Sophia hasn't been conspiring with the enemy. And I feel like a fucking animal, ready to pounce on Harrison's head and rip him limb from limb.

My Angel has been sleeping with the fucking enemy.

My office door swiftly swings open, without warning and without Dana's normal knock. A man wearing a suit and tie comes strolling in like he owns the place, followed by my corporate lawyer, and lastly, followed by Dana who is trying to corral them all out of my office.

"Do you know how to knock?" I bellow at the man who dares to enter this lion's den.

"Mr. Powers, I presume?" he replies arrogantly.

"You barged into my office. You tell me," I challenge.

"Consider yourself served, sir," he says with a smug smile as he hands me an envelope and turns to walk out.

Looking at my lawyer, Cheryl Kealey, I hold the envelope out and yell, "What the hell is *this*, Cheryl?"

Can this day get any fucking worse?

"You're being sued for sexual harassment, Dominic. You and your company are both named," Cheryl says solemnly.

"Sexual harassment?" I ask, bewildered. "Who?"

"Sophia Vasco," Cheryl replies. "We need to talk, Dominic. Alone." Cheryl looks at Shadow and Tucker but neither of them budges.

"Whatever you have to say, you can say in front of them. They are my security professionals and privy to *all* of my information." Especially since this is no doubt why Sophia is linked to Harrison.

Cheryl continues, "This is very serious, Dominic. Those papers name all the employees who have seen and heard inappropriate comments and behavior from you toward Miss Vasco."

Cheryl moves across my office, opening up my line of vision to the hallway outside my office. Sophia is standing in the hallway just outside my door and has apparently witnessed the entire scene.

I don't even see the woman I shared my bed with this morning.

The woman who saved my life is nowhere to be found.

The only person I've allowed to call me by the name that was reserved for my soul mate has disappeared.

Before me now is the black widow who has poisoned me with her venom. She is the witch who put a spell on me and the blinders have finally been removed. She has become the snake who hid in the grass and bit me when I was least suspecting. Sophia's name is now linked to something dark and evil, something wicked that must be eradicated and vanquished.

My stride has purpose and my feet swiftly carry me across my office. When Tucker sees Sophia standing almost in the threshold of my doorway, and my determined gait toward her, he calls out my name in an urgent warning. He needn't waste his breath, though. When I reach the door, Sophia stares at me, speechless, her eyes wide and her lips parted.

Staring back at her and not giving away my intentions, I flick my wrist and slam the door in her face. When I turn back to face the others in my office, Tucker's shoulders visibly slump as he releases the breath he was holding as he waited to see what I would do. Moving to the bar at the other end of my office, I quickly pour four shots and pass them around.

"Now, Cheryl," I speak after downing my shot of whiskey, letting the burn in my chest make my blood pump since my heart has been ripped out, "bring me up to speed."

"Miss Vasco has alleged that you forced her into a sexual relationship with her in order for her to keep her job. She claims that you have placed inappropriate demands on her, of a sexual nature, both in and outside the office.

"She claims that you required her to become your submissive in every way. She is not allowed to wear undergarments, she must wear high heels, she must dress in the way you desire, and she must live in the executive condo where you will have access to her at any time.

"The suit alleges that you have inappropriately touched her on the job, at the condo, and at your house. It also alleges that you coerced her into having sex in your office," Cheryl reads off the list of allegations against me.

She has taken our relationship and turned it against me. The relationship she pursued, that she instigated with her kiss on the plane, and is now attempting to ruin me with it. *That gold-digging, money-hungry, lying, conniving whore!*

In an uncharacteristic display of emotion, Tucker leaps to his feet and vehemently declares, "Bullshit! That's all lies!"

"Well, I'll just tell the court you said so and I'm sure this will just go away," Cheryl pins him with her glare.

"What Tucker is trying to say, Cheryl, is that Miss Vasco and I were in a committed, consensual relationship up until about ten minutes ago or so," I explain much calmer than I actually feel.

"Mr. Powers, I think it's time I share all the information I've found with your lawyer. Most of it will be pertinent to this sexual harassment claim," Shadow interjects.

"By all means," I reply with a wave of my hand.

While listening to Shadow reiterate the entire sordid story, along with a few additional pieces he didn't tell me before, my mind drifts back through all the time I've spent with Sophia. The very first time she walked into my office, our ocean lovemaking session that marked our first time together, introducing her to my parents, and collaring her as mine—all these scenes play over like a movie in my mind.

She ran back into a burning house to save me with no regard to her own safety.

Was that just to make sure that she could get to my money? Is that the only reason I'm still alive?

That can't be it—it doesn't add up. Why put the assassination device on my car then? That was an overt attempt to kill me.

"Dominic, do you agree?" Cheryl asks, obviously not for the first time.

"With what?" I ask, my tone revealing my boredom with this whole conversation. I've checked out.

Cheryl sighs disapprovingly, but restates the pertinent parts I've missed. "Since you've publicly named Miss Vasco as your 'right-hand person,' it makes it difficult for the two of you to continue to work together."

"You think?" I snap.

Cheryl ignores my outburst, "The law is clear that you can't retaliate against someone for claiming sexual harassment. The best course of action is for you to take an extended vacation while your security professionals continue to investigate and gather evidence against her. If you take a leave of absence, it will make you look guilty. However, with your recent wreck, then the house fire, it would make sense for you to take some time off.

"You are not to have any contact with her during that time, Dominic. I don't care what she wants. I will talk to her and she will begin reporting to Darren Hardy while you're away. Whatever work requests she submits will have to be approved by him. Legally, she can't keep you from your own business, this is your livelihood, but this plan keeps everything as uncomplicated as possible. I'm filing a request for a gag order with the judge as soon as I get back to my office."

Cheryl raises her eyebrows at me, clearly expecting a verbal agreement to abide by her rules.

"Fine. I'll take two weeks off and then the third week I will be back onsite in Tennessee. Tucker, call Christine and have her pack all of Miss Vasco's things and have them delivered to her executive condo. If I find anything of hers in my lake house, I will have to burn *it* to the ground, too."

The three of them file out of my office, leaving me alone with my thoughts and my own turmoil. I feel like I'm back in that same spot of trying to fit a square peg in a round hole—the pieces are just not fitting together. All the events are not adding up.

There has to be more to this mystery, though I have no doubt that she's intimately involved in it.

I call Dana into my office with a new resolve— a new spring in my step.

"Yes, sir?" she asks as she enters.

"Dana, I need you to book me a two-week vacation. Have the yacht readied—I'm taking a cruise to Bermuda, the Bahamas, and the Virgin Islands. I want to leave right away, so have Christine pack my things," I instruct and Dana hurries back to her desk to make the preparations.

Moving over to the floor to ceiling window, I continue to mull it over, turning it and examining it from every angle. The only thing that keeps coming back to my mind is how *Harry Dick-man* thinks he's a Dominant. That is laughable—if I wasn't pissed off enough to choke the life out of him. He's only playing at being a Dom, pretending to be something he wasn't born to be.

He accused me of controlling his sister, of abusing her for my own pleasure, and for her death. So he took Sophia, who was young and lost, and made her his sub. But he was wrong about one major point.

He was never her Dom.

Her Dom

If they want to see a real Dom, I will show them a real fucking Dom. Like they've never seen before. Run and hide if you can—the *real* Dom is back.

Epilogue

Sophia

Looking in the mirror, I only see a shadow of the woman I used to be. A ghost has taken her place—gaunt, sick, and bereft of everything that holds any significance. Thoughts plague my mind, nightmares have taken my ability to sleep, and the world that had once been so beautiful, so colorful, has now turned to a drab shade of gray. Nothing vibrant is left in me or in anything around me.

Who am I?

What have I done?

Sophia Vasco is who my DPS badge says I am. Even that reminds me of what I've lost. When I look around, all I see is *him*—the man who is my world. The sounds I hear are all echoes of his voice. My skin feels his touch when he's not there.

He's been away for days now. I can't even catch a glimpse of him at the office.

Cheryl, the corporate lawyer, told me that the court has agreed to a gag order on the sexual harassment lawsuit. I have no one to talk to about it anyway. She also had my office moved off of the top floor. She said it was to protect me, but I'm sure it was to protect him, too.

It's killing me to stay away. I am stricken through and through, and I only have myself to blame. I'm not strong enough to face this. I'm not strong enough to stay away from him. My heart is chained to him, belongs to him, and cries out for him every second of every day.

My Dom has left me and taught me the most painful lesson of all.

The End

About the Author

A.D. Justice is happily married to her husband of 25 years. They have two sons together and enjoy a wide variety of outdoor activities. A.D. has a full-time job by day, with a BS degree in Organizational Management and an MBA in Health Care Administration. Writing gives her the outlet she needs to live in the fantasy world that is a constant in her mind.

Thank you for reading and supporting A.D.'s books! Please take a moment to leave a review of this work. You can find her online at:

Facebook: https://www.facebook.com/adjusticeauthor

Twitter: https://twitter.com/ADJustice1

Web: www.adjusticebooks.com

Email: adjustice@outlook.com

Made in the USA
Middletown, DE
06 July 2015